Fran O'Brien and Arthur McGuinness
established McGuinness Books
to publish Fran's novels to raise funds
for LauraLynn Children's Hospice.

Fran's nine novels, *The Married Woman,*
*The Liberated Woman, Odds on Love,*
*Who is Faye? The Red Carpet, Fairfields,*
*The Pact, 1916* and *The Passionate Woman*
have raised over €390,000.00 in sales and
donations for LauraLynn House.

Fran and Arthur hope that *Love of her Life*
will raise even more funds for LauraLynn.

www.franobrien.net

Also by Fran O'Brien

The Married Woman
The Liberated Woman
Odds on Love
Who is Faye?
The Red Carpet
Fairfields
The Pact
1916
The Passionate Woman

Buy now online www.franobrien.net

# Love of her Life

# FRAN O'BRIEN

*To Norrée, with many thanks Fran*

## McGuinness Books

# McGuinness Books

# Love of her Life

This book is a work of fiction and any resemblance
to actual persons, living or dead is purely coincidental.

Published by McGuinness Books,
15 Glenvara Park, Ballycullen Road,
Templeogue, Dublin 16.

A catalogue record for this book
is available from the British Library.

ISBN 978-0-9954698-0-8

Typeset by Martone Design & Print,
39 Hills Industrial Centre, Liffey Bridge, Lucan, Co. Dublin.

Images courtesy of Jimmy O'Brien
(www.jimmyobrien.ie)

Printed and bound in Great Britain by
CPI Group (UK) Ltd, Croydon, CR04YY.

www.franobrien.net

This novel is dedicated to Jane and Brendan McKenna,
and in memory of their daughters Laura and Lynn.

And for all our family, friends and clients who support our
efforts to raise funds for LauraLynn Children's Hospice,
Leopardstown Road, Dublin 18.

Jane and Brendan have been through every parent's worst nightmare
– the tragic loss of their only two children.

Laura died, just four years old, following surgery to repair a
heart defect. Her big sister, Lynn, died, aged fifteen, less than
two years later, having lost her battle against Leukaemia –
diagnosed on the day of Laura's surgery.

Having dealt personally with such serious illness, Jane and
Brendan's one wish was to establish a children's
hospice in memory of their girls.

Now LauraLynn House has become a reality,
and their dream has come true.

LauraLynn Children's Hospice offers community
based paediatric palliative, respite, end-of-life care,
and the LauraLynn@home Programme.

At LauraLynn House there is an eight bed unit, a residential unit for
families, support and comfort for parents and siblings for whom life
can be extremely difficult.

Putting Life into a Child's Day
Not Days into a Child's Life

## *Prologue*

Liz stood on the landing. The attic door was firmly closed. She lifted the ladder and set it against the wall. Slowly she climbed, slid the door across and stared into the dark aperture. Immediately her instinct was to go back down and put this off for another day but it had happened before and now she refused to allow herself give in to that compulsion again.

She switched on the light, pulled herself up and looked around. She hadn't realised there was so much stuff up here. At a glance, there were boxes. Bags. Chairs. Light fittings. Pictures. A little rocking horse. A child's cradle. Old newspapers. She really should clear it out and get rid of everything, but today she was looking for something particular.

She made herself a cup of tea, pulled the curtains, and felt she was ready. The suitcase was old. Battered. A dark navy in colour. Her mother had given it to her. She lifted the top. Smiling as she picked up the first thing she saw. It was one of her diaries. She had begun to keep a diary when she was thirteen and religiously wrote in the little space every night before she went to bed. At first the entries were about herself and her friends in school, and as she grew older were all about boys.

She leafed through old class books. Opened her jewellery box which held a tangled web of bracelets and necklaces. She picked up a blue glass circle and slipped it on her wrist. To her surprise it still looked pretty. She left it on. Best of all was her first camera, the precious Kodak. She looked through the lens at different things in the room, knowing again that feeling of excitement when she took those first photographs. Now she loved to use a Leica which had been a present from her father.

She picked up an album. Smiling as she gazed at herself aged about six in a paddling pool in the sunlit garden at home. Then more grown up with that shy awkwardness of a young teen. There were lovely shots of the family too and it was very emotional for Liz.

Then she found an extra few photos tucked in at the back of the album. They were landscape shots in black and white. Her first amateurish attempts in that medium. Looking at those old scenic photos set Liz thinking. In the back of her mind was the kernel of an idea which had been lurking there for a long time. It would be so good to gather a collection of various photos which she had taken over the years. Sharp blacks and whites accentuating the images she wanted to portray. Suddenly, she was enthusiastic. Why not?

## *Chapter One*

The door of the studio opened and Sophie looked up to see her sister Brooke come in followed by her two small children. The kids immediately rushed towards Sophie and she kissed and hugged them.

'God, I'm wrecked.' Brooke collapsed into a chair. 'Where's Mum?'

'Out on a shoot.'

'God, those two would drive you around the twist at times.' Brooke watched the children pull open the drawers in the desk and search for the sweets usually kept there for them. They giggled and waved them in the air, delighted with themselves.

'They're not that bad.'

'You can have them.' Brooke pulled off her blue silk scarf and let it hang loosely in her hand.

'I'd love to.'

'I shouldn't have said that, they're my little pets, I love them to bits,' Brooke said. 'Are you going to have any of your own?'

'It's not part of my immediate plan. Have to find a permanent man first.'

'You don't need someone permanent, why not a one-night stand?'

'Come on, Brooke, I'm not that anxious. I've been through quite a few men and I'm enjoying it. Loving the party life.'

'I envy you.'

'Surely you don't want to be back there? You've a lovely husband and two gorgeous kids, what more do you want?'

'You've no idea how tedious it can be. The kids demand so much. I feel like tearing my hair out sometimes. And Rory's no help.'

1

'He works hard so that you can be one of the *yummy mummies* who meet for coffee after dropping off the kids at school. Then you're free to do whatever you like. What a life.'

'You can look after the twins any time. How about later on? Come over and put them to bed, and then I can go out to meet a few friends.' She crossed one slim leg over the other.

'Where's your other half?'

'London, on business, supposedly,' she sighed.

Sophie stared at her, surprised at the sound of weariness in her voice.

'Is something wrong?' she asked.

'I don't know.'

'What's that supposed to mean?'

'If I knew I'd tell you.'

'It sounds as if you don't believe he's on business,' Sophie said.

There were screams from under the table.

'Stop crying you two,' Brooke added to the racket.

'Let's have a drink,' Sophie poured milk for the kids, and made coffee for Brooke. 'When will Rory be home?'

'God knows.'

The studio door opened. A woman came in with a small child in a buggy.

'Can I help you?' Sophie asked, going towards her.

'I want to have a portrait done, you know, a few photos of my son with my husband and myself,' she said, smiling.

'Would you like to take a seat and we can have a chat? How old is your son?' she asked.

'He's just two.'

'He's sweet.' She tickled him under the chin. He giggled.

'The photographs on the wall are amazing, I particularly like that one there.' She pointed.

'You can have either black and white or colour, or both. We do a photo shoot here, or if you prefer, at your home, or any other venue.'

'I'll ask my husband what he thinks. We'll come in and have a look at these.'

'Call me and we'll set up an appointment.' Sophie handed her a brochure.

The children waved at the little boy.

She saw the lady out.

'Thanks for behaving yourselves.' Sophie kissed the two kids.

'I'd give anything for a smoke,' Brooke sighed.

'You can't go back on cigarettes now. You've survived for two whole weeks which is amazing.'

'You have no idea how hard it is to give up something which you really want.'

'Just keep at it. You can't go back on the best New Year's resolution you've ever made. Take it day by day.'

'Sounds so easy when you put it like that. But I'm not the only one with an addiction. You have one as well.'

'What do you mean?' Sophie turned her head sharply and stared at her sister.

'Those cameras over there are your addiction. You're hooked on taking photos. You've been doing it your whole life. And Mum too. You couldn't survive a day without a camera in your hand. It's the way most people are with their mobile phones.'

'At least it won't kill us …sorry, I shouldn't have said that.' Sophie hugged Brooke. 'You know I love you, we all do, we just don't want to see you do yourself harm. Hey, stop that, you two.' Sophie ran over to where the two kids were messing with a tripod.

'I'd better go before they demolish the place.'

'I'll see you on Saturday.'

Brooke looked puzzled.

'Mum's party.'

'There's so much in my head I'd forgotten.'

'And the most important thing is to be on time. It's meant to be a surprise. Have you got a babysitter?'

'I'll organise one. Peggy is always delighted to help.'

'You're so lucky to have a nice mother-in-law. Will Rory be back in time?'

'He'd better be.' Her red lips twisted, and there was a look of bitterness on her pretty features.

'Did you get a present yet?'

'Still have to think of something.'

'She just wants something small, you know she doesn't believe in expensive presents. I'm taking her shopping in the afternoon and we'll have a quick drink somewhere before I bring her back. I've organised a friend of mine to cover the studio for us. And just remember that you'll have to park somewhere else and walk up to the house so she doesn't see the car. What food are you bringing?'

'Dessert I think,' Brooke said vaguely.

'I'll be cooking a couple of puddings as well so there will be a choice.'

'Who's doing the main course?'

'I'll make that nice chicken dish she likes. And a beef curry as well. And Luke is bringing starters and salads.'

'It's all very well for him, he'll probably just get one of his chefs to make them at the restaurant.'

'So what if he does?'

'And we're all slaving over hot stoves. You should have got him to bring the main courses, why do you always end up doing it?'

'I don't mind, Brooke, you know that, I enjoy cooking.'

'Come on kids. Let's go home. Maybe Dad might surprise us and be there.' Brooke dropped a perfunctory kiss on Sophie's cheek. 'See you Saturday.'

## Chapter Two

'That dress is gorgeous,' Sophie said.

'Do you think so?' Liz wasn't so sure.

'Black is always super on you. And that neckline is sexy, I love the cut.'

'Too much black, that's the problem, sometimes I just long for something bright but then my hand always veers to black. What is it about me?'

'You're the same with photographs. Black and white mean so much more to you. If you are going to buy that dress, why not combine a brightly coloured scarf, then you have the choice to wear it or not? I'll have a look for one.' She wandered through the department while Liz went back into the fitting room and took off the dress.

'How about this?' Sophie handed her a long silk scarf in tones of pink and turquoise.

'Such lovely colours, beautiful.'

'It will go with everything. And if you wore the black you could coordinate with coloured shoes.'

'I have those cerise ones, they might look good.' Liz wound the scarf around her shoulders and stared at herself in the mirror.

'Dramatic, no one will forget you in that,' Sophie said with a grin.

Liz laughed. 'How much is this?' She reached for the price tag.

'Tell you what, this is my birthday present to you,' Sophie said, grabbing it.

'No way, I told you, no presents, no nothing, I don't want to even think about my birthday,' Liz said. 'Although it's lovely spending the afternoon with you, I'm really happy.' She kissed Sophie.

'Please let me give you the scarf. I want to.'

'I hope it's not too expensive, sometimes a scarf can be as dear as a dress.'

'This is my treat. Just between you and me,' Sophie begged.

'All right, and thank you.' Liz hugged her daughter.

'How about having a look at shoes?' Sophie asked.

'We both have enough shoes. Every colour in the rainbow. How could you even fit another pair into your wardrobe?'

'I'll throw out a few and make room.' Sophie picked up their bags. 'Come on, let's have a look.' She led the way though the store with determination.

They came out of there some time later, carrying more bags, both having bought shoes.

'Great bargains,' Sophie said.

'You can't resist.'

'No, I'll admit it. But I do love the pleasure of wandering through a shoe shop. Better than sex,' she laughed.

Sophie dropped Liz back home after they had a drink at the Westbury Hotel. 'I'll come in with you,' she said, turning off the ignition.

'Not at all, I'm sure you've things to do, and people to see,' Liz said.

'Just for a few minutes?'

'All right, you know I'm always glad of your company. Is Max still on the scene?'

'No, I dumped him. Remember we had that row in front of you. The cheek of him. So rude.'

'We've all had rows.'

'Not in front of people.' Sophie was angry even thinking about it.

'If he gets on your nerves to that extent it's just as well to say goodbye, and knowing you there will be someone new on the map very soon. But I wish you'd settle for one man. How many have you gone through this year?'

'I've already met another guy, he's kinda nice,' Sophie admitted.

'And he's number?'

'A hundred and ...' she giggled. 'I'm only joking.'

'How quickly did you meet him after you broke up with Max?'

'I just went out the following night with the girls, and *hey presto*.'

'You're too much.' Liz searched for her door keys in her cavernous black leather handbag. 'Why can't you be like your sister?'

'What do you mean?'

'More stable, I suppose.'

'Just because Brooke is married, it doesn't mean I'm not stable. My status is single. I'm out there looking. Casting my net. What's wrong with that?'

'Nothing wrong, love, I just worry about you sometimes,' Liz said, still looking in her bag. 'Why is it I can never find anything in this?'

'Don't worry, I'll use my key.' Sophie turned to Liz. 'Mum, I just want to say it was a great day, I really enjoyed it.'

'Keeping your old mother company, how exciting was that?'

'Don't say such a thing, it was lovely.'

'So what about your latest guy?' Liz asked with a grin. 'Maybe you might try him out for a bit longer. You seem to fall madly in love at first sight and then it fizzles after a week. It takes time to get to know someone.'

'One of these days it won't fizzle and then, who knows?' Sophie eyes were wide with excitement.

'I hope.'

'I'll meet a guy and settle down, all sedate and sensible.'

'That would be great,' Liz said, with a smile.

'But Mum, it's not always about me. Many of them never call again. You've no idea what it's like out there. All sorts and sizes. Most of them are only interested in sex. That's it. Do the deal. If you don't want to jump into bed on the first night then they've moved on to someone else. That's why they disappear so quickly,' Sophie laughed.

'You must be picking the wrong type.'

'I'll have to draw up a questionnaire and get them to fill it in. Name, address, phone number, and intentions.'

'Don't you envy Brooke?'

'What do you mean? She envies me.'

'You're serious?'

'Yea, she told me.'

'When?'

'The other day.'

'How could that be? She has everything. Rory and the kids. A beautiful home. Plenty of money. What more could she want?' Liz exclaimed.

'She wants to be me.'

'I can't believe that.'

'It's true. I think she's a bit lonely without Rory.'

'It must be difficult for her, he travels so much.'

'The kids get her down, they're hard going.'

'I had three of you.'

'But you are *superwoman.*'

'Oh yea?' Liz pulled a face.

'And a great Mum.' Sophie squeezed her arm.

'Go on with you. I went from day to day on skates. Diving this way and that. Hanging on for dear life.'

'You did a good job. Am I not the perfect daughter?' Sophie asked.

'I've two perfect daughters and a perfect son, I'm so lucky to have you all.'

'Although you would like the eldest to finally choose a man and settle down?'

'Only if she wants to do that,' Liz said. 'I just want you to be happy.' She took her shopping bags out of the boot, and walked up the driveway.

'I'll open the door.' Sophie pushed her key into the lock.

Inside, Liz dropped the bags on a chair. Then she went into the living room.

There was a loud shout, and the crowd gathered inside yelled *surprise, surprise* and then launched into a strident version of *Happy Birthday*. Singing loud and long with all the extra bits.

Liz was overwhelmed when she saw them all. Immediately, they were around her. Kissing and hugging and giving her their very best wishes. Someone put a glass in her hand, and champagne was poured.

'To Liz,' they shouted and toasted her.

The house was packed with people. Family, friends and neighbours. Many people she hadn't seen in ages. They were everywhere. In the living room. The den. The kitchen. Chatting and laughing. Liz wandered, trying to catch up with everyone there. As she always insisted, gifts had to be very small, and the boxes and bags piled up on a side table. Brooke handed her a bouquet of flowers.

'Thank you, these are lovely.'

'Not from me though, they're from Chloe.'

'Pity she's so far away.' Liz felt emotional. Her sister lived in Canada and she hadn't seen her for a long time.

Her friend, Celine, pushed a small ribbon trimmed bag into her hands.

'Thank you,' Liz said, smiling.

'Go on, open it.'

Her other friends stood watching her expectantly.

She took a card from the envelope in the bag, and stared at it. 'Girls, this is too much,' she said. 'Ashford Castle?'

'We're all going away for a weekend to be pampered. It'll do you the power of good. You'll feel years younger.'

'Thanks so much.' She hugged them.

'Mum, Happy Birthday.' Her son Luke threw his arms around her. 'Sorry I'm late but the restaurant was packed tonight and I couldn't get away any earlier.' He handed her a small silver bag.

'Thanks so much.' She kissed him. 'You're very good to take time out of your busy night.'

'I can't stay long unfortunately.'

'Why don't you come around for lunch tomorrow?'

Luke threw himself one hundred percent into running La Modena restaurant with his business partner, Daniel. Liz had to admire them.

They were only open for the last year, and so far had yet to turn a profit. But they were talented young men, and both were determined to succeed.

Liz really enjoyed the party, much to her surprise. She had this fear of celebrating signature birthdays. Last time, she had the excuse of being away on business. But this year it had been sprung on her without warning. And as it had approached, she had suddenly begun to feel every bit of fifty. The big *five-o* which meant she was on her way down the hill. After this, sixty, seventy and then what? And would she even reach either of those decades? Would her body wear out much sooner? Thinking like that her single status was suddenly accentuated. Something which normally didn't bother her. She liked her own company these days. It was fourteen years since her husband Ethan had died. A sudden loss which swept the ground from under her feet and left her like a rudderless boat in a storm. At first she couldn't understand why she felt such loss. Their marriage wasn't close and even less so in the last couple of years. But to lose a partner, that person who shared everything with her, was harder than she expected. She had to reconstruct her life quickly, faced with the responsibility of raising her three children on her own.

Her friends suggested she should date someone. She was invited to dinner parties and an extra man always happened to be there. They refused to allow her to fade into the wallpaper. By now Celine was divorced, and glad of it. Megan was still married, just about. Leah was single, reluctantly. Liz didn't have a title for herself. Still she needed a tag line which she was sure the girls already had. She could imagine them saying, 'Liz is her own woman, and wants to stay that way.' They were right. But it sounded so dull. Was she dull?

'We think you have to turn over a new leaf,' Megan was now saying.

'What do you mean?'

'You should attempt challenges in this next decade,' she said with a grin. 'Particularly since you're the first one of us to reach the milestone of fifty.'

'You're not that far behind me.'

'We'll expect you to show us the way.'

'A new decade sounds so long.'

'All the better, gives you a chance to fit as much as you can into it.'

'And make the best of it,' added Leah.

'I'm very busy as it is, not much time left to include any more,' Liz laughed.

'There's a lot waiting around the corner for you. Let's go to see that medium I went to a few months ago. She was amazing,' Celine suggested.

'We all want to go.' The others were enthusiastic.

'She lives in Mullingar, we can stop off on our way to Mayo.'

'No girls, it's not for me.' Liz objected immediately.

'Come on, it will be fun.'

'I'm afraid.'

'What's to be afraid of? Aren't we all with you? We'll arrange it, and you can decide when you get there. How about that?'

'We're all going together anyway, so we'll hold your hand,' Megan said. 'Anyway, don't worry about it now. This is your night, so enjoy!'

## Chapter Three

Liz wandered around the house. There were still half full glasses tucked in unusual places, plates under tables, cutlery down the sides of cushions. Still, she was glad to have something to do. After all the company in the house the previous night there was a strange quiet about it, the rooms empty now, her footsteps echoing.

As she worked, she listened for other sounds. It was something which happened occasionally. Imagining the girls upstairs screaming with laughter. The blare of their favourite music being played too loud. Always too loud, she had complained. Doing the mother thing. In the kitchen the noise of pots and pans. Clinking and clanking. When he was young Luke spent his time in there. Cooking up all sorts of dishes. Most of them inedible at first. Although occasionally, he produced a rare treat. And that was wonderful. But her children had moved on and left her behind. Suddenly she wanted out. Into the fresh air. She pulled on a heavy jacket, and automatically picked up her camera as she passed the hall table.

She walked towards the sea. The day wasn't too cold for January. The breeze whirled tiny particles of moisture into her eyes and caught her straight dark hair as she followed a narrow track which meandered along. The house was built on a height although very few people came this way and she was surprised to see a man walking ahead of her. She didn't know who he was and wasn't inclined to get into conversation with a complete stranger. But unexpectedly he stopped and she was forced to do the same. He raised his arms and she could see him taking photographs. She bent her head and drew closer.

'Hi ...' he said.

She muttered a rude word to herself, but was left with no choice but to look at him.

He stared at her.

She went to pass.

'Liz?'

She stopped.

'Liz Sheeran?'

She was taken aback. It was a long time since anyone had used her maiden name.

'Scott ...Scott Fenton. Good to meet you again,' he smiled, and held out his hand. Automatically she took it and only then she recognised him. She knew his name, but thirty years had passed and he had changed. The thin gangly guy she knew at college was gone, replaced by a well-built man, his face fuller, hair shorter and sprinkled now with grey.

Liz stared at him with astonishment. 'What are you doing here?'

'My aunt died and I came up for the funeral,' he explained.

'I'm sorry to hear that.'

'She had been ill for a while.'

'It's always tough when you lose someone. My parents are both gone now.'

'Mine too.'

There was a pause for a few seconds. She felt awkward.

'I can't believe you're standing in front of me, such a surprise to meet you after all these years.' He touched her arm. It was just a soft sweep of his hand. The handshake had been perfunctory, but this was a renewal of friendship. And what that had meant in their youth. She stepped back a little. Feeling she was standing too close to him. He smiled, blue eyes dancing. 'My Liz.'

A giggle burst out of her and developed into a laugh. 'You're something else. I can't believe you even remember me.'

'Why wouldn't I? My first love. The woman who broke my heart.'

'I didn't break your heart surely?' Guilt swept through her.

'Oh yes.' He nodded.

Her eyes moistened. She couldn't help it. Always in tears at the slightest thing.

'What was it all about?' he asked.

'I don't even remember. Some row about Ethan I think,' she had to admit.

'He wanted to get me out of the way and you let him.'

'I'm sorry,' she was aware of a slight trace of bitterness in his voice and was saddened by his accusation.

'Liz, I'm so sorry for mentioning it. I shouldn't have. I can see I've upset you. The first time I meet you I put my big foot in it. Can you forgive me?'

'Old rows should be left in the past,' she smiled. 'Forgotten.'

'That's a relief,' he said with a smile, his voice more upbeat. 'I've just realised I'm probably delaying you.'

'No, I'm only going for a short walk.'

'Would you mind if I join you?'

She could have found some excuse. But didn't.

'What are you doing now, Liz?'

'I live up there, that red-bricked one.' She waved back in the direction of the house.

'It's in a wonderful position, such a view. My aunt's family live in Raheny and as it's a nice day I decided to take a drive out here.'

They walked along the path. Waves crashed on the rocks below, the sound musical.

'I live near the sea too,' he said softly. 'Kinsale.'

She didn't reply. Just stared down.

'I took a few photos,' he indicated the camera in his hand.

'I have mine as well, carry it everywhere with me.'

'I take most of my photos on the phone these days, and I don't often use a regular camera, I just happened to have it in the car.'

'We use digital in the business, this camera is my hobby.'

'The business?'

'Photography, my daughter Sophie and I work together.'

'It's an art, good photography. Where is your studio?'

'We're in Ranelagh, on the main street.'

They came down into Howth Village.

'Would you like to go somewhere? Maybe have a drink or a coffee?' he asked.

Liz hesitated. Unsure whether to accept or not. Would it be a step too far? There had been no men in her life since Ethan. Although she had an odd invitation over the years, she never had the interest or confidence to accept. But this was different. Scott had whirled her back in time to those days when he had been the only person who mattered to her. Their friendship had lasted from her first day in college and developed into love very quickly. They were inseparable until their final year. But that was when Ethan made his move. Taking over Scott's place in her life when he went to do further studies in engineering in England. While they had kept in contact by letter and phone, Scott's jealousy of Ethan signalled the end of what had been a beautiful relationship.

They went into a café. 'Do you still drink your coffee black?' he asked with a grin. 'And enjoy muffins for breakfast?'

She laughed. Through a veil of maturity youth was revealed in his face. In those few seconds she was drawn in and suddenly knew him again. The years contracted.

They talked then, reminiscing.

'I have to admit I missed you when we split,' he said. 'And you got married.'

'Ethan died quite a while ago.'

He seemed taken aback. 'I'm sorry to hear that, for your sake.'

'Tell me about yourself?' Liz asked.

'I got married and we had two sons. They're both involved in our company.'

'What business are you in?'

'Aircraft supplies.'

'Is your wife with you today?' she asked.

'We're separated. She left when the boys were young.'

'That was tough on you.'

'Yes, I suppose, but it was harder on the boys. They lost their mother.'

'She left without her children?'

He nodded.

'I can't believe that.'

'There was another man, although I only heard that in recent years from her mother.'

'I suppose my children had to get used to a single parent as well when Ethan died.'

'How many children have you?'

'Two girls, Sophie and Brooke and a son, Luke. I love them to bits.'

'How strange that both of us were in a similar position,' he said slowly. 'If only ...'

Her phone rang.

'Do you mind?' She took it out of her pocket and saw that it was Brooke.

'Not at all, take it.'

She went outside.

'Can you babysit this evening? Peggy can't come over,' Brooke asked.

'I'm out at the moment,' Liz said.

'Where are you?'

'Meeting a friend.'

There was silence at the other end of the line.

'Could Sophie help?' Liz asked.

'I can't get her on the phone.'

'What time do you need me?'

'If you could be here before five? We're going over to see friends.'

'But that only gives me half an hour.'

'If it's one of the girls, they won't mind.'

'All right,' Liz gave in, knowing somehow that it wouldn't be a good idea to mention she was having coffee with an old flame.

She went back into the cafe. 'I'm sorry, but I have to go. My daughter, Brooke, needs a babysitter urgently,' she explained to Scott.

'That's all right,' he stood up. 'I'll walk you back,' he offered.

'No thanks, I'm going to have to fly, sorry.' She was already at the door, creating a distance between them. Strangely glad of that.

But he kept up with her. 'It's been lovely to meet you again Liz, would you like to have dinner one evening?'

'I'm not sure,' she was about to say she didn't go out with men these days, but that sounded so odd she said nothing more.

'Maybe you might give me a call?' He took a business card from the top pocket of the navy jacket he wore.

'I must go,' she said, accepting it from him.

'I look forward to seeing you soon.' He reached and clasped her hand.

She pulled it away. 'Bye, thanks for coffee.'

## *Chapter Four*

The next time Sophie saw Max after their row, he stood at her door and handed her a colourful bunch of flowers.

'What are you doing here?' she demanded.

'I wanted to apologise, I just lost the head.'

'It was so embarrassing to have a row in front of my mother. And it was ridiculous too. I don't even know what it was all about. Anyway, I think I remembered that I said I didn't want to see you again.'

'I thought you might have calmed down. And anyway, I'm sure your mother has seen enough rows in her time.'

'I like to keep my private life private,' she snapped.

'I want to be part of your life.' He stepped into the hall. 'I love you.'

'You don't always show it.' She closed the door.

'Forgive me?' he smiled, in that disarming way of his. He was such an attractive guy, those blue eyes had made her heart leap in excitement that first time she had met him in Davy Byrnes.

'I'm seeing someone,' she said.

'Already?'

'Yea.'

'How could you do that?' He put his arms around her, and pulled her close to him. 'You know how I feel about you.'

'Max, please go. It's finished between us.'

'Let's just ignore what happened. We'll put it behind us. Please? I've missed you so much,' he whispered. 'Three long weeks without you. I thought I'd lost you.'

'You have lost me.'

'Don't say that.'

'It's the truth.'

'Give me another chance?' he begged, and got down on one knee.

'Get up, Max. You're being ridiculous.'

'I want you.'

'I'm not available. I told you already.'

'You're so cruel.' He seemed crushed.

She almost felt sorry for him, but stiffened her resolve. 'Please go.'

'I'll call you,' he said.

'Don't.' She opened the door. 'Out.'

He went through, head down. She stood watching as he made his way to the lift and pressed the button. He looked around at her, a sheepish look on his face, but she closed the door, threw the flowers into the bin and rushed to get ready for her date.

This guy was nice. Chatty. Easy going. They had a few beers in a quiet bar and he told her a lot about himself. Quite open really about his life, previous relationships, opinions on politics and his interests. He was into athletics, and trained regularly for marathons, travelling all over the world to participate. She was interested and later in the evening took him to a music venue to meet her friends. 'Are you into rock?' she shouted as she lead the way through the people gathered inside.

He grinned. She didn't know whether it was a yes or a no but went on down to the bar which was pumping with the sound of heavy metal music, a large crowd in here as well. She put her hand back and grabbed his as she pushed through searching for her friends. Eventually she found them in their usual corner swaying and singing along to the song that was being blasted out of the speakers. Her best friend Robyn threw her arms around her as soon as she appeared, followed by Lucy and some other people they knew, all of them had had quite a few drinks by this stage.

'I'll get the beers.' She shouted in his ear.

He shook his head, pointed to himself and disappeared in the direction of the bar.

The girls crowded around her.

'Who's he?' Robyn asked, using simple sign language. The music was at such a pitch they often had to rely on communicating in that way when down here. Having a regular conversation with anyone was impossible.

Later, they all came back to Sophie's apartment.

'Help yourselves to a drink if you want, it's in the kitchen.' She sat down on the couch. Lucy passed her a tablet. She didn't even know what it was but certainly she preferred something like that rather than any more beer or vodka at this time of the night. Someone told a joke and then one led to another. They laughed wildly. She put on a CD. The music boomed out but she immediately turned the level down, careful not to have the volume too loud. She was on the top floor and knew the neighbours on either side were away so wasn't too worried about noise. They danced and she let herself go with the heavy rock rhythm.

'Where's your guy?' Robyn asked when she took a breather.

'I don't see him.' Sophie looked around.

'A few people have left.'

'Must have gone.' She shrugged.

'He didn't say goodnight?'

'No.'

'Pain in the ass. He was a bit too quiet for you, Sophie.'

She was disappointed. He was nice, different. She wouldn't have minded another date with him.

'Let's dance.' Lucy jumped up.

What of it, Sophie thought. There are plenty more where he came from.

## Chapter Five

In the kitchen of La Modena Luke barked out directions. The sous chef sizzled a small fillet of beef on a pan. One of the commis chefs prepared a mix of red and yellow peppers. Another plated up the various dishes which had been ordered by the diners. It was busy this evening and there was a general air of frenzy about the place. Presentation and service was everything to Luke. He had trained in various Michelin starred restaurants, doing stints in London, New York and Paris, and it was his dream that La Modena would achieve the same level of excellence. He let a shout out to one of the commis chefs who was presenting a dish which was not quite to his satisfaction. He went over, grabbed the plate and threw the contents into the nearest bin. The young man began all over again as fast as he could.

Luke's partner, Daniel, ran front of house and between the two of them they offered a varied menu most of which had a basis in French cooking. He came in, and had a look at the list of orders still unfulfilled. Luke raised his arms in the air and shrugged. Then he checked the plates which were ready, and gave them the seal of approval. The waiters picked them up and rushed out through the swing doors, followed by Daniel.

The business was mostly done at the weekend. The numbers of people who came in during the week was small, and it was very difficult for Luke to know exactly how much food he should order, and often he was forced to throw it away because it wasn't quite as fresh as he liked. Luke's standards were very high, and it was the source of many an argument with Daniel lately.

'We're not doing the turnover,' Daniel complained one night when they returned home. It was after one o'clock and they were both exhausted.

'We're only a year in business, it'll take time,' Luke said, opened a bottle of red wine and poured a glass.

Daniel made himself a cup of coffee. 'The bank account isn't looking very healthy,' he pointed out. 'I don't know if we'll manage to pay the staff next week.'

'What?' Luke exploded.

'I told you last week.'

'How could that be? We've had a couple of great weekends.'

'But think of how much the staff have to be paid not to mention ourselves. Then there are the basic costs, bank loan, rent for the building, rent for equipment, rates, insurance, light, heat, phone, etc. Our food is very expensive, all Irish and organic. The wines we serve are quality, and our margins are narrow.'

'Maybe we might have to get by with less waiting staff,' Luke said.

'But that affects the service which is one of the assets of the restaurant.'

'What do you suggest then?'

'Maybe cut back in the kitchen.'

'No way, I can't manage in the kitchen without a full complement.'

'I suppose I could do a little more myself. Give the part-timers less hours.'

'Then when we want them they won't be available.'

'We could reduce our own salaries.'

'How would we live then?' Luke asked.

'And we're trying to save for the wedding,' Daniel added.

'We haven't chosen a date yet. Maybe we should use that money for the business, it might get us over the hump. How much have we in the fund?' Luke asked.

'About fifteen thousand.'

'Great, that'll cover the wages bill for a while.'

'But it's for the wedding.'

'We'll be able to start saving again later, don't worry about it. We can get married down the line, it doesn't have to be this year.' Luke was dismissive.

Daniel looked crushed.

Luke didn't seem to be aware of that. He lay on the couch and stared up at the ceiling rolling a mouthful of wine in his mouth as if he were a wine taster and would spit it out any moment and pronounce how good or bad it was.

'What if we closed mid-week and just opened at weekends?' Daniel suggested.

'It won't do our reputation any good. It will be obvious we're having problems.'

'Who are we worried about? The public or other restauranteurs?'

'We won't get a *Michelin Star* if we're only offering a partial service.'

'We won't get a star if we're out of business.'

'We'll work our way through it, you'll see, and we can start by getting rid of some of the waiting staff.'

'So I have to carry the can?'

'Spread the available hours around,' Luke suggested. 'Maybe none of them will have to go. And do a bit more waiting yourself.'

'Thanks.' Daniel finished his coffee, stood up and left the room.

'Hey?' Luke followed him upstairs. 'Don't be so ...this will just be a temporary thing.'

'You've changed,' Daniel accused.

'I have not,' Luke said.

In the bedroom they stood staring at each other.

'The business is affecting everything else in our lives. We're not the same,' Daniel said.

'What do you mean?'

'I feel we're going in two different directions. It's all work. Our personal lives are gone. Can you even remember when we've been out for an evening? Just the two of us, alone?' Daniel asked.

'We have to make sacrifices. A business like this is extremely demanding.'

'I hope it's worth it.'

'It will be, give us another few months and we'll be coining it. We've already built up a good base of patrons and all we have to do is to keep them happy and talking about us. That's what it's all about, word of mouth.'

'I suppose.' Daniel seemed down.

'Maybe we should borrow some more working capital from the bank,' Luke suggested.

'No, we'd be stretched trying to repay that on top of everything else.'

'You're too cautious, Dan.'

'You take too many chances, Luke,' he laughed.

'Opposites attract and that's why we work well together.' Luke put his arms around Daniel. They stood there, holding close. 'It will work out, don't worry so much.'

## Chapter Six

Celine's car was ticking over in the driveway. Liz climbed into the back beside Megan, and clicked on the seatbelt.

'Right, have we all got everything? No last minute requests? Visits to the loo? Drinks of water?' Celine asked.

'No, Miss,' they chorused.

'Right, we're off,' she pressed the accelerator and drove out of the gate.

'Does the GPS woman know where we are going?' Leah asked.

'Of course she does. But I have a fair idea myself. It's a bit out of the way, but once I remember the turns we should find it.'

'You made the appointment with the medium?'

'Of course I have.'

'Will we all go in together? Or one by one?' asked Liz.

'It's a group sitting. I thought it would be more fun and then we can all remember things about each other's experience.'

'I thought we would be on our own with her,' murmured Liz.

'No, and that means it won't be so scary. Anyway, she won't say anything nasty.'

Liz didn't want to meet with this medium at all but was reluctant to spoil the weekend for the girls.

'It will be fun.' Megan poked her with a pointy elbow.

'I'm looking forward to making contact with someone from the other side,' Celine said in a low gloomy voice.

'Stop that,' Liz ordered.

'Do you believe in the spirit world?' Leah asked.

'I do,' Megan replied promptly.

'This woman is good,' Celine said. 'She's a lovely person and does healing and cleansing and it's all very spiritual. I won't explain too much, you'll see for yourselves. But you have to take it very seriously, there can be no giggling.'

'And did you speak with a spirit?' asked Liz.

'My mother.'

They fell silent.

'I told you that, don't you remember?'

'I do, but I didn't want to know about it at the time. I seem to recall shutting you up very quickly.'

'Do you ever see a spirit? Would a ghost appear?' Leah asked.

'I didn't, but I think people can.'

Liz shivered.

'Keep your camera at the ready, if one of us is communicating with a spirit then the camera might pick up the image.'

'I'm sure she wouldn't allow that.'

'We can ask,' giggled Megan.

'I'll be so terrified I probably couldn't even focus the camera.' Liz shivered.

'It'll be fun. It's all part of our weekend. Now let me concentrate on the road.'


A short time later they were standing outside a large detached bungalow. Celine rang the doorbell. Liz felt very nervous now, and actually had a crazy urge to go back and sit in the car. But she didn't get a chance as the door opened and a pleasant middle-aged woman stood smiling at them.

Celine introduced them to Niamh and she shook hands with each in turn. 'Come in, it's lovely to see you all. A cup of tea or coffee after your journey might be just what you need,' she said. 'I'll take your coats, and if you want to use the bathroom over there please do. Now I'm just going to put on the kettle. Come on in to the kitchen when you're ready.'

Liz was amazed. It certainly wasn't what she expected. This person was so ordinary. The decor in the house was modern, minimalist. Just lovely. She didn't feel so nervous now. Niamh brought them through into the kitchen and invited them to sit down around a large natural wood table. Poured tea and coffee, and cut generous slices of fruit cake.

When they had finished, Niamh stood up and went to a door off the kitchen. 'I do my group readings in here.'

They followed her.

The room was furnished with a number of easy chairs and a table covered by a dark cloth. Light was provided by the soft glow of lamps and flickering candles. There were two packs of cards on the table. In the background, Liz could hear a hint of music with an oriental tone.

Niamh sat at the table. 'I'm sure Celine has told you how I work, but I'll just run through a few things. I do different kinds of spiritual healing, so if there are any health problems I can focus on them and channel energy to you which helps healing. Spiritual cleansing can deal with negatives in your life. If you want to leave behind something which has caused you some distress this method of cleansing is good. Then there is the communication with the spirit world. I can't always choose to talk to a particular person, but often the spirits sense who is here and make their own contact through me.'

Liz was anxious to say that she didn't really want to participate, but somehow didn't get the opportunity as Niamh had closed her eyes and seemed to have begun the session. Liz was afraid to even look at any of the others who all sat quietly watching and listening. There was no question of anyone laughing under these circumstances.

Suddenly, Niamh spoke. 'I have Anna here. She's looking for Megan.'

Liz stiffened and clasped her hands tightly together. There was an increased air of tension in the room.

'That's my grandmother,' Megan whispered, and burst into tears. Celine put her arm around her.

Niamh sighed deeply. She said nothing else for a while.

Liz hoped that this was the end of it. She longed to get out of the

27

place.

'Anna says that she's happy. You should look after yourself, and she'll be watching out for you,' Niamh said.

Megan nodded, distraught.

Then Niamh spoke again, in a rather rough gravelly voice, deeper than before.

## *Chapter Seven*

Scott Fenton had a narrow life, or so he thought himself. Since his wife, Ciara, had left him he had met various women from time to time over the years but he had never fallen in love again and a relationship without love just didn't appeal to him. His own family used to suggest that his boys needed a mother, and that he was just being selfish, but he could never have asked someone to live with him for the express reason of looking after his children. It wouldn't be fair on any of them. So they remained a threesome. His next door neighbour offered to look after the boys with her own children while he was at work. The boys seemed happy enough about that, and he was very grateful to her. In the early years he often talked about Ciara just to remind them of her, and kept the family photographs in the same position they had always been.

Ciara had left him without warning. The letter she wrote was very brief.

*Scott,*
*I am leaving you and going to live somewhere else.*
*Ciara.*

In the days following it was tough going. The boys were inconsolable. Ryan was three years old, and Cathal was four, and every night they cried for her. Refusing to sleep in their own beds, both of them in the large double with Scott. It was that way for years.

All the time they asked for her. Little voices alternating. He could never get the sound out of his head.

'Where is Mam?'

'Why did she go away?'

'Dad, is she in town?'

'Is she at Gran's?'

'When is Mam coming back?'

'Will she be here tomorrow?'

'The next day?'

'Soon?'

They spent their time looking out of the windows. Often imagining that they saw her outside.

'There she is.' Cathal would rush to the door. 'Let me out.' He reached for the handle, usually followed by Ryan. But there was always disappointment.

'Boys, it's not Mam,' Scott would say gently.

They took little notice of him, broken-hearted.

On and on it went. Day after day. And it was months before he noticed that they began to stop asking quite so often about Ciara.

He didn't want them to forget her. But knew that if she wasn't going to come back into their lives those boys would have to grow up without her. Which they did. There was never a call, or a card or any contact whatsoever. He often asked her mother, Kathleen, if she knew where Ciara was living, but the boys were grown up before she told him that Ciara was living with a man in London. When he tried to persuade her to give him the address, she always closed up.

He often wondered if the boys would enquire about their mother when they were older, but there was never a mention and he said nothing either. Was that decision wrong? Should he have talked about her more often and asked them if they would like him to make enquiries as to her whereabouts? That question haunted him. Now the boys were strong independent young men in their twenties and involved in the business. He was glad that they were both interested in working with him. The company needed young men at the peak of their careers who would bring new blood into it and regenerate.

Then yesterday he had met Liz again. Such a shock to see this woman he had known so long ago. She was hardly changed. The dark hair style was shorter, and hugged her classic features. The soft fringe framed her large brown eyes. She was still as beautiful as that first day he saw her.

## *Chapter Eight*

Sophie stared at Brooke. Shocked. 'I don't believe it.'

'It's true. I've been suspicious for ages, and knew there was something going on.' She dabbed her eyes with a tissue.

'But Rory of all people, he loves you to bits. What possessed him to go off with someone else? Who is she, anyway, the bitch?'

'A colleague.' Brooke was bitter.

'The old story.'

'They're so much together. She travels with him occasionally to meetings and I don't know whether she needs to do that or he brings her along so that the two of them can have a bit of fun together.'

'Has he told you he's leaving?'

'Last night. After I had put Cian and Jess to bed, and we had dinner.'

'What did he say exactly?' Sophie asked.

'Just that he was going to move in with her.' She sniffled.

'Has he gone?'

'He went straight upstairs, packed a bag, and left.'

Sophie was silenced for a minute. Then she hugged Brooke. 'I don't know what to say to you. I'm no help.'

'Thanks for coming over, it's so good to see you. I don't know how I'm going to get through this. I'm dying for a cigarette. I'll have to go out and buy some. I didn't sleep a wink last night. I took the kids to play school and collected them and couldn't even talk to anyone. I've had a couple of texts from my friends who were wondering what's going on with me but I haven't been able to explain. I hate the thought of people finding out. Imagine telling Mum? She's going to have a fit.

She won't understand how I could let something like that happen.'

'It wasn't your fault. Anyway, Rory could just suddenly realise that he's done something really stupid and that your woman isn't quite so attractive when he's living with her, and has to look at her across a desk as well. He'll begin to feel very trapped in no time. Bet you anything. If he came back all contrite and said he didn't realise what he was doing and how much he's going to miss you and the kids, would you forgive him?'

'I don't know.'

Sophie was very upset for Brooke. While she had questioned her own experience with men, for Rory to have walked out on a marriage so suddenly was something she couldn't have imagined. Sophie had had some long term relationships, but none of those men had moved in on a permanent basis although she had been tempted once or twice. Now she was glad she hadn't taken the plunge.

## Chapter Nine

'Do you think we've received a bad review?' Luke asked.

'Possibly.'

'It might be on line, a blog perhaps?'

'I'm going to look.' Daniel opened up the laptop and googled the restaurant.

Various reports and reviews came up on the pages but there was nothing to indicate the cause of any change in the business.

'Are we getting repeat bookings? Is there some way we could check that?' Daniel asked.

'Maybe go through the diary?'

'That would be very tedious.'

'From now on, let's ask if they've been with us before, chat and do the PR thing.'

'Good idea. It can't do any harm.'

'Maybe we should discontinue the lunch time sitting?' Luke sat on the couch with a deep sigh.

'We need to do as much turnover as possible. We've reduced our staff costs but that doesn't seem to have worked. And even some of the wedding money has already been sucked up. It won't last long at this rate.'

'And I still haven't come out to my family,' Luke said.

'How do you think they'll react?'

'The girls will be all right about it, but I'm not sure about Mum.'

'But she's quite broadminded, isn't she?'

'You know what mothers are like about their only sons,' Luke grimaced.

'Do you think any of them have guessed?'

'I don't know, they've never said.'

'Maybe you should drop the bomb regardless, then we can be more open. And if we decide to get married then everyone will be delighted for us. I know my crowd will.'

'I dread it.'

'Don't be a wimp.'

'Every time I think about bringing up the subject I feel sick. I try to imagine what I might say to Mum, and just have a blank.'

'You can't prepare for it. You just have to pick your moment and then go for it. That's what I did.'

Luke hadn't admitted to Daniel exactly how worried he was about coming out. They both worked so hard there simply wasn't time for much more, and it was easy to push the subject off his agenda. But he loved this man and knew that he wasn't going to wait forever. Daniel found their relationship restrictive, and longed to be able to walk along the street holding hands, and kissing openly if they felt like it. For Luke, that was out of the question. Weirdly, he was almost glad that they needed to put the money Daniel had saved for the wedding into the business. It pushed their marriage plans further down the road and gave him more time to pluck up enough courage to tell his family.

## Chapter Ten

Liz sat there, her heart racing. Candles glimmered in combinations of reds, golds, and purples, creating shadows which danced around the room.

'I have someone here who wants to talk to you, Liz,' Niamh said.

She was speechless with fright.

'His name is, I can't quite catch, it's unusual.'

Liz listened but really didn't understand what she was saying as the woman's voice was so husky.

'There are a number of other people here too, a woman wants to talk to Leah. She says she is your Auntie Kathleen.'

Leah seemed frozen.

'The man for Liz is back. His name is Ethan. Do you know a person by that name?' She was breathing deeply now, and the sound filled the room. *'Liz? It's me.'* Niamh's voice was loud and she sounded as if she was going to choke.

*'You have a chance for a new life.'* The woman's breathing increased in volume.

Liz was immobile. Like a statue. Her brain in a state of shock.

*'Take it,'* Niamh said, bent her head and held it in her hands. She stayed in that position for quite a while.

The girls waited silently. Eventually Niamh raised her head up. Tears coursed down her cheeks.

'I'm sorry, it is very emotional for me to talk to the people who love you. He was so anxious I had to let him in. There were relatives for you too,' she said to Celine. 'But I did not have the energy to talk to them.

Come back to me another time and then I promise you that I will help you to meet them again.'

They sat into the car, silent. Celine turned on the ignition, and they snapped on their seatbelts. 'That was something else girls, wasn't it? Being together was even more powerful than when I was there on my own.'

'Imagine she talked to my aunt,' Leah whispered. 'I don't know what my mother is going to say. She won't believe it.'

'And Liz, Ethan actually spoke through Niamh, how do you feel about that?' Celine asked.

'It was so frightening.' Tears filled Liz's eyes.

'I think she's genuine. How could she know Ethan's name? It's certainly unusual.' Celine hadn't driven off yet.

'I'm stunned, I can't believe it.'

'What do you think Ethan meant by saying you had another chance? And that you should take it. Was that what he said or have I got it wrong?' Megan asked.

'No, it was something like that. What does it mean to you, Liz?' Leah asked excitedly.

'Not much,' she said. 'I can't help being sceptical.'

'Come on, it must mean something.'

'Maybe it will happen in the future?' Megan asked.

'Let's get going,' Celine said, and pulled away from the house.

Liz looked out over Lough Corrib, the water sparkling in winter sunshine. 'It's so beautiful here.'

'And wait till you see the castle, it will be coming into view any minute now.'

'I'm looking forward to this,' Megan said, her eyes sparkling.

'Three days of utter luxury,' Leah sighed, leaning back in her seat. 'Let me at it.'

'There's the castle,' Celine was excited as she turned into the avenue.

'It's wonderful.'

'Thirteenth century.'

'Imagine what it was like in those days.'

'Soldiers on duty on the battlements, watching out for the enemy. Others on horseback. Prancing about. Lords and ladies taking the air wearing wonderful clothes. Satins. Laces. Gold. Silver.'

'That's us.'

They were welcomed by a uniformed porter, checked in quickly and were brought upstairs in the lift to their room. A suite with two bedrooms.

'Let's draw lots to see who shares with who.'

'I don't mind, but I do love this red one.' Liz wandered into the first large room.

'That's your choice then, *birthday girl,* I'll share with you.' Celine followed her.

'Leah and I will sleep in the blue room,' Megan said, posing in front of the cheval mirror.

'I feel we should wear medieval clothes, just to match the rooms.'

Leah threw herself on the chaise longue dramatically.

'Hey, champagne and chocolates,' Liz spotted the ice bucket on a side table.

'I'll open it.' Megan pulled the cork with a pop and poured four glasses of bubbly.

'To a great weekend and a happy birthday to Liz,' Celine raised her glass.

'Let's check out the castle, search for secret passages, go down into the dungeons,' Megan suggested.

'I'm keen to have a look around the spa, does anyone else feel like a swim?'

'My hair will be a mess.' Megan ran her fingers through her short blonde hair.

'They do a great afternoon tea here, it's delicious.'

'I'm hoping to lose a few pounds in the spa, so no cakes for me,' Liz said firmly.

'It's going to be a gorgeous experience,' Celine said.

'Let's hope the masseur will be a fabulous hunk,' Megan grinned.

'I'm looking forward to it.'

'This must have cost you the earth girls, I must pay my share,' Liz insisted.

'It's your birthday present, do you think we're going to let you fork out?' Megan scoffed.

'But it's so expensive here.' She waved around at the opulent surroundings. The heavy gold silk damask drapes and beautiful antique furniture were magnificent, but most of all the view from the windows over the lake was something else.

'We're splashing out, a once off, and we're going to enjoy ourselves, so no more talk about paying?' Celine hugged Liz.

'Thanks so much girls, you're amazingly generous.'

'We just want you to enjoy yourself.'

'I will, don't worry,' Liz assured them. The experience with the medium was still in the back of her mind, but she tried to forget it, convincing herself that Niamh was a fraud, had to be.

## Chapter Eleven

Scott parked on a side street, and walked back into Ranelagh. He hadn't heard anything from Liz, but since they had met again he couldn't get her out of his head. So when he had a business meeting in Dublin, he had decided to call to the studio in the hope of seeing her again. He had checked the address on the website, and found the corner shop close to the turn for Appian Way, with a series of dramatic black and white and colour photos in the windows. He pushed open the door suddenly realising that he didn't know what he was going to say to Liz if she happened to be there. A bell rang and a girl appeared. Immediately he knew that here was her daughter. She was so like Liz it was uncanny. That same dark hair and eyes. He was taken aback.

'Can I help you?' she smiled.

'I called in some time ago and talked to Liz.' He was making it up as he went along. 'I want to have some photographs taken, and she said I could make an appointment.'

'Why certainly, she'll be here next week, probably Tuesday.'

'Could you give me her number please? I'd like to talk to her.'

'I can make an appointment now if you like?'

'I do have to check with the family so maybe you might give me a card and I will phone?'

'Certainly, here you are.' She handed it to him. 'And this is a brochure which will give you an idea of what we do.'

'Thank you, I'll be in touch.'

'We look forward to that.'

He left. Disappointed that Liz hadn't been there. Outside, he glanced at the business card. There were two numbers there, the studio landline and Sophie's mobile. A pity, he thought, no number for Liz.

He drove to Raheny and called in to see his uncle for an hour before heading back to Cork. As soon as he arrived into the office he was immediately caught up with what was happening. It was busy, a huge demand for the aircraft parts they produced in the factory which were exported all over the world.

'Dad? I was looking for you earlier.' Cathal appeared in his office.

'Sorry, I had something to do this morning.'

'Could you have a look at this order for Brazil. There are some items which we still cannot supply, and we want to bang heads together in the UK because they're holding us up at their end. We've committed ourselves by a certain date on the contract so Brazil have already been on the rant.'

Scott was immediately in business mode. It was what he enjoyed most and for now at least Liz was pushed to the back of his mind and he could concentrate on something else. But she was still there in the background. He didn't know whether she had any interest in knowing him again, but hope had escalated almost within minutes of talking to her and he had been swept back into the past when he had loved her so much. Now he decided to write to her, and took a sheet of his personal notepaper from the drawer.

*Dear Liz,*
*It was great to meet you recently. Since then memories have swept back, clear as if it was yesterday. I'd love to meet you again and maybe we could spend a little longer together this time.*
*I look forward to hearing from you.*
*Scott.*

He posted it the same day before he began to have any doubts as to whether he should have written at all.

## *Chapter Twelve*

Brooke listened for the car engine but the narrow road on which they lived was silent. She still hoped to hear Rory's key in the lock, but time passed and she lay there sleepless, knowing that she was fooling herself. She hadn't seen or heard from him since he had walked out and it was obvious that he wasn't coming back. Tears filled her eyes and she turned to lie on his side of the bed. Emotionally she was a wreck. It was so hard to put a brave face out to the world. Her sister, Sophie, was still the only person she had told and she was very supportive, calling around regularly to see her, but it was obvious that she couldn't do anything to help other than to give her encouragement.

While she needed that, there were practical things to take into account too. Rory had a very well paid job and Brooke hadn't needed to work but now the money in her bank account was diminishing and she would have to insist that he support her and the children.

In the morning she rang him and to her relief he answered immediately.
'Rory?'
'Yea?'
'It's me,' she said.
'I know who it is,' he snapped.
'I need to talk to you.'
'About?'
'The children.'
There was silence.
'They miss you and I miss you.'

He said nothing.

'When will I see you?'

'I don't know.'

'But Cian and Jess don't understand where you are.'

'Tell them I'm away, they'll get used to it.'

'It's not fair on them.'

'You wanted the kids, not me, so now you have them don't ask me to be responsible.'

'I thought you wanted them as well.' Tears welled up in her eyes.

'I suppose the idea of having kids was attractive, but then they arrive and it's all that squealing and bawling, drives me mad.'

'They love you.'

'I know they do.'

'Couldn't you come over this evening?'

He sighed.

'Please?'

'All right, I'll try.'

'Thanks. Will you have dinner with us?'

'No, don't bother cooking. I'll just drop in for a few minutes.'

'I could do tandoori chicken, you like that.'

'There's no need. I won't be staying long.'

'Come before the kids go to bed, they'll want to see you.'

'If I can, but I must go now.'

He was gone, and she stared at her phone. Left wondering why.

Brooke spent the day cleaning. Since Rory had left home, her mood had been such that she simply couldn't motivate herself and the condition of the house showed that. Now she wanted everything to be spic and span. Dressed the children in their best clothes and herself too. She had this idea that she was in competition with that bitch, and was determined to win. She would get him back from her. A sudden resolve swept through her, and she was strengthened.

But the waiting was difficult. Time crawled by. She cooked the dinner and made his favourite dessert of ginger pudding. Even opened a bottle of red wine. Everything was ready. She gave the children their tea. But didn't eat herself. It was six o'clock. Six thirty. Seven o'clock. She was impatient. Where are you, Rory? You promised you'd be here for the kids. She muttered to herself, becoming angry. She was about to call him on his phone when she heard the key turn in the front door lock. She rushed down the hall. 'Rory?'

He went straight ahead of her into the playroom. The two children rushed towards him. 'Daddy, Daddy.' They threw their arms around him.

He lifted Jess into his arms and Cian clung to him. 'Daddy, lift me up.'

'All right,' he smiled.

At least his attitude towards the kids was the way it should be between a father and his children. As for herself, his expression when he came in was hostile to say the least.

'I'm going to take you two up to bed now.' He lifted Cian as well and went upstairs with both of them in his arms.

Brooke followed.

In the twins' bedrooms, there was much fun between them as the kids resisted being put to bed. Suddenly, Brooke felt it was like any normal evening. Maybe he had changed his mind about leaving? Perhaps it hadn't worked out with that one. She hated even saying her name.

'Right. Lights off.'

'Daddy, Daddy,' Jess screamed excitedly. 'Tell me a story.'

'I can't, I haven't time.' He waved at her from the door. 'Night, Jess.'

'Go to sleep,' Brooke kissed her.

She hated leaving them like this, they were high as kites and probably wouldn't sleep. But she needed to talk with Rory and try to persuade him to give them another chance.

She followed him downstairs. 'Will you have dinner?'

'I told you not to bother. I'm not hungry.'

'A glass of wine?'

'I'm driving.'

'At least sit down for a while, I want to talk with you,' Brooke said gently, her hand brushing his, using all her persuasive wiles.

But he just stood and crossed his arms.

She took a deep breath. 'It's about practical things, I have very little money in my account.'

'I pay the mortgage, the insurance, electricity, gas, pretty well most of the utilities. There's not a lot left for you to cover.'

'I have to feed and clothe the kids, and myself as well.' She hated this. 'And there is the jeep, diesel and other things too. I just don't have enough.'

'You'll have to get out there and work.'

'That's not easy. It's difficult with the children, I could only work part-time.'

'So you expect me to pay for everything?'

'I could try to find work, but in the meantime I must have money, I have nothing to live on.'

'I'll give you something to tide you over but I'm not going to continue giving you money. You'll have to make an effort to earn some yourself. I'll transfer five hundred euro into your account tomorrow but you'll have to make that last. Apart from the mortgage and utilities there will be nothing more, after this you're on your own.' He turned on his heel and walked down the hall. 'I'll call around later in the week and pick up the rest of my stuff,' he stated bluntly, opened the door and closed it behind him, leaving her gasping with shock.

## Chapter Thirteen

Sophie sipped her beer, and danced to the rhythm of the music. Tonight there was a big crowd in the bar and they were listening to a live band playing. Her friends gathered around her. They shared some Ecstasy tablets.

'I love the drummer, look how his eyes roll in his head, and that hair, he's amazing,' Robyn shouted, waving her arms in the air.

Lucy joined in.

'Hey girls, how's it going?' A group of guys pushed their way through.

Introductions were shouted and Sophie found her hand being grabbed by a tall lanky guy. 'I'm Josh,' he shouted into her ear.

'Sophie,' she did the same.

'Good to meet you.'

She nodded with a grin.

More drinks were ordered.

Josh took her hand and brought her towards the back of the bar where the noise wasn't quite so loud. 'That's a bit better,' he gulped his beer.

'Yea.'

'They're a great band, I know the lead singer.'

'Are you into music yourself, do you play an instrument?' Sophie was interested.

'I strum guitar. A few friends and I had a group but it was difficult to keep it going with people going off to work in various places.'

'What was the name?'

'*Cool Dudes,*' he laughed. 'Although there's nothing much happening at the moment, we're defunct.'

'Pity.'

The rest of the crowd gathered around them. Singing loudly to the number the band played. Sophie really enjoyed herself. They came out of there later and headed over to a late night place for coffee and burgers. That kept them going. Josh stayed with her, and they found out a good deal about each other over the night. He was a pharmacist and worked in the family business. A profession which didn't really match his rather rough appearance which consisted of scruffy jeans, trainers, and a black shirt. But there was something attractive about him which she liked. So she was delighted when he asked for her number.

Sunday was her lie-in day, and it was after one when she finally surfaced. She texted Liz and hoped she was enjoying her weekend in Ashford Castle. She was delighted that her friends had arranged it for her. She smiled to herself thinking about that fellow she had met last night. He was quite nice, she thought, although she had preferred the previous guy more. She had liked Max at first too, the man before him, but had tired of him after that row they had. Why did she meet so many guys who only stayed in her life for a short time? Ships that pass in the night. Just a couple of dates if that even happened. Mostly, they met once and she heard no more. One night stands. Her friends were the same. Enjoying the excitement of sex with someone new. While Robyn and Lucy hadn't much interest in permanent relationships, Sophie was tired of the casual nature of hers. Now she wondered if her approach frightened them off? What was she doing wrong?

But Sophie didn't ponder for too long on these questions which probably had been prompted by her chat with Liz on that day they were in town together. She was a happy person and things generally didn't get her down. That afternoon she headed out for a run, doing an easy few kilometres along the coast road, forgetting all about the men she had met recently, persuading herself that she would meet the right guy when she was least expecting it.

## Chapter Fourteen

Liz lay on the bed in the treatment room as the therapist gave her a facial. This morning she had enjoyed a full body massage, and now she felt absolutely wonderful. Such an experience. According to the brochure, this place was a sanctuary of calm and contentment where the cares of the world could be forgotten. And as they promised, Liz had put everything out of her mind and enjoyed being pampered.

'How do you feel, Liz?' the girl asked softly as she cleansed her skin once more.

'Really good, thanks,' she murmured.

'I'm going to use some aromatic elixirs of herbs to re-energise your skin and you will feel amazing.'

When they met later the girls swopped stories, all of them vowing that they would make this a regular thing.

'We need to pamper ourselves,' Celine reminded. 'Us girls deserve it.'

'Particularly the one who's on the way down the hill,' Liz said, laughing.

'We're all heading that way. Who's next?' Megan looked around at them suspiciously.

'I'm December,' Leah said.

'I'm next year, and I'm not even going to mention the month,' Celine said, with a wide grin.

'I think we all know it already,' Liz laughed.

'It's unlucky to even say it.'

'And I'm the youngest of us all. The baby. The lucky one,' Megan stared at herself in the mirror and preened. 'I'm only twenty something. Born on the twenty-ninth of February, you'll be old age pensioners when I reach fifty.'

'Seriously though, we're lucky to be able to enjoy our lives the way we do. I've my two and they keep me on my toes. We've got jobs which means we can stay somewhere like this without breaking the bank. But what's ahead of us all? That's the question. Liz is the first one of us who has reached the milestone and she'll have to report back and warn us of all the pitfalls up ahead,' Celine said.

'Megan is the only one who has a husband who supports her.'

'But the big question for me is when am I going to find a man?' Leah asked.

'You don't need a man, Leah. Celine and I are perfectly happy as single women. We have our own independence, and that's everything,' Liz pointed out.

'Yes, life is good. We're all so lucky. We have our health and that is the most important thing of all,' Celine added.

'I suppose that is true,' Leah agreed.

'Let's lighten up, girls, I saw a couple of guys in the foyer,' Megan giggled.

'Were they taking treatments?'

'I don't know, but men do have facials and massage too. And a lot of them use cosmetics. Moisturising creams. Day cream. Night cream. Have their eyebrows tinted. Wax their bodies from top to toe. And tan. They enjoy looking after themselves as much as we do.'

'What did those guys look like?' Leah asked.

'Not bad,' she said, with a grin.

'Right girls, glam up, tonight's the night for a bit of diversion,' Celine announced.

'I feel a million dollars.' Megan stretched her arms above her head.

'I'm massaged to within an inch of my life,' Liz smiled.

'It's been fantastic,' Leah said.

'I feel years younger,' Celine breathed.

'My skin is as smooth as silk.'

'Let's come back next week,' Celine suggested.

'Yea, and take a loan out to cover it,' Liz said, laughing.

'I'm going to save up until I have enough money.'

'And we can go to see Niamh on the way again. That session was amazing, wasn't it? I couldn't believe how the spirit of Ethan spoke through her.' Leah hugged a white velvet robe around her.

'Have you any idea what Ethan meant when he spoke to you through the medium?' Celine asked.

Liz shook her head.

'What did he say again?'

'I can't remember.' She shrugged. 'And I don't want to talk about it, girls, I'm going to shower and change, what about the rest of you?' Liz went into the bedroom.

It was their second night, and they were determined to make the most of it. They ordered another bottle of champagne and later they went down to the bar. To their surprise the two men Megan had seen earlier in the day were already there, and before long they were chatting, and accepted their invitation to join them for dinner. It was a very pleasant evening and rounded off the weekend. The following day they left after lunch, did some sightseeing in the area, and headed home.

Liz went into the house. She felt ill at ease and was surprised at that. She should have been over the moon after such a wonderful weekend, but wasn't, somehow.

She made herself a cup of coffee, and then went upstairs where she took a shower, and climbed into bed. In spite of the amount of drink she had consumed on both nights they were away, her mind was sharp and wouldn't let her drift off to sleep. Thinking over the events of the weekend and in particular that session with the medium, she glanced at a photo of Ethan which stood on the small bedside table, one she had taken just shortly before he died. She picked it up. 'How could you talk to me from wherever you are?' she whispered aloud.

Back at work, Liz opened the post. Choosing the handwritten envelope first. She pulled out the single page, and glanced at the signature at the end, surprised to see that it was from Scott. She smiled and read the few lines inviting her to meet him again, feeling unexpectedly happy.

Her first clients were a large family. Liz focused the camera, arranged their positions and worked through the photo shoot. She was happiest here and wanted to make her clients look as good as they imagined they should. Older faces anxious to appear younger, teenagers who wanted to look older, more sophisticated.

She watched the interaction. The reluctant grandfather. Togged out in his best clothes. Complaining about the length of time it was taking. The delighted grandmother with all her children and grandchildren around her. Smiling. Happy. The sons and daughters trying to control the young ones. Get them to stay in one place. Smile at the camera. And say *cheese*.

Later it was a couple on their own. Just married. She wore a white silk dress, with a dramatic feathered creation on her blonde head, a small posy clutched in her hand. He was a handsome dark haired devil, Liz had to admit, in a navy suit with a white rose in his buttonhole. She felt grateful they allowed her to share in their special day, almost envious of their happiness. Little snippets of a life absorbed into her mind and were imprinted on the lens of her camera.

At home in the evening, Liz took out the photographs she had found in the attic, and laid them out on the bench in her developing room. Then she had a look through others which she had taken since then. There was a varied selection of landscapes, many of rivers and lakes, calm stretches of water slashed with streaks of light. She chose some of her favourites, grouped them together, and pondered on the possibility of publishing a book.

But as she looked at them, she was reminded of Ethan, always there in the background of many of those photos. Her marriage wasn't exactly how she had expected when she made her vows in the church. Liz had realised very soon that she had made a mistake, and there was a distance between them which grew wider each year. The arrival of her children made it easier. She didn't feel alone then and managed to hold it together. For years, conversation consisted of basic remarks around the everyday. Affection diminished. He never kissed her. She never touched him. They had no sexual life. That lack of affection was something which got to her. She was by nature a touchy feely sort of person and to hold herself back from even putting a hand on his arm was difficult. Those last couple of years were the worst. Since he died she had never been close to another man.

'Liz, you're a virgin by choice,' Celine said.

'A virgin by fate,' Megan added.

'Would you know what to do if a man touched you?' Leah asked with a giggle.

'Maybe I'm out there more than you imagine?' Liz had quipped.

'Leaving us behind?' Celine screamed.

Liz shrugged.

'What do you bet she's got a guy already?'

'Go on, tell us?'

'Is there someone?'

They pestered her.

'No,' she denied, laughing.

'Maybe she fancied one of those guys we met at Ashford?'

'The tall one had his eye on Leah.'

'He wasn't bad,' Leah admitted.

'Both of them live in London, not much use to you here,' Megan said.

'Doubt if we'll see either of them again.'

'Well.' Leah had a mysterious look in her eyes.

'Well what?' Celine demanded.

'Harry will be over on business in a week or two and he wants to meet up.'

'Why didn't you tell us?' There was a cacophony of voices.

'What's his background? Is he single?' Liz asked, relieved that the conversation had switched to Leah.

'I never asked. Everyone has baggage. Look at me?'

'Does he come over regularly?'

'Apparently.'

'What's his business?'

'Retail something.'

'You didn't ask him?'

'There wasn't much chance to get personal, was there?'

'But he asked you for your phone number?'

'Just as we walked out of the bar. He put it into his phone. For God's sakes, girls, this is like an interrogation.'

'Never know where it might lead,' Liz said.

'Yea, I'm looking forward to hearing from him. It would be nice to have dinner, and maybe a few jars.'

'And a bit of the other?' Megan quipped.

'Well, might say no, might say yes. Don't jump the gun, girls, first he has to ring.'

'I wish I was waiting for someone to ring,' Celine said.

'What about one of those guys you met on line?'

'They're all shits.'

'It's hard to meet someone.'

'You can meet *someone,* but they're not worth talking about. Not worth a damn,' she said vehemently.

'In time, Celine,' Megan said gently. 'Look at me, girls, I have a husband but it isn't all sweetness and light. We go around each other in circles. I reach out to touch him but he's always going in the opposite direction.'

'Maybe you should try harder,' Celine said.

'I do,' Megan insisted.

'Hold on to him. Don't let go whatever you do,' Leah advised. 'Do you want to be like me?'

'We're getting morose, girls,' Celine said.

'Grab every day you have with both hands and enjoy,' Liz said with a broad grin.

'The only one around here who doesn't seem to want a new man in her life is our Liz.'

'Career woman. Workaholic. Happy with her own company.'

They laughed.

Liz sipped the last of her gin and tonic, and didn't respond to that remark. Had the girls got it in one, or ...

## Chapter Fifteen

The light from the house shone across the garden. Brooke thought how its luminosity distorted plants and bushes into strange unidentifiable shapes. She whispered the word. Unidentifiable. And knew immediately it was how she felt. She had no place in the world. Was no longer a wife. Her place usurped by that bitch in Rory's office. He was so uncaring, and all he was interested in was working out the detail. I'll pay this. You pay that. Go get a job. No love left for her any more. It was all reserved for that other one. Brooke was like a child who was lost and couldn't find her way back home.

'Mum?' Cian stood at the door. 'Can I have a drink?'

She poured him some water.

'When is Dad coming home?'

'I'm not sure, baby, he's at a meeting.' She searched for a suitable reply.

'In the middle of the night?' He stared up at her. 'Where is he?'

'America.'

'Will he bring me a present?'

'I'm sure he will.' She hunted him up the stairs. 'Back into bed now.'

He climbed in.

She pulled up the duvet. 'Go to sleep.' She leaned down and kissed him. 'I love you, my little boy.'

Tears filled her eyes as she left the room. Leaving the door open just a little. Cian hated the dark, so even a chink of light would reassure him.

She went into Jess's room. The little bedside lamp glowed pink in the darkness. In sleep, her daughter hugged a teddy in her arms, and dark eyelashes brushed plump cheeks. Brooke reached to touch a silky curl.

Later she called Sophie.

'I don't know what to do,' she wailed. 'He's coming around this evening to pick up the rest of his things.'

There was silence at the other end of the line.

'Sophie, can you help me?'

'I'm sorry Brooke,' Sophie said softly. 'What arrangement have you come to?'

'He's still paying the bills, but I have to feed and clothe myself and the children. He suggested I get a job, would you believe?'

'It's a good idea. It will give you independence.'

'I only worked for a couple of years before the twins arrived.'

'I'm sure you'll find something.'

'Do you expect me to work in some burger joint or somewhere like that?'

'You could do a course and then it might be easier to find a job.'

'It's so hard on my own.'

'You'll be better off without him, he's a bastard.' Sophie was firm. 'Let him go.'

'I don't want to do that, I love him.'

'What will you do then?'

'I want you to tell me.'

'I can't do that, are you mad?'

'You're no help.' Brooke was suddenly irritated with her sister. 'I'll talk to Mum. She'll understand.'

'I thought you didn't want to tell anyone?'

'I suppose it will have to come out eventually although I know they will all think I'm such a fool.'

'That's not going to happen, everyone will be very supportive.'

'Don't you tell anyone,' she warned.

'I won't. We'll be going around to Mum for lunch on Sunday, tell her then.'

In the bedroom Brooke went across to the mirrored wardrobes and slid a door open. Rory had taken some of his clothes but quite a number of suits, jackets and trousers still hung there. Some of his shoes were neatly positioned on the shelf at the end. She leaned in and brushed her face against a soft wool fabric. His aroma was all around her. Traces of aftershave reminded of his embrace. His arms around her. His lips on hers.

What did that bitch have that she didn't? Brooke wondered. Her relationship with Rory had always been so good. Their sexual life was exciting. Impromptu. Highly satisfying. Grabbing a moment here and there to kiss and touch intimately out of sight of the children. How had he become bored with her? Had this other woman thrown herself at him and he couldn't resist? Typical man. Weak. Easily distracted. His loyalty to her thrown out the window without the slightest thought.

She went around the house then and looked at various things belonging to him. He must be bringing a van, she thought, if he's taking everything. All his surfing gear and clothes and goodness knows what else. It seemed so final. Each time she talked to him in her heart of hearts she became imbued with hope that he would come home despite his appalling attitude towards her. She kept expecting a miracle but when she heard his curt replies it was like another nail being studded into her coffin.

Any love he had felt for her had long gone it seemed. Tears flooded her eyes. How would she live without Rory? He was her life and the children's too. It was just impossible to contemplate.

Anxious to look attractive, she re-did her make-up and changed. I won't let him see how I really feel. I won't give him the satisfaction. Unexpectedly, anger began to creep around the edges of her mind, like tiny ants nibbling. She couldn't shake it off. Even saw images of the creatures. How dare he do this to me and the kids. I'm not going to take this lying down. By the time he arrived she had built up to a crescendo and when the door opened, she immediately hurried down the hall as if she was about to attack him. But, of course, she stopped short of that and just stared at him. Silent.

'I'll take my clothes,' he said, brushing past her.

She put out a hand to his back longing to touch, to demand, to say something at least. But couldn't. He went up to the bedroom. She stood at the door and watched. He crossed to the wardrobe and lifted the hangers which held his suits. He laid them over his arm.

'Would you carry some of the jackets for me?' he asked.

She gasped. The cheek of him. 'I will not. What do you think I am, a porter?' The words burst out.

'Don't bother then, Brooke. At least my clothes won't smell of cigarettes. It will be a relief to get away from the awful stench. It's everywhere.'

'How dare you?' she shouted furiously. Having a crazy urge to guard her bedroom. Her house. Her children. Against him. As if he was a stranger.

'It's the truth, Brooke, just accept it.'

He went up and down carrying the rest of his stuff. He filled suitcases with shoes, sweaters, sports gear, and even cleared the bathroom. Eventually, he glanced at his watch. The one she had bought him for their fifth anniversary. She felt like asking him to return it. Although she remembered then that it was bought with his money.

'I'll come back for my surfboard and golf clubs,' he said.

'You are such a pig,' she yelled.

'Very polite, Brooke,' he smiled wryly.

'How could you treat us like this. You didn't even look in on the children. What have they done that you should treat them in such a way? And what have I done?' She stood blocking his way, hands on hips.

'You're boring, Brooke. I want more out of life and I think I've found it.'

'How dare you? I hate you.' She ran at him, banging her fists against

59

his chest, like a crazy person.

He reacted violently. Pushed her away from him and down on to the bed. 'Never do that again, or I won't be responsible for my actions,' he yelled, holding her there.

'Daddy?' Jess cried.

## Chapter Sixteen

Liz collected the photos in a file and showed them to Sophie who had a keen eye for the particular and would immediately identify those which were most suitable for the book.

'I love them all, Mum.'

'I don't know, so many of them include water scenes.'

'And they're beautiful.'

'I just love water, it means fertility, life, and that's the message I want to send out to people,' she said. 'Do you understand what I'm getting at?'

'Of course I do. It's a lovely thought.'

'How many photos will we include?'

'Let's have a look at some other books. See what they've used.' Sophie went to the bookshelves and searched for something similar. 'There's about thirty in that one. It might be enough.'

'I've about fifty-three.'

'You could introduce each photo with a few lines about it. Where it was taken and when. Were you on holidays? Was it work and you just took a few shots as you were passing through, or whatever.'

'Good idea. It would make it more personal. People like to have the background to something. It's like a painting, you'd love to know why the artist painted a particular image.' Liz was enthusiastic.

'Right, let's choose.'

Liz spread them out on the table.

'First, I love those old ones.' Sophie pointed to them.

'Are they good enough?'

'Of course and I'm sure you have a history attached to all of them.'

'Yea, that was taken in Midleton when we were on holiday. It must have been in the early eighties, and that's when I got my first camera.'

'And this one here?'

'On the Shannon. Your grandfather loved to sail and a lot of my shots were taken on Lough Derg.'

'You could write about that.'

'I think that's Connemara.'

'It's lovely. How do you remember them so well?'

'I just do.'

'What year was that?'

'I can't remember exactly, I was in college at the time, and we used to head off on a motorbike to Cork and Kerry.'

'Who's we?'

'A boyfriend.'

'What was his name?'

'Scott.'

'Is that him there?' she picked up a photo.

'It was a long time ago.'

'A serious relationship?'

'We were very close,' she smiled.

'What happened?'

'Your Dad and I ...'

'Did you ever see the guy again?'

'No,' she said, and wondered what Sophie would say if she knew that her mother had already met her old boyfriend.

'You went one way, he went another. If you're anything like me, there's a lot of those guys lying in the ditch.'

'I had a couple of boyfriends when I was at school, but nothing serious, then I met Scott on our first day in the library, and we were together right through. When we graduated, he went to England and that was that.'

'Dad was the lucky one.'

'Yea.'

'Do you think you'll include Scott?'

'No, I couldn't.'

'Just make an oblique reference. It makes it slightly mysterious, people love anything like that.'

'No, I'm only going to use landscapes.' Liz gathered them up.

'You'll have to say something, they're wonderful, nostalgic, and about a special time in your life.'

'Youth,' Liz laughed. 'When we were all crazy.'

'What was it like then, back in the eighties, Mum?'

'Not much different to now except I suppose we had to fight harder against our parents.'

'They didn't want you to think for yourself I suppose.'

'Not mine anyway.'

'Did they force you to do anything?'

'The main thing was that they wanted me to go to college and I didn't. I was like you and wanted to get out there and take photographs. That's all. I didn't think it needed a degree in social studies which I never used anyway.'

'That's the difference I suppose. Although you never minded that I didn't go to college?'

'I wanted you to be happy. To follow your heart. Pushing you into something just wasn't going to work. You'd have resisted no matter what and I'd have lost you.' She put her arm around Sophie's shoulders.

'Thanks Mum, for letting me do my thing.'

'Since I wasn't allowed to do what I wanted, I could hardly force you into the same narrow straitjacket.'

'You're an amazing person,' Sophie whispered. 'I don't think anyone appreciates what you are. Even Dad didn't.'

Liz was silent.

'Did he love you, Mum?'

'Of course he did.' She was immediately on the defensive.

'He never showed it. I don't think I ever saw him kiss you.'

Liz wondered had she overdone the mothering to make up for Ethan's lack of affection to herself and the children.

63

'I was thirteen when he died. Did you love him?'

Liz looked at her, taken aback.

'Or did you always love that other guy?'

She took out the photographs which had been gradually whittled down between herself and Sophie. Over the weekend she looked at them again and again. Each time eliminating one or two so that now she was almost at the final number which she intended to use. She wasn't confident that they were any good, and couldn't imagine them in book form.

She opened up the laptop and put her mind to writing the pieces about each photo. Should it be like a poem or just a descriptive piece of prose? She wondered. But went ahead, typed a few words and gave the piece a title. It took a lot of time to try to wind stories around the images and she still wasn't happy.

She had made an appointment with her printers, Martone Design and Print, for the following week. They had done all their printing over the years and she was confident that Martin would produce exactly what she wanted. As regards the cost, she would dip into her savings account, and hoped sales of the book might go some way towards covering it. She was excited now about the whole project.

Later, she read the letter from Scott again. When they met that day, he had asked her to contact him but she hadn't even considered doing that. It just wasn't something she would do. Now, she was in a quandary. Maybe it would be nice to meet again. She simply didn't know. It was strange that Sophie had asked if she still loved him. Her question echoed. But the instant she heard her words, Liz's immediate reaction was to deny. How could she still love someone she knew so many years ago? He was a different person. She was a different person. They didn't even look the same. But yet her reaction to his kiss had touched a nerve. Part of her wanted to see him, but at the same time, there was fear there too.

## *Chapter Seventeen*

In the bar, Robyn held out a small bag of tablets to Sophie and Lucy, then swallowed one herself.

'What are they?' Sophie asked.

'Not so sure, but enough to get us high. Isn't that all we want?' she laughed.

'No thanks,' Sophie refused, although she would have given anything for one. In an effort to reduce her intake, she hadn't used today.

'What's with you?' Robyn asked.

'Don't feel like it. I'll have another beer instead.'

'You'll have a head in the morning if you keep drinking.'

'I'll chance it.'

'Please yourself.'

'Feeling all right?' Lucy asked.

'I'm trying to give it a miss for a while.'

'What?'

'Drugs,' she said. Glancing around her and hoping nobody overheard.

'You won't get our jokes then.'

'I will of course.'

'But that's so uncool, did you hear the one about?' Lucy went on to tell the story, and Robyn exploded with laughter.

It was true, Sophie didn't really get it.

'Are you coming to the club with us tonight?' Robyn asked.

'No, I mightn't bother.'

'For God's sake, what's got into you?' Lucy burst out.

'Busy.'

'But it's Saturday night? Are you working tomorrow?'

'I've to do some stuff with my mother and I don't want to be too tired. I've to make decisions which are important.' It was an excuse. She hated letting the girls down. They were her closest friends and she knew that tonight wasn't the time to try to explain exactly how she felt. They wouldn't understand. On the other hand, her mother wouldn't understand either if she found out about the drugs. Sophie would be so ashamed. How to explain to her why exactly she tortured her body in this way. Torture. She thought about the word. It was the exact opposite to the effect of the drugs.

'Come on, Sophie, have one, you'll feel so much better then,' Robyn persuaded.

'We're going to have a blast tonight, without you it won't be the same.'

'Sorry girls, but I'll have to go.'

Robyn pulled a face.

'Come back if you change your mind,' Lucy urged.

'Maybe. See you soon.' She pushed through the crowd.

'Sophie?' A voice echoed to her left.

She turned.

'How are you?'

It was Josh. That guy she'd met recently. The pharmacist.

'Drink?' He waved his glass of beer.

'No thanks.'

'Are your mad friends here tonight?'

'Yea sure.'

Leaning over her, one arm against the wall he kissed her. Heavy. Wet. Sloppy.

She stepped back.

'Come on, Sophie?'

She tried to get away from him but the people crowded around them.

'Baby.' His hand reached for her.

'Josh, please, I must go.'

'You're not going to leave me, are you?' His fingers slowly worked their way down to the neckline of her tee shirt.

'Take your hands off me,' she burst out furiously.

'What's with you?'

She ducked under his arm and forced her way towards the exit. But found herself going the opposite direction, twisting and turning until she didn't know which way she was going.

'Sophie?' he shouted from somewhere behind.

She was in tears now. Frantic. Unable to find her way. 'Robyn, Lucy?' she screamed. Her eardrums buzzed. She wasn't able to breathe.

'Hey, where you going?' someone asked.

'Watch it.'

'F off.'

'Stupid bitch.'

'Sophie?'

She could hear Josh's voice close by, and almost hysterical now, she tried to escape from where she thought he was. Suddenly, the world turned upside down and she fell. Tumbling among the legs around her, feet stamping, stilettos twisting. She cried out. Caught in the dark. So afraid.

Someone caught hold of her. She resisted. Crouching on the floor.

'Sophie?' It was him again. 'Stand up.'

'Get away from me.' She pushed herself to her feet and finally found a break in the throng of people. Hurrying through until she reached the exit, able to catch her breath at last in the cold night air.

'Are you all right?' Josh asked, keeping up with her.

'I'm fine,' she snapped, and ran into the crowds on Grafton Street.

Sophie didn't feel so good the following morning, still a trace of that strange experience the night before. The feeling of panic swept through her again. Perspiration gathered on her forehead, the back of her neck and the palms of her hands. She pushed herself up out of bed, anxious to get a drink of water. But as she stood on her feet, a wave of dizziness forced her to sit down again. She bent her head between her knees. The dizzy spell eased.

What is wrong with me, she wondered. Have I picked up some bug? Maybe I should stay in bed. She swung her legs back in and lay there, shaking. She pulled the duvet over and slept after a while. When she awoke again she felt decidedly better.

It was Sunday and as usual her mother was making lunch, but Sophie didn't feel up to it but if she told Liz she wasn't feeling well then she would only fuss over her. As she sat there wrapped in a towelling robe, she went through the events of the previous evening. Had anything particular happened to cause this. She only had a few beers and no drugs. But maybe her drink was spiked. That could be it.

Eventually, she showered, dressed and headed over to Howth. Brooke and the children were already there and Liz was in particularly good form.

'Lunch is almost ready.' She went towards the kitchen.

'Can I help?' Sophie asked.

'Sit down and relax for a few minutes, I'll give you a shout if I need you,' Liz said.

Sophie sat beside Brooke. 'Did Rory come back?' she asked, in a whisper.

'No.' It was a dull reply from the normally vivacious Brooke.

'Has he taken all his stuff?'

'Pretty much.'

Sophie didn't know what to say, but put her arm around her sister. It was a loving gesture, but Brooke didn't respond and instead sharply rebuked Jess. 'Stop fighting with your brother, let Cian play with his tractor.'

'It's mine,' she insisted.

'Nana Liz will be annoyed.'

The two ignored her. Brooke pulled a face and shrugged.

'Lunch is ready,' Liz appeared wearing an apron, her face slightly flushed from the heat of the kitchen.

'Thanks, Mum.' Sophie took Jess's hand. 'I'm going to wash your hands, little missy.'

'No.' She pulled away.

'Yes,' Sophie insisted, lifted her up and carried her wriggling body into the downstairs loo.

'No dinner if you have dirty hands,' Liz warned.

Brooke washed Cian's hands and soon they were all sitting at the table.

'Luke isn't coming today?' Sophie asked.

'No, he's busy.'

'We don't see so much of him these days.'

Liz served.

Sophie was reminded of how she felt earlier, and thought perhaps she should detox. To just drink water for a while, and cut out the drugs and alcohol. It could be good for her body in general. Since the episode last night she had remembered a couple of other incidents which had occurred recently, although they had not been as severe. She wondered if perhaps it was connected with stress.

'Sophie?' Liz drew her attention back to the conversation. 'Where are you?'

'Sorry, my mind drifted,' Sophie excused herself, embarrassed.

'We were talking about Luke.'

She nodded.

'Both of us think he's not his usual self.'

'He's just busy, I suppose.'

'There's something I have to tell you, Mum,' Brooke said.

Liz looked at her.

'Rory and I have separated.'

'What?' Liz stared at her in surprise. Then she stood and put her arms around her daughter. 'When did this happen?'

Brooke looked to where the children played, and softly explained the situation.

'A colleague?' Liz whispered. 'My God, I never would have

expected that. Rory is such a nice guy, I thought he was devoted to you and the children.'

'So did I.' Brooke was bitter.

'When did this happen?'

'A few weeks ago.'

'Why didn't you tell me before now?'

'It's hard to admit you've been dumped by your husband. I suppose I was ashamed.'

'Never feel like that, Brooke,' Sophie said. 'He'll get fed up with her. So many men go off and only then realise the mistake they've made.'

'In the beginning I thought my heart was broken, but now I'm not having him back,' Brooke said vehemently. 'He can just stay with her. His attitude to Jess and Cian is unbelievable. It's almost like they're not his children. He said he never even wanted them in the first place.' There were tears in her eyes.

'I don't believe it,' Liz said.

'It's true.'

'Will he support you and the children?'

'He is paying the mortgage and most of the utilities, but I have to cover everything else.'

'We'll be able to help.' Liz patted her hand.

'I don't want you to have to do that,' Brooke said. 'I intend to stand on my own two feet.'

'What about the house?' Liz asked.

'I'm not leaving my beautiful house. I've created every last bit of it,' Brooke was defiant.

Later, in the kitchen Liz made coffee in the percolator. 'I'm worried about Brooke and Rory, it's such a tragedy,' she said to Sophie. 'They seemed like the perfect couple. I can't get my mind around it.'

'Me neither.' Sophie took out cups, saucers and plates.

'The last time I saw him was at my birthday party. But I was high as a kite that night and wouldn't have noticed anything,' Liz said.

Sophie had to admit her mother was unflappable. Her reaction to the news was amazingly calm and there were absolutely no accusations of any sort, or suggestions of making a go of it if Brooke could persuade Rory to come back. Sophie wondered how Liz would react to hear of her dependency on drugs. While she thought of her habit as recreational, and a replacement for alcohol, she did drink quite a lot as well so it wasn't as if one replaced the other. An unwelcome thought drifted into her consciousness. How dependent was she?

# Chapter Eighteen

Liz took a sheet of notepaper and began to write.

*Hi Scott,*
*Thanks for your letter. It was nice to meet you recently and if you*
*happen to be in Dublin do give me a call ...*

she hesitated. She would have to give him her number, and that would
mean allowing him into her own private space, a place she held dear.
Still she remembered what he was like when they were young, and
reminded herself that she had never loved Ethan the way she loved
Scott.

Quickly, she printed the digits of her phone number in brackets
beside her name, folded the sheet of paper, put it in the envelope and
addressed it.

When Scott went to study in the UK, Ethan and Liz became closer and
spent more time together. It seemed natural. They were good friends.
Then Scott returned unexpectedly one night and called to Ethan's flat.
She had opened the door and hugged him immediately. He hadn'
expected to see her there, and she had struggled to allay his suspicions
that there nothing was going on between her and Ethan, which was true
at that time.

Their voices swam around her, adding to her rush of explanations.
In that second a fuse was lit. And a flame crept slowly along, spitting
and hissing, until Scott turned from them and left, banging the door

behind him.

Liz had no patience with Scott's jealousy and in a flush of youthful disregard she turned to Ethan who was only too pleased to draw her further into his life. He asked her to marry him in a matter of weeks and still smarting she agreed. Ethan had been offered a position in UCD, and his family were wealthy and quite willing to finance the deposit for their home. She was carried on a wave of excitement. Her parents scraped enough money for the wedding reception and within six months Ethan and she were married and living in the house in Howth. She didn't know how she got there exactly. One day she was a very young college graduate of twenty. And a year later she was a married woman with responsibilities.

'You're so lucky. A husband, a home and independence,' Celine said.

Her friends were envious.

That word *independence* meant most of all.

'But I've been independent since I started college,' she protested.

'Your parents have no control over you any longer,' Leah stressed. 'Your husband owns you now.'

'No one owns me.' She imagined a parcel wrapped in brown paper and twine. Handed to Ethan to hold in his possession for as long as he wished. 'I'll never be anyone's property,' she argued. 'Anyway, who makes that decision?'

'Society,' they laughed.

What was society? Nameless, faceless individuals who set down laws of how people should behave. Her own parents were examples of that. Devout Catholics. Expecting their own children to follow in their footsteps. She had done exactly that and they were pleased. Her sister Chloe was delighted to be bridesmaid. Such a flurry of excitement among the family. Dresses to be made. Hen party and stag night to be arranged. Flowers. Music. Honeymoon. She had no control over it. She enjoyed her temporary job but as soon as that gold wedding band was on her finger Ethan insisted that she give up work and become a home-maker.

'But I want to work. You know, go out every day. Nine to five,' she insisted.

'You are my wife. I can provide everything you need.'

'What will I do every day?' she asked, astonished.

'Look after our home.'

'I'll go crazy. That will be done in an hour.'

'You'll find something to do.'

She didn't know how she hadn't found out his feelings on the matter before they were married. It was as if he had changed into someone else. It was the old story. She had been caught in a trap. Like an animal. A delicate ankle chain imprisoning her.

## Chapter Nineteen

Having told Liz about her separation from Rory, Brooke felt a weight had lifted from her shoulders. She went home with her children, into that house with its pale minimalist colour scheme of greys and whites. She looked around and suddenly realised it was like a dull day, and wondered why she had allowed a designer to have such a free hand. The only rooms which were rich in colour were those of the children. Up there it was a different world. Like stepping into a rainbow. Wispy pinks and lilacs for Jess. Red, greens and yellows for Cian.

The two children went on with their lives unaware of the drama going on around them. Brooke longed to be a child too. Simple. Uncomplicated. While they spent their time playing with each other and their toys, she watched from a distance. Like a manager of a team on the side lines of a match. Shouting orders. Screaming encouragement. One day she took a step forward. Another, it was two steps backwards. Someone had taken her heart. A Valentine's Day heart. Red satin. Lace trimmed. She had one among the cushions on a chair in the bedroom, it was held by a small white furry teddy, embroidered with the words *I love you*. Rory had given it to her the previous year. What had it meant? A symbol of love? Or an excuse for not loving her?

She tried to remember when things had changed between them. Was it a gradual winding down which she hadn't noticed. Or had it happened on one day. A moment between them when the light in his eyes went out and he looked beyond her into another world.

Brooke began to hate her home. All her attention on Cian and Jess. She longed to get away. Anywhere. One day while they were at school, she went into the guest room and struggled to move the two divan beds closer together. Then she transferred all her clothes, shoes and other stuff into the wardrobes in that room and closed the master bedroom door. She would let the dust settle on everything in there before she slept in that bed again.

Aware that she shouldn't waste money, she was unable to stop herself buying small tins of paint in bright rainbow hues. A brush. A roller. Then she went back to transform the guest bedroom, painting each wall a different colour. The rainbow hues took her into a dream state and the nightmares receded. But Rory still crept around the house like a spirit. Sometimes she felt a swish of air across her as if he had just passed by. Images of him in photos jumped out at her immediately reminding of happier times. In the kitchen, she put away his favourite mug. The chair where he sat. But she couldn't escape from Cian's eyes and Jess's smile.

Slowly she drifted. Life was quiet. Most of her friends were Rory's friends and she wasn't invited to socialise with them any longer. And she couldn't afford to join the wives for coffee or lunch and was abandoned.

Now she spent more time with her mother and sister. She wouldn't have minded going out on the town with Sophie but no invitations were forthcoming. She wondered why. Before she met Rory, Sophie and she had occasionally gone out for a night together between rows. But really now she couldn't afford such an extravagance. That thought reminded that she must do something to earn money. She bought the newspapers Checked on line. Went into an employment agency. Asking vaguely about jobs. Most of the positions available were at the lower end of the scale. The upper end needed highly qualified people. So choices weren't good for a mother with twins.

Brooke sat at the white kitchen table. She sipped a glass of juice pensively and stared around the room. It was almost too bright. Spring sunshine beamed in through the glass patio doors. Slanting shadows across the floor were like pointers showing the way to go. Straight ahead, left, right.

On the table were piled various papers. Bills mostly. Electricity. Phone. Insurance. She picked up her bank statement and saw that her credit balance was fast diminishing.

There too was a pack of cigarettes which she had bought today. She picked it up. Opened it. And took out a cigarette, her hand shaking. She brought the narrow white tube up to her nose. Longing swept through her. But suddenly the aroma disgusted her. Remembering Rory's comments, she pushed the cigarette back into the pack and threw it into the bin.

She called him. He answered. His blunt *yes* was abrasive.

'Will you call around? We need to talk.' She tried to hide the desperation in her voice.

'About what? There's been no change.'

'Money.'

'Brooke, you think of nothing else.'

'I must look after the children. It's not for me.'

'I told you that I wasn't giving you any more money.'

She gasped.

'And there's something else. I want to put the house up for sale. It will be better for both of us. Prices are rising and we should do well when the mortgage is paid off. Then each of us will have some money to start again. Do you agree with that?'

'I don't know.' She stared at the pile of bills in front of her. Some of them were on direct debit and covered by Rory, but others she would have to pay herself.

'I'm giving the house to an estate agent and hopefully we'll get a quick sale. He will be in touch with you to inspect it, take photographs etc. And if he brings some prospective buyers around to see the house, make sure the place is spotless.'

'Is the house ever any other way?' she asked, suddenly angry with him. But he had already put down the phone. He did that lately without even saying goodbye as if he couldn't bear to talk to her for a second longer.

Shocked, Brooke dropped the phone, and stared out through the window. The young man they employed to keep the garden in order was trimming the bushes at the end. She would have to tell him that she didn't need him any longer and hated doing that. He was a nice guy. She heard the snip of his shears in the quiet. Saw the glint of the blades. Branches tumbled on to the grass. She felt as if parts of her were being chopped off and she would flutter helplessly to the ground as well. She wondered what Rory would think then. Such an event would not suit his plans. She was a vital cog in his wheel. Going around and around as it spun. Keeping it balanced. Looking after his children. So that he could enjoy himself with his new love.

## Chapter Twenty

Liz's phone rang just as she came in the door, and she put down her briefcase on a chair in the hall and answered it. It was Scott. She didn't say anything for a few seconds, her pulse racing.

'Thanks for your letter, Liz, it was great to hear from you.'

They chatted. Just the usual lightweight stuff.

'Would you like to have dinner, I'd love to meet you again,' he asked.

'Sure, why not?' Her acceptance came out in a rush, without even thinking about it.

'I'm coming up next week, which evening would suit you?'

'Let me check my diary.' She put down the phone, and had a look. 'How about Wednesday?'

'Yea, that's fine,' he agreed. 'I'm really looking forward to seeing you. Will I pick you up?'

'I'll meet you,' she said abruptly. Liz didn't know why she was so curt.

'Where would you like to go? Do you have a favourite restaurant?'

'I'd prefer to choose somewhere different,' she said immediately, reluctant to take the chance of bumping into someone she knew.

'There's a new place on Dawson Street, it's called Chambre Bleu. I read a review. It sounded good.' He seemed enthusiastic.

'Let's go there.'

'Eight o'clock?'

'Yes, that's fine.'

'It will be really nice to catch up.'

'See you.'

Wednesday dawned. A pleasant day. Liz rose earlier than usual, unable to sleep. Work dragged. Sophie was out on calls. She checked her watch more than once until at last the hour for her hair appointment finally approached. Leafing through the newspaper in the salon she found it hard to concentrate, a terrifying shiver inside. Of anticipation. And something she couldn't identify. By the time she was stepping into the new black dress, she wanted to phone and say she couldn't be there. Make up some excuse. Doubt swept through her as she clipped on a silver chain. She stared in the mirror. Brown eyes wide. Frightened. But she reminded herself that he had driven up from Cork, and it would be very rude to cancel at this stage. As she sprayed perfume, she noticed her hands were shaking. The time was seven sixteen on the clock radio.

On perilously high stilettos Liz climbed the steps and pushed open the glass door of the restaurant. She was a few minutes early and wondered would he even be here. But that thought was immediately dashed as she saw him walk towards her, a broad smile on his face. His hands held out in greeting.

'Liz?' He drew close and kissed her on the cheek. 'You're looking wonderful, thanks for coming. I was having doubts that you mightn't be able to make it, perhaps some last minute emergency, and I was like a young fellow on a first date. Would you like an aperitif? I'm just having a beer.' He ushered her over to where he had been sitting on a low couch and waved to the waiter.

'A toast to us,' he said with a smile, leaning forward towards her.

Sitting on the other side of an L shaped couch his knees almost touched hers. She inched away.

'We've a lot of catching up to do, Liz, it's been thirty years, hard to imagine.' He sipped his beer.

'I almost got cold feet,' she admitted. 'But the thought of you driving up from Cork stopped me from looking for an excuse.'

'I'd have been very disappointed I can tell you,' he said, smiling.

The waiter called them to their table, and the next while was spent choosing from the menu and eating. They caught up with the present to some extent, but the chat between them went back further.

'Remember that day we met in the library, sorting out books and making so much noise the librarian came over and asked us to be quiet,' he asked.

'I was a complete idiot in those first days at college, I didn't know what I was at.'

'I wish we were back there again.' His eyes looked into hers and held them.

'The parties. The drinking sessions. Great times.'

'Have you kept up with any of your friends, Liz?'

'Only a couple, Leah and Celine, do you remember them?'

'Was Celine the red haired girl, a real stunner?'

'Yea, and Leah was a madcap, always in trouble.'

'Most of our crowd went abroad and stayed in various places so I lost touch. Opportunities in engineering were really overseas.'

'Did you stay in the UK?'

'No, I qualified and luckily got a job back here in aviation. I wasn't too pushed about going further afield, I'm a bit of a home bird as you probably remember. What about you?'

'I had a job for a few months but Ethan wasn't keen for me to work.'

'Strange how we dropped out of each other's ambit so quickly, almost like we'd never known each other.' He was serious.

'That happens, there are people I knew in those days who lived in Dublin but I've never met them since.'

'And odd how we met on that day near your house,' he said. 'Who could have predicted that?'

'I met a medium a few weeks ago, I should have asked her what was coming up in the future,' she laughed.

'Are you into that sort of thing?' He seemed surprised.

'No, but Celine and the girls persuaded me to go along.'

'Did you communicate with anyone on the other side?' He put on a ghoulish expression.

'The woman said she was talking to Ethan. It was peculiar. I didn't believe her.'

'What did he say, I mean, what did she say?'

'Something vague, it didn't mean anything to me.' She suddenly realised that perhaps she shouldn't say any more.

'So no earth shattering predictions?' he asked with a grin.

'Nothing as dramatic as that.' She glanced at her watch and looked around. 'We are almost the last people here.'

'So what?'

The waiter came over with two drinks which were on the house. Scott asked the man for the bill.

'I love this lemon liquor.' She sipped it.

'Cheers to a lovely night.' He raised his glass.

'Let's split the bill, please?' she asked.

'Thank you Liz, I know we used to do that in the old days, but I think I can manage to scrape enough money to pay it.'

'Thanks.' She gave in. It was a gesture which she didn't expect him to accept anyway.


They stood outside the restaurant.

'Let's stroll?' he suggested. 'It's not too cold for you?'

'No,' she said, and they walked slowly along South Anne Street chatting. On Grafton Street, a group of girls and fellows hurried out of a side street and almost bumped into them.

'Hey,' Scott put his arm out to shield Liz.

One of them apologised, and the others turned to look. And there was Sophie among them.

'Mum?' she exclaimed.

Liz didn't know what to say and just stood there, silent.

They smiled. She knew some of them.

'What are you doing in town, Mum?' Sophie asked in a high-pitched voice. 'We're just going on to another bar for a few drinks.'

'Want to come along?' one asked, and Liz could hear some of them snigger.

'Sorry, we didn't mean …' Sophie said.

'This is my daughter, Sophie,' Liz introduced her to Scott.

He held out his hand.

Sophie took it. 'You're welcome to come along with us although it might be a bit noisy,' she offered.

'We have our own plans, haven't we Liz?' Scott said.

The girls looked at each other, eyebrows raised.

Liz felt she would never get away and began to steer him further down the street. 'Thank you but we'll head on, enjoy the night,' she said.

'Bye,' they chorused.

'They all seem high on something,' Scott said, serious now as they continued on.

'Just a few drinks probably,' Liz said.

'It's more than that.'

'How would you know anyway?' She couldn't help the tinge of annoyance in her voice.

'I did some work with …' he began, but then seemed to change his mind. 'I wouldn't worry, your daughter is a lovely girl.'

She was suddenly concerned by what he said. Surely he couldn't mean that Sophie and her friends were taking drugs? She was horrified.

'Would you like to go somewhere else?' There was a glint in his eye.

'Probably bump into Sophie and her gang there, no thanks. I'll grab a taxi and go home.'

'I really enjoyed meeting you again, Liz.'

'Me too, and thanks for dinner, that was a really nice restaurant.'

'We might go back there again sometime?'

'Maybe.' She left it vague, unable to commit herself.

He hailed a taxi. It pulled up. 'I'll go with you.'

'Where is your car?'

'I left it at my uncle's house in Raheny, I'll stay the night with him. He's always glad of the company.'

They didn't talk much during the journey. Somehow meeting Sophie had put a gloom on the evening for Liz. The car stopped outside the house. She opened the door and turned back to him. But he was already walking around the car. He helped her out, and told the driver to wait. At the front door, she took out her key and pushed it into the lock.

'When can I see you again, Liz?' he asked.

'If you want to give me a call when you're up in Dublin, I'll see if I can make it.'

'Next week?' he looked down at her.

'Perhaps.'

'Please?'

She didn't answer.

'Wednesday again?'

She nodded, and laughed.

'See you then, but I'll call you in the meantime.'

She wasn't sure how she felt. It was like a step back in time to sit opposite him tonight. To look into his eyes. He was very close to her now and they were illuminated by a shaft of moonlight which peeped out from behind a cloud. To her surprise, suddenly she longed to reach out. Touch him. Ruffle his hair.

He stepped closer. So familiar. His lips were soft on her cheek. It was only a second. Just that. But enough to remind her how much she had loved him.

## Chapter Twenty-one

It was after three in the morning when Sophie arrived home. She flung herself into bed and slept heavily. It was only the following morning when her alarm went off on her phone that she remembered meeting her mother and some man the previous night. Who was he, she wondered. And why was her mother walking down Grafton Street with him. The images became clearer as she drove into the studio. One particular recollection as he put his arm through Liz's when they walked away. It was a possessive move. How dare he? She exclaimed out loud. Then suddenly she remembered. He was that guy who came into the studio looking for her. And the man she mentioned knowing at college, Scott, yes, that was him.

She reached the studio and opened up. Liz had said she had a meeting with her printers, Martone. Sophie checked the time, anxious now to see her. To ask about last night.

But there was no opportunity to talk to Liz as they were very busy during the day and it was only as it came close to five that they had a few minute's break. But Sophie didn't have to say anything, as Liz brought up the subject herself.

'Did you enjoy last night?'

'We went on to the *Crazy Horse*, it was good.'

'Was it a late night?'

'Yea.'

'I don't know how you manage to work on so little sleep. I'd collapse I think. And you don't even show it. You're as bright as ever.'

'I try to hide it, Mum. About last night, that was the guy you knew at college, wasn't it? Scott Fenton?' Sophie asked in a teasing tone. 'You seemed very friendly. Are you seeing him?'

'We're old friends, Sophie, that's all,' Liz said.

'It has been a long time, what did you say, first day in college when you met?'

'Yea.'

'Do you like him.'

'I do, he's a nice guy.'

'Is he keen?'

'No, it's not that way, Sophie. I'm not looking for a man at my age, I'm middle-aged, it's the last thing on my mind,' Liz said, laughing.

'Mum, I don't think of you as being middle-aged, you're incredibly young. Look at yourself in the mirror. Wish I had skin like yours. Smooth as a baby's bottom. Not a line or a bag to be seen. Have you had work done, Mum? Go on, admit it,' Sophie teased.

'No, I have not had any work done. And I have no intention either. And if you took off your rose-tinted glasses you'd see lots of lines as I do every morning.'

'But what about him? He seemed very possessive.'

'You're imagining things.'

'You were very close to him, and just mentioned him recently. Isn't it a surprise he suddenly turns up,' she giggled.

'That's my private business,' retorted Liz.

'It's hardly business?'

'No, not exactly.'

'I didn't think so. It was a big date and we all thought you looked a million dollars in that new black dress.'

'Thanks for the compliment,' Liz said.

'Have you written the pieces for your photos yet?'

'Some of them, I'll show you.' Liz brought them up on the laptop 'What do you think?' she asked nervously.

'I like them. But they might need a little editing.'

'I've talked to Martin, and he's come up with some good ideas.'

'What about a title?'

'I wondered about *'Memories'?* Liz asked, tentatively.

'It's perfect, and it will be wonderful to have your photos out there in book form, you might even make some money.'

'I'm not really interested in that, although if I could cover most of the cost I'd be happy.'

'You'll definitely make some money, we'll all be out there flogging them.'

Liz smiled. 'This is a new venture, something I've never done before. To publish a book of my work is mind blowing.'

'It will be a great success.' Sophie hugged her.

'There was something I wanted to run past you, to see what you think,' Liz said.

'About the collection?'

'No, it's Brooke.'

'Has something happened?' Sophie was suddenly concerned.

'No, but her financial situation is bad, and I wondered if we could do something for her,' Liz said. 'Like giving her a job?'

'I did think about that, but I wasn't sure that she would be interested.'

'We could train her to take a decent photo. She has a good eye so she might surprise us.'

'She's making an effort to find something but she hasn't had any luck.'

'Do you want me to mention it? Or will we do it together?' Liz asked.

'We'll make it a joint thing so she doesn't think one of us is putting the other under pressure,' Sophie suggested. 'Although I know she'll definitely think it's you leaning on me.'

They met a couple of days later in a new restaurant near Brooke's home.

'Thanks for asking me to dinner Mum, and you too, Sophie, I haven't been out in ages,' Brooke smiled.

'We wanted to treat you. Give you a break.'

'This is more like normal life again. Almost,' she admitted.

'It's lovely to see you happy,' Liz clinked her glass against those of her daughters.

'If you could call it that.' A shadow darkened her eyes, and lines appeared on her face which hadn't been there before.

Liz nodded.

'No one knows what I'm going through.'

'We understand.'

'You haven't a clue.'

'Probably not, but we want to help you, and we'll do this more often,' Sophie said. 'Get you out of the house.'

They enjoyed the meal and the tension eased. By the end of the evening they were regaling anecdotes. Who did that. Who said what. Remember. Remember. When we were young. Even Brooke had shed her low mood.

'We, that is Sophie and I,' Liz was saying. 'Have had an idea. We don't know whether you'll be keen on it but we wondered ...' Liz glanced at Sophie. Her large brown eyes twinkled.

Sophie let her continue. She really wanted her mother to say this to Brooke rather than herself. A spark could suddenly flash between them, a fire would take hold and the pleasant atmosphere would be incinerated.

Brooke paid attention. She squeezed her hands together. Sophie noticed she still wore her engagement ring and wedding band.

'We wondered if you would like to come and work at the studio, Liz asked.

'What would I do?' She seemed astonished.

'If you trained at the studio, it will bring in a wage, you must have money to support yourself and the children.'

'I'm looking for a job,' Brooke said defensively.

'It will be hard to get something part-time. You must work around the children so you could be flexible at the studio.' Sophie felt like giving Brooke a thump.

'I know nothing about photography.'

'Well, at first you could help with the admin, appointments, that sort of thing, and later on you can learn how to take good photos,' explained Liz.

'I know how to take good photos, I'm always taking the kids on my phone, I'm good, everyone says so,' Brooke exclaimed.

'We know you're good, it's in the blood,' Sophie said with a grin.

'But how would we get on together? I can imagine us arguing the toss over every tiny thing.' Brooke drained the last of the wine in the bottle into her glass. She was skittish.

'I think we've matured a bit,' Sophie said.

'We've all matured, me included,' Liz admitted, waving to the waiter for the bill.

'What do you think?' Sophie asked.

'I don't know,' Brooke sighed.

'I thought you were looking for a job?' Sophie asked.

'I am.'

'Well, you try and find something, in the meantime, are we going to get someone in?' Sophie looked at Liz. She intended to scare Brooke as really the position was created solely to help her.

'There was someone on last week looking for work,' Liz said, as she put in her pin number into the machine.

'Why don't you think about it,' Sophie suggested, taking her large handbag and placing it on the table. It was a final gesture. An end to the evening. She was putting it up to Brooke. Did she really want to have her bumbling about between her mother and herself in the studio. Liz and Sophie got on really well, and she could imagine the problems which would ensue once Brooke put her head in the door. But she was her sister and in trouble and they were honour bound to help.

Like many sisters, Sophie and Brooke had fought incessantly right through childhood. Too close in age, just a year between them, they squabbled over their toys, their books and comics as they grew to school-going age, and later, their clothes. Wearing exactly the same size, dresses, skirts, jeans and other stuff often disappeared into one another's wardrobes much to the annoyance of the owner who rightly claimed that this pink blouse or blue jeans was their most treasured possession.

Now, even still, some gripe lay buried. Never forgiven. And neither remembered exactly what it was about, but it could often raise its ugly little head and poison the air they breathed.

## Chapter Twenty-two

Liz met her friends on Saturday night, and they had a delicious meal in their favourite restaurant, El Guadeloupe.

'Right, give us the news. Bring us up to date,' Leah demanded.

'My pain in the ass has gone off to the States on business. Left me to my own devices. What do you say to that?' Megan asked.

'Plenty of opportunities,' they smiled knowingly.

'I'm not hanging around here, I'm off to Spain. Anyone want to come along?'

'Work has priority in my diary. I don't have a sugar daddy supporting me,' Celine said, laughing.

'Me neither,' Leah added.

'And Liz?'

'I can never drop out of sight without warning, you know that. Any break must be planned well in advance. And I'm busy with my book. It's with the printer now so I'll have to be here to check proofs and that sort of thing.'

'I think it's so exciting to be publishing a book,' Celine said.

'It's fantastic to get your photos out there, and let everyone see your work.'

'I mightn't sell any.' Liz wasn't confident.

'Course you will. We'll all buy one anyway, won't we, girls.'

'And sell one to everyone we know.'

'Thanks a mill.'

'Any news from the English guy you met at Ashford Castle?' Megan asked Leah.

'Yes actually,' Leah was coy. 'He's coming over in a couple of weeks' time and wants to meet. Do you think I should?' She was the only strictly single one of the four. Never been married at all. And her only wish was to reach that status. That above all else. Be able to tick *married* on a form. Wear a wedding band on the third finger of her left hand and know that it was put there by a man who loved her.

'You fancy him, don't you?' Megan asked.

Leah nodded.

'Then go ahead. Why not? Life is for living.' They were unanimous.

'And wear that blue outfit you bought recently. You'll look great.'

'Get your make-up done.'

'And don't wear floppy knickers like *Bridget Jones*, whatever you do, it must be something really sexy underneath,' Celine added.

They screamed with laughter.

'How about black lace?' Megan suggested.

'And maybe you should lose a couple of pounds in the meantime?'

'More than that I think,' Leah screamed with laughter.

'Starvation diet.'

Liz thought that the advice should have been directed at her. She wasn't quite as svelte as she used to be so perhaps some toning would be in order. Although there wasn't much improvement that could be made between now and Wednesday so Scott would have to put up with the way she was now. Anyway, what did she care?

She felt guilty that she hadn't divulged Scott's existence to the girls They would have loved it. A man in Liz's life. My God. Astonishing. Tell us all about him. Go on, tell, tell. Leah and Celine had been in college with her and knew Scott back then too, so she kept him to herself like an entry in that diary she had found recently. Scott hadn't yet found his way into those nightly episodes. The secret pulses of a young girl's imaginings. He came later. And now she was keeping secrets again. A woman afraid to speak out.

'Let's go to the theatre next week, I've got a voucher for the Gate, Celine asked. 'How's Wednesday?'

'What's on?'

'Chekhov.'

Someone made a face.

'Boring.'

'It's supposed to be good.'

'What's the name?'

'Can't remember.'

'Doesn't say much.'

'I don't want to waste the voucher.'

'We can use it again.'

'I have it for ages, it might go out of date.'

'The Gate are very good about vouchers.'

'Come on, let's go, it will be an enjoyable night out.'

Hands were raised.

'Liz?'

'Can't make it. Sorry.'

'What are you doing?'

'Work.'

'Can you change it?'

'No, it's been arranged for ages.'

'Let's make it the following week.'

'You go ahead, girls,' Liz said.

'We'll miss you.'

Liz felt embarrassed. She wouldn't have minded going to the theatre. But now Wednesday had already been pencilled into her diary. There the entry glimmered in red like traffic lights. Was it a warning? 'There's something I must tell you,' she said hesitantly, deciding she may as well.

'That sounds serious,' Celine said.

'What is it?' Megan squealed.

All their attention was on her now.

'Come on? Explain?' Leah demanded.

'I have a date on that night. I apologise that I said it was work but it isn't.'

'With a man?' Celine asked, very slowly and distinctly.

'Yea.'

'Who is he?'

'It's someone I knew years ago.'

'What's his name?'

'You might remember him, Celine and Leah, he was at college with us …it's Scott Fenton,' she admitted, feeling a blush steal over her cheeks.

'Scott?' they repeated together.

She nodded.

'When did you meet him?'

'Just a couple of weeks ago.'

'Have you been out already?'

'Once.'

'And is he single still?'

'Not exactly.'

'What does that mean?'

She had to explain.

'All those years since the wife left, sounds safe enough.'

'Make the most, girl. Enjoy.'

'Two of our merry little band are suddenly talking about new men in their lives. It leaves Celine and I out in the cold,' Megan pouted.

'You're not in the market, Megan, so you shouldn't even be thinking about the possibility.'

'I'll tag along with you two,' Celine said. 'Maybe there will be a few friends hanging around.'

They laughed. The possibility of new men appearing always raised their spirits.

## *Chapter Twenty-three*

Luke tried out some new dishes for the menu at La Modena. And anxious to drum up some late night business they decided to extend the hours at the weekend, as they already had the various licences needed. He could supply a tapas menu and prepare it himself so the kitchen staff wouldn't be needed. And they arranged to employ a pianist to play jazz, and a singer who could double up as a waitress. They were taking a chance but thought it was worth it for a few weeks.

But he couldn't avoid that elephant in the room and still dreaded telling Liz he was gay. Luke couldn't bear the thought of being criticised. And had a terrible fear of being expelled from the family.

Get out of this house.

You're no longer acceptable.

What will people say?

You have shamed us.

And the door banging.

Behind him.

With a crash.

Loud.

Final.

No longer loved.

That was the way it was for some people he knew. Those very words used by parents who were supposed to love their sons and daughters. By siblings too. So Luke spent less time with the family, afraid they would notice his preoccupation. Although the Referendum had changed everything, he still held back from telling his family that he was gay.

He knew he should talk to his mother. He remembered when he was a boy. There were so many opportunities to tell her then. Walking the beach together. In the kitchen as she taught him to cook. He remembered the delicious recipes they tried out together. His mouth watered. Taste buds were activated. Those times were so dear to his heart. He could have explained how he was feeling then, a teenager attracted to another boy at school. But it never happened. And the secret remained buried deep, like a tiny nagging stone in his shoe.

Unexpectedly it was busy that night. The waiters passed through the orders and they were pinned on a board. Once complete Luke struck a line across. When they had opened up the restaurant, they had considered going the hi-tech route with waiters wearing mikes, and orders picked up on the computer in the kitchen. But they didn't want to spend the money initially, so kept to the old ways.

Daniel ushered people in and reorganised the tables when necessary. Front of house was very important and they certainly weren't going to hand that initial contact over to an employee. They had half a dozen waiters and waitresses who whizzed through the swing doors which led to the kitchen and returned bearing trays. Luke and Daniel's secret was to offer an excellent service and the quality of the food was as high as possible.

Luke reached for Daniel's hand. They had little time to themselves these days and he missed the opportunities for intimacy which were swallowed up by their tough working schedule. They kissed slowly.

'Let's plan the wedding,' Daniel murmured.

'We've no money now.' Luke moved closer.

'We'll just have a simple ceremony. We can scrape enough for that. The honeymoon can be deferred for now.'

Luke opened the buttons on his shirt.

'We could arrange it in a few months. How about after Christmas when it's slack? I'll get the diary.' Daniel went over to the desk and came back with it. 'How about the end of December? We won't open again until New Year.'

Luke kissed him.

'If we don't get married this year then it might never happen. Come on, I'll make all the arrangements,' Daniel encouraged. 'You won't have to do a thing.'

Luke looked at Daniel. He did love him and wanted to live with him. To be married. Properly. In the eyes of the State. They had equality with everyone else in the country which was an amazing achievement. Many of their friends had already got married. Weddings varied from colourful events with music, flowers and all the trappings, to the simple two witness ceremony and a low key dinner afterwards with only close family in attendance. But Luke had always wanted a splash. To make a statement about his sexuality.

He remembered Brooke and Rory's wedding. It had been such an amazing day, although he had felt out there on the edge of it all. Men handsome in tuxedos. Woman in drifting chiffon and feathered hats. But he was neither one thing or the other. Unable to tell everyone that he wanted to be next. That he had a partner. Someone he couldn't introduce to his family. Daniel was right. They had to commit to a date, and all that meant.

## Chapter Twenty-four

Sophie had an evening appointment with a family of four in the studio. They burst in the door, a group of excited people, mother, father, son and daughter.

'We're the Taylors, here for the photo-shoot,' the wife giggled, as did the daughter.

She poured coffee from the percolator. They sat down. The daughter close to her father, his arm around her shoulders. They chatted among themselves while she prepared her cameras. Setting up the tripod. Repositioning the backdrop. She noticed how affectionate they were with each other. The son particularly so with his mother. His hand cupped her cheek for a few seconds, then softly slid down her arm and held her wrist gently.

'Would you like to come over and take a position?' she asked.

They stood in front of the screen. The son slightly behind his mother, his hands touching her arms. He dropped a kiss on the back of her head more than once. The girl snuggled into her father.

For one crazy moment, Sophie wondered if they were two couples. The older woman with the toy boy. The man with the young girl.

She took a few shots. But however hard she tried to change their positions, she couldn't quite manage it. They insisted on staying as two couples. They were very strange. Always touching and clinging in various poses. Grouped together. Full length. Head and shoulders. Laughing. Serious. Sitting. Standing. They were keen to use the various chairs and tables she had. Particularly the chaise longue. Shoes were taken off. The men unbuttoned their shirts. And the women gradually showed much more cleavage as the session progressed.

When the photo shoot was finished, she asked for their details so that she could print out an invoice.

'There's no need for paperwork,' the man said.

'We always make out an invoice.'

'We prefer it this way.' He handed her a bundle of notes.

'You don't have to pay in full until you receive the final prints,' she protested. 'I'll need your email so that I can send you all the photos and you can choose the ones you want.'

'I'll call in to collect the prints of all of the photos.'

'You want all of them?'

'Yes, that will be fine. If we owe you any more then I'll pay the balance on collection.'

'All right.' Sophie was puzzled, it was unusual.

'It was a very pleasant experience. We enjoyed it,' the mother said. The others nodded and laughed, arms still around each other as they went out.

Sophie fingered the notes, and wondered if she …

# Chapter Twenty-five

Brooke called into the studio.

Sophie immediately appeared from the office. 'Oh, it's you,' she said. It was a blunt unwelcoming response.

'Yea, I wanted to chat,' she said awkwardly, aware of the coldness of Sophie's expression.

'We're busy.'

'I'll wait until you're finished.'

Liz came from behind. She kissed Brooke. 'How are you?' she enquired softly. 'And the children?'

'Grand thanks.'

Liz was so gentle a glimmer of tears filled Brooke's eyes. Immediately, she felt like throwing her arms around her mother and crying out loud like one of her own children might do. The loss of Rory was so close to the surface. Her despair infinite. Abandoned by the person she thought loved her above any other.

'We're just finishing up.' Liz led her through into the office. 'But this could be timely, I'm thinking,' she smiled and pulled out a chair for her. 'Have we much more to do, Sophie?'

'We just need to confirm the appointments in the diary.'

'We've a busy week ahead of us.' Liz entered names.

'Can I still accept your offer of a job please?' Brooke asked hesitant. Nervous now. Aware that Sophie wasn't pleased that she hadn't taken up their offer immediately. She clasped her hands tightly. Her fingernails were perfectly manicured and painted a soft pink to match the padded jacket she wore. 'Is it still available?'

'Yes it is,' Liz replied, smiling.

'I was wondering what you would like me to do exactly?'

'We need help in lots of areas,' Sophie said. 'We don't expect you to go out on photo shoots immediately.'

'Thanks for that.' Brooke was grateful. She relaxed and sat back in the chair her body softening underneath the bulky shape of the jacket. The tense lines around her mouth disappeared.

'First, I thought you might be able to help us with the admin,' Liz said, with a smile.

'I'm sure I could.'

'It's just general stuff. You know, keeping account of deposits and balances, invoices, statements etc. We have a very simple system, so you should have no difficulty. I'll go through it with you in detail. Also, when we're out, you could deal with people who call in, give them some info, make appointments, sell our services etc. How does that sound?'

'I hope I can manage, the job doesn't sound as scary as I first thought.'

'Did you feel nervous about it?' Sophie asked.

'Of course, what did you think?'

'I thought you just weren't interested, and that it was altogether too boring for you.'

'No, that wasn't it.' She couldn't explain that her confidence was at an all-time low. That she was scared of accepting the job. How would she compare with Sophie in her mother's eyes? Would she make a mess of everything? The thought of working here was daunting.

'Well, you're coming to work with us and that's the main thing.' Liz hugged her.

'I'm glad, Brooke, we need help, you need a job, so it's perfect,' Sophie added.

'Great. What days would you like to work?' Liz asked, picking up her pen.

'I could work mornings while the kids are at play school, but I'd need to be able to finish before lunchtime so that I can pick them up,' she offered.

'That would be fine.'

'And I could do some work on my computer at home as well if you like?'

'Sure, we're absolutely flexible about that.'

'Thanks for asking me to come and work for you. It means so much. I don't know where I'd have found a job.' She wanted them to know how grateful she was.

'When would you like to come in?'

'Tomorrow?'

'We'd love that, wouldn't we Sophie?' Liz smiled.

'Sure.'

'Have you seen Rory?'

'No, but he was on the phone.'

'That's positive,' Liz murmured.

'I don't know about that, he wants to sell the house.'

They gasped. Together. In shock.

'But he can't do that, it's your home?' Liz exploded.

'Maybe it might be for the best,' Brooke admitted. 'I've been thinking that if I refuse to agree to the sale of the house, then I'll have to pay the mortgage and all the bills.'

'But he has to support you,' Liz said vehemently.

'He's being very difficult, and I can see myself having to take him to court to force him to support me and the children. And I don't think I could take the stress of all that. Having to bring him back to court time after time when he falls down on the payments would be just too much.'

They listened sympathetically.

'So to sell the house might be the better option?' Liz asked.

'You could buy a smaller house with the proceeds,' Sophie said.

'We'll help you find somewhere nice,' Liz was suddenly enthusiastic

'Prices are going up all the time. I might have to get a mortgage.'

'And as you haven't been working or saving in a bank or building society that may be difficult,' Sophie pointed out.

Brooke realised that she was right, and suddenly the idea of buying her own home looked bleak.

'The kids must miss Rory,' Liz said.

'They do. It's tough on them.' She had tried for their sake not to break down quite so often. How could she ever tell them their father had left home. Her little babies. She still thought of them in that way.

## Chapter Twenty-six

Luke called over to Howth to see Liz on Sunday morning. All week he had braced himself questioning why he dreaded the thought of talking about his sexuality with someone he loved. Who loved him so much. It was the most natural of relationships. Without barriers. Why did he fear this baring of his deepest self to his mother. He accused himself of weakness.

'Liz hugged him close. 'It's been too long. Tell me why I haven't seen you. What have I done?'

'Nothing at all. It's me. Work has taken over.'

'I can understand that. Is there an end in sight when you might begin to think of yourself?'

The question slid through him.

'I'm thinking of myself now,' he said. Years of hiding his true nature wouldn't disappear just like that. He remembered growing up. Those teenage years. Why he was different to other boys in his class, because he wasn't interested in football, but played anyway so as not to stand out. It wasn't until he was in college that he made those first hesitant friendships with others of similar persuasion. Frequented gay bars and finally came out to himself.

'I worry about you.' She looked at him keenly.

He twisted his hands tightly. Knuckles white. 'The business isn't going well.'

She was sympathetic. 'It takes a couple of years to achieve profitability in any business.'

'I know. Yet it's what I've always wanted to do.'

'But there's no time for a social life by the sound of it.' It was a pointed remark.

He flinched.

'What about girls? Where do they fit in?'

'They don't.' It was his ideal opportunity but he didn't take it.

She smiled, knowingly. 'There will always be someone, Luke.'

'I want you to come over for dinner to the restaurant soon, bring the girls.'

'We'll have to pay.'

'No, I've invited you.'

'I don't know how you can make a profit at that rate.'

'This is a once off.'

'No such thing. We won't come unless we pay,' she said. 'And that's that.'

He could never win with his mother.

'Are you staying for lunch, have you time?' she asked. 'I'm putting it on now.'

'No, I'll have to go, I just wanted to see you.'

'We've missed you, it's been ages.'

'I've missed you too.'

'Please come more often.'

'There's something,' he said, making a huge effort to explain what was in his heart.

'Yes?' All her attention was on him.

'I've never told you this, or anyone in the family, but I have to do it now.'

She waited. Her eyes met his, and he felt reassured.

'I'm ...gay,' he said hesitantly. He wondered if she could even hear him.

'Luke, I know you're gay, and I have known that for a long time.'

He stared at her, astonished. 'How?'

'I'm your mother, Luke,' she said softly. She stood, put her arms around him and held him close.

They were silent. No need for words any more.

A huge weight lifted off him. He couldn't believe this.

'There were times I felt I should say something, but it really had to come from you.'

'I should have told you long before this.'

'Even when you were a teenager I knew.'

'So many lost opportunities,' he admitted.

'A hint would have been enough.'

'Imagine how scared I was,' he said, smiling. 'Even these last years I couldn't summon up the courage.'

'And I presume Daniel is the man in your life?'

He nodded. 'We want to get married now so it was very important that we tell everybody. I don't feel so worried about Sophie and Brooke.'

'They both know as well, so you don't have to say anything. Try and come around when we're all here together, maybe next Sunday, and you can just tell us you're getting married to Daniel, and bring him along as well.'

'You are wonderful, I love you to bits.' He flung his arms around her.

'And remember that I love you, and you should never worry about telling me anything, whatever it is,' reassured Liz.

## Chapter Twenty-seven

The estate agent called. Brooke was taken aback. Suddenly she was being pushed into the sale of the house before she had even decided whether she would go along with it. He wanted to make a viewing appointment the following morning. But she said no. It would have to be the afternoon. It felt good to be busy and anyway why should she facilitate Rory by being too obliging. She knew enough about Family Law to know that she was a vital part of it and he couldn't sell the house without her agreement. But the fact that he had threatened not to pay the mortgage was enough to force her into agreeing with him.

The man called. She brought him around watching while he photographed, measured and made various notes about the house and garden. She had already moved a lot of personal items out of sight. Hating the thought that people would be staring at her personal space in the newspapers and online.

Rory called around later that evening and his first question was about the estate agent. No mention of the children, and how they were, or herself either. That infuriated her.

'Is there any way I could keep the house?' she asked, although she already knew the answer.

He laughed, a sarcastic titter. 'Not unless you can buy me out.'

'And you'd want half?'

'Of course.'

'Would you take less?' she ventured.

'Are you stupid?'

'I'm just discussing my options.'

'You don't have any options.'

'I have a job now,' she was defiant.

He turned to look at her. A look of surprise on his face. 'That was quick.'

'I'm working with Mum and Sophie.'

'That's good. Now you can pay your way. Amazing what you can do if you put your mind to it. Approach the bank anyway, but you have no track record and they're unlikely to give you a mortgage.'

'I'll do that,' she said stubbornly, knowing in her heart of hearts that he was right. But she decided to open a new bank account immediately and save as much as she could so that when she wanted to buy her own home she would be able to do it.

'Work away. In the meantime, we'll be showing the house, and you'll be expected to be out when prospective buyers arrive.'

'Goodness knows what they will be doing, poking and prying into everything.' She shuddered physically.

'If you're not here, you won't know about it.'

'They could even steal things. I've heard of that.'

'Then don't leave anything about the place.'

'But I can't move everything.'

'Brooke, you'll have to deal with it yourself.' He turned to leave.

'I wish you could come around to see the children? You're not away every week,' she said, trying to be gentle. 'And they really miss you.'

'Claire doesn't have time for children.'

'But take them out yourself, to the park, the playground, anywhere at all.

'I'll see.'

'Are you still living in her place?'

'What's this inquisition, Brooke?'

'I'm just wondering where we fit in.'

'You don't fit in anywhere.'

'You're so callous.'

He shrugged and went into the hall.

She followed.

'Daddy?'

She stared at Cian who ran down the stairs.

But Rory was already closing the front door.

She gathered him up in her arms.

'Where's Daddy gone?' he asked.

'He had to rush off.'

'Will he come back?'

She tucked him up in bed. Then she kissed him. 'Go to sleep now.' He closed his eyes. She sat on the bed for a while until he eventually fell asleep. It was so unfair on the kids. She wondered how she had ever loved Rory. He was so different now compared to the man she had met and married. By leaving her for another woman she had thought her heart would break. But as time passed and she could see the other side of his personality her love for him had become blunt as a used knife.

Brooke left the house. Feeling like she was saying goodbye. In an hour's time, the estate agent would begin to ferry a series of people into her home. To stare at her precious possessions. The items she had bought for the various rooms over time. Those things which reminded of a marriage which had gone wrong. The paintings Rory and herself had chosen together. The work of contemporary artists which they hoped would increase in value down the line and be a pension plan for the future. Would Rory give most of their collection to her, or insist on dividing it up piecemeal? She hated the thought of that. One for me. One for you. And so on until everything was allocated. It made her sick.

She climbed into the jeep and took a glance back as she waited for the automatic gates to swing open. It was a cold day. Tall trees surrounded the house. Shadows dipped under the eaves like eyebrows over mullioned windows. The walls were painted white. The front door a shining black. The gravel driveway circled around, an entry on one side, the exit on the other. She pulled out on to the road. She didn't know where she was going. She had dropped the children out to Peggy, who was delighted to look after them for the afternoon. So upset, she really couldn't have gone into the studio to face her mother and sister, or to meet any friends. Not that Brooke had seen many of them lately, somehow she had fallen out of the circle. She wondered whether they were ever friends. She drove out to Donabate. Parked the jeep and walked along the beach. There was no one around. She put her face into the cold wind and strode out, her hands pushed into her pockets. She tried not to think of the invasion of curiosity currently taking place in her home. Foreign shoes bringing dust and mud on to her highly polished wooden floors. Fingers lifting a piece of her delicate Lladro, examining it, and putting it down again on a glass table with a sharp crack. Eyes looking from one to another. *Like this. Like that. Don't like this. Don't like that. This house is too expensive. Not worth the money they're looking for it.*

Later, she picked up the children from Peggy. 'Thanks so much for looking after them.' She hugged her.

The children sat watching cartoons on television.

'They don't want to go home now,' Peggy said, laughing. 'Can I get you anything?'

'No thanks, but there's something I want to tell you,' she hesitated. Not knowing whether Rory had told his mother how things were between them. 'I've got a job with Mum and Sophie, I'm joining the business.'

'That's lovely for you, it will be nice to have something to do. What does Rory think?'

'He's happy enough,' she said awkwardly.

'You're great to go out to work. As the kids are at play school it will give you a chance to do your own thing. And next year it will be regular school, so you need to be busy.'

'I'll be going in mornings only, and then I can work at home if I want.'

'It will be a new challenge for you. And don't forget I'll look after the children any time you need me.'

'Thanks, Peggy, you're a pet.'

On her return, the house seemed the same. Still white. Pristine. But it wasn't the same. To Brooke it had been tainted by the breath of strangers who hadn't been invited. She could feel it in the hall the moment she opened the door. Since she had given up smoking, she immediately noticed the slight whiff of a smoker which was carried in the air. A strange perfume clung to the drapes. The children followed as she went through the house searching for something which was out of place. Opening doors. Looking behind furniture for someone who hadn't left yet. She even went down to the shed at the end of the garden. The kids immediately demanding to play with some of the toys they spotted in there.

'No, not today,' she said, and wouldn't give in. She had too much to do. Checking. Re-checking. Examining. Counting. It seemed as if it was all there. Although a vase was nearer the edge of the mantle than it should be. She moved it to its correct position, and immediately rushed to wash her hands, fearful of contamination.

Rory phoned. 'Were there many viewers?'

'I don't know, I wasn't here. Ring the auctioneer.'

'I expected seven or eight, and we might even get an offer out of that lot.'

So quick, she thought, with a sense of dread. She had hoped it would take much longer than that. She wasn't ready to leave yet. To find somewhere new to live. To settle her children's hearts. Tears flooded her eyes. She struggled to hold back. Reluctant to let Rory know how much she cared.

'Let me know if anything happens,' he said.

Before she had time to think of a reply he was gone.

She wondered about finding a house. It would certainly be nowhere like her home here. But she wanted to stay on the north side of the city near her mother. Her mind took her closer to Howth. Maybe she might find somewhere out there. Loneliness stabbed like a knife cutting through delicate skin. It felt like a brutal attack by a husband who coveted another woman.

## *Chapter Twenty-eight*

Liz showered and changed. She was nervous, unable to make up her mind what to wear for her date with Scott. Finally, as she had worn black the first time they met, she chose a pale grey skirt with a silver top and matching scarf.

She took a taxi into Dawson Street, and the car pulled up outside Chambre Bleu. She paid and stepped out, pushing up the umbrella to protect herself from the rain. She dashed for the entrance door and went inside. Someone came in behind her, a swirl of wind hurtling through as the door was opened. She glanced behind her.

'Liz?'

It was Scott.

They stared at each other. He moved closer. His eyes met hers. His hand reached to cup her face. His lips touched. Soft. Warm. So familiar. She responded. Their bodies clung to each other. But they had to part almost immediately as the door opened behind them and a group of people pushed in. They went into the restaurant, which was crowded with diners. The manager came towards them, smiling.

'We've a reservation for Fenton, table five in the window,' Scott said.

The manager took their coats and they were seated. 'I think this calls for champagne.' Scott took her hands in his and held them tight.

'A celebration?'

'Definitely.'

The waiter came over, and Scott ordered.

The champagne arrived, and the wine waiter pulled the cork from the bottle with a pop. He poured the sparkling liquid into their glasses and Scott raised his and clinked against hers.

'To us, Liz.'

For the first time she felt totally relaxed with him. That kiss at the door had whirled her back in time to the way it used to be when they first met. The evening had a mystical quality about it. They ate slowly, talking all the time, but she wasn't even aware of the taste of the food. She must have finished it as she vaguely noticed that when the waiter cleared the table her plate was almost clean.

Scott poured the last of the champagne, and she stared into his eyes. Deep blue. She was caught in their glance. He smiled. She couldn't resist. His fingers caressed hers. Softly massaged her skin. Slowly. Tenderly. She gripped the stem of the glass and sipped. His touch was electric. She trembled. Some deep upheaval erupted inside her. A volcano. Nothing else existed. Only Scott.

'I still love you, Liz,' he whispered. 'Never stopped, I couldn't.'

'I love you too.'

He leaned nearer. Their lips met in soft recognition. Her head swam.

He shared the taxi home with her as before. She took her key and opened the front door. The alarm beeped and she hurried into the hall to insert the code. He followed. She turned around to face him.

He took her into his arms. She let herself go as naturally as ever. Easing close to his body. Feeling the contours. The broadness of his chest. His strong arms encircling. His thighs touching hers. She closed her eyes. They stood there oblivious of anything else. The waiting taxi. The wind whipping around the house and causing the heavy front door to slowly move back and forward on its hinges.

'Will I let the taxi go?' he asked. A slight tremor in his voice.

'Yes,' she said.

He took his time, kissed her again, and went out. She stood waiting at the front door, smiling at him as he came back up. She closed the door and locked it.

'*Fort Knox*?' he laughed.

'Would you like a drink?' she asked. Walking ahead of him into the living room.

'No thanks, I just want you.' He put his arms around her and drew her close again.

Her heart fluttered. She couldn't believe this was happening.

He kissed her. Their lips clasped. His tongue searched for hers. Deep. Her senses screamed. His touch so familiar she responded to him with a sexual need she had not known since they parted all those years ago. Ethan had never lit such a flame within her. It was only now that she realised what she had missed.

Scott's hands curved around her back underneath her top and found soft skin. She shivered. His fingers fumbled with her bra fastening. She giggled.

'Sorry, I'm out of practice.' His sudden smile reminded of how he looked when he was young.

She opened it.

'God,' he groaned, pushed up her top, and delicately traced the curves of her breasts.

'I've missed you so much.'

She ran her hands through his short hair. It was silky. Then she pulled her top off and the rest of her clothes. Urgently he did the same and they lay on the couch.

'My love.' His lips touched hers and then moved down her body. The point of his tongue drawing damp designs on her skin until at last he slid his hands around her back and held her upwards into him. Slowly she gave of herself and they knew each other at last.

Liz awoke later. They were curled together. At her movement, he tightened his embrace. She kissed his forehead. 'Let's go upstairs,' she suggested.

He opened his eyes.

'It's cold down here.'

'I don't want to let you go.'

'The bed's cosier. Come on.'

They went up. To make love again. And sleep again. Only finally waking when her radio switched on. They smiled at each other.

'I thought this might have been a dream when I first opened my eyes.' He pushed her fringe back from her forehead. 'What joy to see you.' He cupped her face. 'I love you, Liz, so much, you've no idea.'

'I love you too, Scott, it's like I'm seventeen again.'

'It's wonderful to be here with you.' Scott stood behind Liz and put his arms around her.

She giggled as she mixed scrambled eggs and slid them on to two plates. Then crisp bacon, mushrooms, tomatoes, and golden buttered toast. She put their plates on the table, poured coffee, and sat down.

'You always were a great cook,' he smiled.

'Not bad yourself I remember, could do a mean beans on toast.'

'That was about all I could do, all we had back then.'

She was quiet for a moment, remembering those early days in his flat in Rathmines. Dreamy almost.

'Tell me about your boys,' she asked later.

'They're doing fine, we work together. Cathal is our Sales Director and Ryan handles the production end of things. Cathal is living with his partner, Gillian, but Ryan is still on his own, as far as I know,' he said, and laughed.

'It must have been tough when Ciara suddenly left like that.'

'We managed.'

'Were things very difficult before she left?'

'Not so much. I didn't know that she was so unhappy. I was a workaholic, intent on building up the business, and I suppose I didn't give her what she wanted. I wasn't there a lot of the time. I couldn't blame her.' He picked up the coffee pot and refilled their cups. 'No one would have put up with me, even you, Liz.'

'I wasn't much different.'

'Maybe it's just as well we didn't meet again before I'd matured a bit and realised there is more to life than business and money,' he said with a wide grin.

'It's all very well saying that but when you're trying to support a family you just give it your all. While our mortgage was paid off, I had to raise the kids, and all the costs that go with that. Education. Utilities. Food. Clothes. If I didn't get out there and work I don't know where we'd have been on Ethan's pension, it was miserable.'

'How is your daughter, Sophie? I remember we met her with her friends on Grafton Street last time.'

'Not so well, she has some sort of bug and is on antibiotics.'

'I hope she's all right, give her my regards.'

'She was very curious about you and quizzed me the following day. When I was choosing photographs for my collection I happened to mention a boyfriend and let your name slip. Sophie is quite sharp and we got serious for a bit, she even asked me if I loved you.'

'What did you say?' he laughed.

'I don't think I replied.' Liz couldn't remember exactly what she said to Sophie.

'I'm disappointed,' he said. 'But now that we're sitting here opposite one another, fully sober, can I believe that last night actually happened and it meant as much to you as it did to me?'

'Of course it did. It's the first time I've been with a man since Ethan, so there has only been one person since you and I.'

'The same for me, though you probably find that hard to believe.'

'No, if you say so, I believe you. Anyway, there is no point in telling a lie about something at this stage, it wouldn't be a good start.'

'Are we starting?' His eyes searched hers and he took her hand.

'I think I made that decision last night,' she said softly.

'How will we work things out, how often am I going to see you?' he asked.

'Since the two of us are workaholics that might be difficult.'

'Let's get together at weekends. I'll come up and maybe you might come down? And if I can I'll drive up during the week. I love you, Liz.

You've made me so happy.' He kissed her again.
'I love you, Scott.' They hugged close.

## Chapter Twenty-nine

Sophie felt guilty. All of the money she had received from the Taylors had been spent on drugs. She knew it was a very unfair thing to do on her mother, and she shouldn't have done it. She thought about her recent efforts to come off drugs which had proved ineffective, and now realised that the panic attacks had something to do with that, and weren't a result of stress or the spiking of her drinks. As well, her balance was affected sometimes, and her work was definitely substandard. So she had given up trying to reduce the quantity she normally took. It was just too difficult.

She received another call from the Taylors. Could she do another session? There had already been quite a few and she agreed immediately. Why not?

This time they were even more dramatic. The women wore floating silk gowns, and the men wide brimmed seventeenth century hats. They had brought a blow air heater with them, and it caused the women's dresses to whirl in the air. They relaxed languidly on the chaise longue. The women fluttered beautiful lace fans. Peeping out from behind them in a teasing fashion. The men tied on masks. Reminiscent of Carnival in Venice. She found it hard to focus. Their movements grew more and more sensual. Suddenly she wanted to stop. To tell them that she didn't want to do this. But couldn't.

She excused herself for a moment to bring in another camera and quickly took a tablet. Ecstasy and sometimes other drugs were essential to her everyday living. To get through the daily grind.

She wound up the session. They were pleased. Keith Taylor paid her in cash as usual. He arranged another session. It was such a help to her. She could use this money to finance her drugs and no one was aware of it.

There was a new man in her life. Clayton played in a band. They had hit it off famously. He was divorced. So no problems there. And he was in much the same circle. Drank a bit. Used a bit. Nothing too sinister. He moved into her life easily. Came home to her apartment after gigs and stayed over. Often still there when she arrived home after work the following day. He had his own place but much preferred hers. His friends called regularly too. She enjoyed their company, and often hung around his dockland warehouse where he had his music studio.

'There's something about that job you did the other day,' Liz said.

'Which one?' Sophie asked.

'The family with the new baby.'

'Oh?'

'The quality wasn't great in some of the shots.'

Sophie stared at her mother, feeling embarrassed that Liz had noticed.

'Which?'

'The baby on her own. They were a bit soft focus. I'm not sure what we're going to do about them.' She stared at the photos on the computer screen.

'What's wrong exactly?' Sophie was suddenly worried.

'As I said, they're soft, look.' She pointed.

'I don't see anything.'

'Come on, Sophie, they're not up to your usual standard.'

'Maybe it was the camera?'

'The settings mightn't be correct.'

'Do you think they'll be acceptable?'

Liz stared at her, shocked. 'Of course they won't.'

'What will we do?'

'They'll have to be re-done. Perhaps the whole photo shoot, we can't pick some of them out and re-do them. There's a vitality about the family groupings.'

'I'm sorry, Mum,' Sophie couldn't say any more.

'Call them, admit there was a technical problem with the lens and make another appointment,' Liz suggested. 'Really, it's not like you at all.'

Sophie was upset, and couldn't understand how it had happened. Normally she was as particular as her mother regarding the quality of their work.

'And we will have to compensate them in some way. It's a nuisance to ask the family to come into the studio again. Give them some discount on the overall job.'

'How much do you think?'

'It would have to be at least twenty percent anyway, a decent amount.'

Sophie agreed, almost expecting her mother to say that the amount would be taken out of her salary. Something that would probably happen if she were employed in any other company. But she didn't, of course, much to Sophie's relief.

She rang the client and re-arranged the photo shoot. But to her surprise they particularly liked the soft focus shots of the baby, and wanted to keep them. But Sophie took more photos anyway and gave them two lots from which to choose. In the end, it worked out fine and she insisted on giving them the discount.

'I should repay that money,' Sophie said to Liz.

'Don't worry about it.' Her mother continued with what she was doing. 'Oh, I have the proof of the book, Martin sent it this morning. What do you think?' They looked at the screen together.

'It's really great. The simple black cover with your name and the title in gold, I love it.'

'And this is the way he's set out the photos inside. They're positioned at different angles with the text following. The backgrounds are in different hues, greys, pale blues, and that very soft pinkish tone. I think it works quite well and brings some colour into the collection and doesn't highlight the black and white element.'

'It looks super.' Sophie scrolled down through the different pages.

'Martin will have it printed by the middle of March. How about some time in April for the launch? We need to give ourselves plenty of time to send out invitations.'

'I'm looking forward to it.'

'Thanks a mill, I don't know what I'd do without you.' Liz hugged Sophie.

But as she returned her mother's hug, Sophie thought the same. Where would she be without Liz?

Sophie uploaded the photographs she had taken at the last session with the Taylors. Now she worked on them at home, aware that if she did that at the studio Liz could easily look over her shoulder and question the nature of them.

She was in the middle of it when Clayton arrived.

'Ready?' he asked.

'For what?'

'We're meeting some friends, remember I told you?'

'You did?'

'We're heading down to Wicklow, the others are in the car outside.'

'Sorry, I can't go.'

'What?' He stared at her, decidedly put out. 'But it's a formal do.'

'I'm sorry.'

'For God's sake, Sophie, how many times have you done this?'

'A few, I suppose, but that's the way my work is. I'm always busy.'

'You can't expect me to be the one to *kowtow* to your schedule every time.'

'Your own life isn't exactly nine to five.' Immediately, she regretted the irritable snap.

'Maybe you'd rather not be involved in it anymore?'

'Clayton, I've enjoyed our times together.' It was a stiff reply, but she didn't go as far as saying she loved him. Although at odd times when they had sex she sometimes whispered those words, as he did. But now she wondered if there was any truth there. Make love. Say you love. Was it an automatic response? Like the meaningless lyrics of one of the songs he sang on stage?

'I'd better go,' he said.

'Enjoy yourself.'

'Will I call you?' he asked, sounding unsure.

'If you want.' She let it lie there. That option.

He stood looking at her. His eyes quizzical.

She felt she could control the situation now.

'I must go.'

'See you.'

He cupped her face in his rather large hand. And kissed her.

She stood there making no response, and accepted his kiss apathetically.

He left then. The door swung closed after him. Soft. Silent.

She took the notebook from the drawer, and drew a line through his name.


Brooke called.

'Have you done all the invites?'

'As many as I can think of.'

'When will we send them out?'

'About two weeks before. Not too early and not too late.'

'Luke will organise the wine. Is your guy, Clayton, doing the music?'

'I don't know.' Sophie felt guilty. She had asked him and he had agreed, but after their rather strained conversation earlier she doubted that he would.

'Pity.'

'Maybe we'll put on a CD, at those kind of events you can't hear a thing anyway.'

'They were only going to play at the beginning as people wander in, so it doesn't matter that much.'

'We had an argument.'

'Was it serious?'

'I suppose.'

'Want to talk?'

'He's not worth it.'

'Then we'll just put on some music to add a bit of atmosphere. By the way, one of my friends asked me to approach you with a proposition.'

'What sort of proposition?' Sophie was curious.

'Don't jump the gun, think about it,' Brooke warned.

'Yea, I usually do that, don't I?' Sophie laughed.

'You said it.'

'Go on, tell me.'

'Do you know Paula? She has long dark hair, tall, thin.'

'I think so, but I'm not sure.'

'She's going to have a baby and wants to have the event caught on camera.'

'But surely, they can take a few shots themselves. The husband perhaps?'

'She feels that her husband will be so caught up with the whole birth process, he won't be able to focus on anything else.'

'Probably right. They're usually pretty useless around that time.'

'So, would you be willing to do it?'

Sophie was surprised. 'I don't know. I've never seen anyone have a baby. I'd be scared stiff.'

'It's not that bad.'

'You only know it from the inside, to watch it from outside is a completely different thing.'

'Paula wants someone she knows.'

'Brooke, what did you say to her?'

'I just said I'd ask.'

'Where is she having the baby?'

'At home.'

'I suppose that's better, I had imagined trying to work around nurses and doctors, anyway I wouldn't have thought they'd give permission.

'There will only be a midwife.'

'I'll have to talk to Paula before I agree, see what she wants exactly.'

'I'll text you her number.'

Sophie was astonished. Was this some new-fangled notion among the *yummy mummy* crew? Photos of a birth. She had a vision of bloody mucus and her stomach heaved. She wasn't good around stuff like that. What if she fainted? How embarrassing would that be? No, she decided to avoid this particular job.

## *Chapter Thirty*

'We've got an offer,' Rory sounded excited.

Brooke wasn't able to say anything.

'Although the estate agent thinks we might do better.'

She couldn't understand his enthusiasm. How anxious he was to hand their home over to someone else. Their home. So full of memories. Of happy days. Bringing up their children. Friends around at weekends. Laughter. Love.

Tears filled her eyes.

'You might start looking for somewhere else to live.'

'If we accept the offer, how much will I get?'

'Probably about a hundred thousand after our mortgage is paid off, and auctioneers and legal fees are covered.'

'That won't buy a house.'

'It'll go some way towards it. And if you start saving then eventually you might be able to get a mortgage. But you have to be ready to move out. Start packing up your stuff. It could all happen very quickly and I don't want any delay in closing the sale.'

She was being evicted. It was hard to believe. Evicted. A hard hearted landlord was telling her to get out of her home. A person who professed to love her such a short time ago. A man who brought her red roses. Gifts of perfume. Jewellery. Surprising her with tickets to a show. A night away. Just the two of them. The ultimate in romance. How was it that he had changed so much? Had this new woman turned him against her. The bitch saw more of him than she did. All day, every day. The ideal opportunity to get her claws into him and drag him away from his wife and family. Furious, Brooke longed to grab hold of her and let her know how she felt.

She wondered about refusing to agree to the sale of the house? It was an interesting possibility. She smiled, thinking of Rory's reaction to that scenario. But if she wanted any support, she would have to play his game. If she stalled the sale, then he would certainly make sure to get his own back. It probably wasn't worth it. She hated being pushed into a corner. But had she always been pushed into corners? Had he bullied her from the beginning? And had she given in for the sake of peace between them?

It was an unpleasant truth and reflected who she really was. A wimp.

At the studio, Brooke looked at the screen. She was checking through the list of payments lodged into the bank account going back over the past months. Comparing it with job cards, and appointments in the diary, which according to their accounts procedure were always meant to be compatible with each other.

But one name cropped up in the diary which appeared to be a firm appointment. But there was no job card, or bank lodgement. She puzzled it out, but couldn't quite find a reason why this should be. There was a telephone number and she decided to make a PR call. It wouldn't do any harm and if they hadn't done any business then it might encourage them to come in for a session. She made a note of the number.

Brooke still worked the mornings, and a few hours later in the day as well. She was so thankful to her mother and sister for giving her the opportunity to join the company. And she was saving hard too, watching her own spending carefully.

Her phone rang. It was the estate agent.

'I've some more people who want to see the property, will tomorrow morning suit?'

'Yea, sure,' she agreed, and gritted her teeth. More people to come around her home and gaze, and examine, and touch. The thought of it made her feel sick.

She made the call to the client, Mr. Taylor.

'Yes, we've been around to the studio on a number of occasions,' the man said.

'Have you been happy with the results?'

'Delighted. Sophie has been particularly accommodating as regards the time, fitting us in after she has finished for the day.'

'When is your next appointment?'

'We were in last week, it's usually every two or three weeks.'

'Good, we look forward to seeing you again,' she said, and put down the phone. She sat there. Unsure of what to think. Was something going on? But then she dismissed the suspicious thoughts. She would have another look at the diary. See if the Taylors were booked in. It was probably just an error. Something small.

In the office the following morning, she was on her own. Both Liz and Sophie were out on calls, and she had a chance to check dates in the diary. She flicked through the pages. But there were no other appointments with anyone named Taylor in recent weeks, or job cards in that name, or bank lodgements either. She was puzzled.

## Chapter Thirty-one

Scott drove up to Dublin and met Liz for a drink at the Merrion Inn. As soon as she appeared he kissed her softly. 'I've been longing to see you, every minute of every day you've been in my mind. I can't explain why that is other than that I love you more than I've ever loved anyone.' His lips gripped hers. She responded immediately, and her arms wound around him, pulling him close to her. 'Remember this place in the old days?' he asked as they sat down.

'I certainly do, we had some great nights here,' she smiled.

'Would you like a drink?'

'Gin and tonic.'

'I'll just have a coffee and a sandwich. Unfortunately, I've to go back tonight, I have a meeting in the morning.'

'It will be tiring.'

'It's easy, mostly motorway.'

'Why not come back with me and go early,' she suggested, with a cheeky grin.

A short time later, they drove back to Howth. Inside the door, without a word, she turned to him. Her lips on his. Filling his mouth with their sensuality. Their bodies cleaved together. He lost all sense of place. In the darkness he knew only Liz. His fingers moved across her body. He could feel the undulations. So delicate. He was carried away by the scent of her. Breathing deeply. Each intimate fold. Longing to take her with him. And keep her. For ever.

This time he didn't sleep. But watched her as she lay in his arms.

Like a child. Eyes closed. Long dark lashes brushed luminous skin. Cupid bow lips pursed. Full of promise. It was the start of many other nights like this.

He couldn't believe it was happening. That this woman whom he had adored since the first moment he set eyes on her actually felt the same way about him. He was in a dream. While he went through the motions of everyday living. Talking with his sons. Going to work. Making decisions. Dealing with clients. Communicating with staff. Meeting friends. All of this happened in a different sphere. Where Liz was, he wanted to be, and nowhere else.

Her eyes opened.

His arms tightened around her.

She curled into him.

He bent his head and kissed the corner of her ear.

She giggled. 'Tickly.'

He did it again. She wriggled.

His moist tongue found its way inside.

He drew closer.

His body became taut.

She responded, clinging. 'If we keep this up we're going to collapse,' she said, smiling. 'We can't survive without sleep. How do you work?'

'I can do anything when I know I'm going to see you.'

'I'm surprised I can even focus the camera.'

'We do spend a lot of time in bed,' he laughed. 'But it's wonderful, the only place I want to be with you. Will I see you this weekend?'

'Sure.'


Liz went out to the car with him. It was still dark and she sat in.

'I hate leaving you,' he said, kissing her.

'See you Friday.'

'I have something for you.'

'What is it?'

'A little gift,' he said, and reached across to open the glove compartment. He handed her a black box.

'Thank you so much, Scott.' She was taken aback.

'I hope you like it.'

She opened the wrapping, and then the box. She stared at an exquisite gold pendant and earrings nestling in black velvet.

'Scott, they're beautiful, I love them, thank you.'

'I'm looking forward to seeing them on you.'

He kissed her slowly. Thinking how much his life had changed since they had met. Such happiness was like something out of this world. He could hardly believe that it was actually happening.

## Chapter Thirty-two

'That new dress looks great, Mum,' Sophie sat on the bed. 'Black is so your colour.'

'It will do fine. Plain. Simple. I'll wear my diamond pendant.'

'And earrings?'

'I've matching ones.' She opened a drawer and took them out of a box. They were long gold chains with a diamond at the end.

'They're beautiful.' Sophie stared in admiration when Liz put them on. 'When did you buy those? I haven't seen them before.'

'They were a present.'

'I think I can guess who gave you those?' Sophie said, with a wide smile.

'I couldn't get over it,' Liz admitted.

'He's obviously very generous, they're expensive.'

'He always was.' Liz stood in front of the mirror, and turned around.

'You look wonderful. And now, just to finish off, you need the heels, very high.'

'I've got them.' She slipped her feet into soft black suede shoes.

'You'll put us all to shame tonight, Mum.'

Liz laughed. 'Keep complimenting your old mother, she loves it.'

'Old mother, don't be ridiculous,' Sophie kissed her. 'Now could we run through the plan for the evening so we've got it right? The first people will probably arrive just after six. The writer, Michael Feeney Callan will be here at seven to formally launch the book.'

'Michael and Ree are such nice people,' Liz said, smiling.

'We were lucky to get him, he's under a lot of pressure himself writing his latest book. Luke will send over a couple of his staff to serve the wine, and they'll bring glasses, tables, tablecloths, and he's even doing some finger food as well.'

'He's great.' Liz dabbed perfume

'Now let's head, we don't want to be late.' Sophie glanced at her watch.

'I'm a bag of nerves,' Liz admitted.

'Don't be silly, you're the star of the show.'

'We'll sell the books over here as people come in.' Sophie moved a table nearer the door of the studio.

'Have we got some change?'

They stared at each other in horror and immediately began to search in their purses.

'Don't worry, girls, it was the one thing I thought of myself.' Liz produced a roll of notes.

'You sit down here beside us to sign the books.' Brooke moved a chair.

'Yes, Miss. This is like being in school,' she laughed.

'Now, smile please.' Sophie picked up her camera and began to take a few shots. 'Head left, head right, you know the drill. Look at me. Over my shoulder. Full on. At the camera.'

'Don't zoom too close, Sophie, or every line I have will be obvious.'

'What lines? Anyway, if there are one or two smiling ones it just shows character,' Brooke said, watching. 'That's you.'

'Let me see the photos.' Liz reached for the camera.

'No way, you'll see the final result tomorrow and we'll print up a few, some of them might even be the basis for another collection.'

'I'm not going to publish another book with photos of myself in it,' Liz exploded.

'No, but there might be a couple of interesting ones.' She looked at the screen on the camera. 'And some of these are very nice. The camera loves you.'

'Let's get through tonight first.'

'Here's someone coming in.' Sophie put down the camera.

It all happened very fast after that. In a short time the studio was crowded with people standing around sipping glasses of wine.

Sophie and Brooke were busy selling books, and almost everyone there bought one. Liz had a pain in her wrist from signing. Michael and his wife Ree arrived, and he launched the book, saying a few words without any reference to notes. He was very entertaining and Liz was delighted when they decided to stay on, have a glass of wine and mingle with the crowd for a while.

'This is amazing,' Sophie said with a grin.

'Unbelievable,' Liz turned to the woman who had just bought the book and asked for her name. There were plenty of people here that she knew, friends, and family, but lots of strangers too. More excitement then when a journalist and photographer from the Irish Independent arrived to talk with her and take more photos. And screams from her own friends when they arrived and threw their arms around her.

'This is fantastic. You're a great success.' Celine hugged her.

The waiter came over carrying a tray of glasses of wine, and offered them to the girls. They all helped themselves.

'Sign this for me, will you Liz?' A low voice drew her attention.

'Scott?'

'Sorry I'm late, but I had a meeting which went on a bit longer than I anticipated. The book looks wonderful.' He flicked through the pages. 'Congratulations.'

She stood up and kissed him, and didn't care who noticed. 'Thanks so much for coming up. I appreciate it.'

'You've got a great crowd in.'

She glanced at the queue. 'I can't believe it. But I'm going to take a minute to introduce you to Brooke and Luke, you've already met Sophie.' She made the introductions, and then took him over to where Celine, Leah and Megan girls stood. And then she continued signing A crazy exhilaration within her now.

The high point eventually diminished approaching nine o'clock and people left gradually.

'Let's head over to Luke's place,' Sophie handed Liz her jacket and handbag.

'I hope you can join us?' Liz asked Scott.

'Love to,' he accepted her invitation.

'Girls, you'll come as well, won't you?'

'You don't have to ask us twice.' Celine, Megan and Leah were enthusiastic.

'I can't believe it's all over,' Liz admitted when they had arrived at La Modena.

'Mum, you're still on a high, I can see it in your eyes,' Brooke exclaimed.

'I suppose I am.'

'A night of excitement which is well deserved. Congrats, you sold a lot of books, and I must give you the money, although I haven't counted it yet.' Sophie reached for her handbag, took a roll of notes and handed it to Liz.

'My God, this looks like an enormous amount.' She stared at it.

'You can count it when you get home.'

'It's such an achievement, Mum,' Luke said, as Daniel brought over a couple of bottles of champagne and glasses. Luke pulled the corks and poured. They stood up.

'To Mum.' They raised their glasses.

'Thanks everyone, you've made this night so wonderful, I couldn't have done it without you. I can't thank you enough,' Liz said and hugged them.

She was still on cloud nine when she arrived home with Scott.

'It was so great to see you tonight, an ideal opportunity to introduce you to the family and friends.'

'You'll have to come down and meet my two soon.' He kissed her.

'I'd love that,' she said, smiling.

'I feel I've found my other half, you know.' He took her hand.

She felt suddenly shy, not knowing what to say.

'Liz, I long to be with you. I know we've lost a lot of years but the future is ours and I want to make the most of it. I'm going to see my solicitor next week about divorcing Ciara, and I'm hoping there won't be any problems with that as she's been gone for so long. So as I'm not into playing around, this is a formal proposal. Will you marry me, Liz?' he asked. 'When I'm free?'

'Yes,' she said.

# *Chapter Thirty-three*

Sophie worked on her phone. Deleting information which she didn't need to keep. But one text jumped out at her. It was from Brooke giving her the phone number of her friend, Paula, who wanted photographs of the birth of her baby. She had already decided against doing it, but suddenly thought of her mother. She shouldn't say no to a client without running it past Liz. Maybe she would be interested. And there were a few messages from Clayton.

But she had decided to cut him out of her life. If he couldn't put up with a genuine excuse, then there wasn't much hope for a future with him. She was saddened. Not so much about Clayton particularly, but her seemingly unending search for someone to share her life. Maybe she was going for the wrong type of man? But what was that? Every man she met was quite different. Initially, she was always attracted to the guys. That tingle of excitement made her footsteps lighter. She felt life was good. Looked forward to sharing birthdays. Christmas. Holidays. But that initial thrill never lasted. Sometimes not much longer than a couple of weeks. This time Clayton fitted into her life for over a month but now she was disillusioned and knew that she would let him go on his merry way. Another one down.

'It's an awkward one, Mum,' Sophie explained about Brooke's friend Paula wanting photographs of the birth of her baby.

'Very unusual. I've never heard anyone ask for that before.'

'Seemingly it's becoming popular.'

'Are you to be there for the whole thing, the labour and the birth?'

Liz asked.

'I'm not sure.'

'Why don't you give Paula a ring? As she's a friend of Brooke, it's only polite to get back to her. You can't make a decision without any information.'

'Would you do it?'

'I'm not sure.'

'How much would you charge?'

'I haven't a clue, it depends on the number of hours.'

'I wish Brooke hadn't suggested me,' Sophie sighed. She really wasn't in the mood for tackling something so unusual.

'You'll have to talk to the girl. It mightn't be as difficult as you think,' Liz said firmly. 'And don't forget, if you just refuse without discussion it doesn't reflect well on the company.'

A couple of days later she went to see Paula. She welcomed her in warmly and immediately Sophie could see that she was about to give birth very soon.

'My first child was born in hospital and I really didn't enjoy the experience and thought I'd never get out of there. My second child was a home birth and there was simply no comparison. I have a lovely midwife who helps me along at every stage. My husband can be there, and the children too, and we all welcome the new baby into our family the moment he or she arrives.'

Sophie was taken aback. She had never heard of anyone doing such a thing. And as for having the other children there, that was something else. Any friends of hers who had babies all went into hospital. 'It sounds idyllic,' she had to admit. 'But what if something goes wrong?'

'My midwife is wonderful. She'll know immediately if there's anything out of the ordinary happening and I'll be whipped off to hospital like that.' She clicked her fingers. 'So, what do you think, will you do it for me, Sophie?'

She was unable to refuse. 'I hope I don't faint, it will be a first for me.'

'You won't. You will be so fascinated you won't even have time to faint.'

'I wish I had your confidence. Now, tell me roughly how long you will need me?' she asked, taking out a notebook.

'The last labour took about eight or nine hours and the birth itself was very fast. But don't worry, we don't call the midwife until I'm well on in labour, and we'll give you a call at the same time. I can judge how I'm getting on myself.'

'So it might be just three or four hours?' Sophie asked.

'Or even less.'

'Of course, I'd have to be on standby, ready to jump in the car and get over here hot foot,' Sophie said, suddenly finding herself more enthusiastic. The other girl's excitement was infectious.

'So you're going to do it?' Paula asked.

'I will,' she said.

'Thank you so much.' She stood up and kissed her.

'Oh, there is the matter of cost, I'm not too sure how much it should be,' Sophie said, feeling awkward now, and hoping that Paula wasn't expecting her to do it as a favour.

'I'm sorry, I should have discussed that before. I've a friend in London who had a photographer around when she had her baby, and she tells me the average over there is about five hundred pounds, and that includes photos and some video. How would that be for you?'

'It sounds fine,' Sophie said. She didn't really want to make a huge amount of money as Paula was a friend of Brooke's, but if that was the average then she would accept it. She still didn't know how she would handle the whole experience, and prayed it wouldn't be a disaster.

# Chapter Thirty-four

Liz was really happy with the book launch. She was inundated with emails and texts of congratulations from people who hadn't been able to make it on the night, promising to order the book on line. And in a short time she had to place another print order, her bank account reflecting a healthy profit. After the excitement, it was difficult to fit into the normal everyday. But slowly she managed to do that. Scott came up from Cork as often as he could although he always stayed the weekends with her. She couldn't believe he had asked her to marry him so quickly, and that she had accepted without hesitation.

It was busy at the studio, and there were a lot of sessions entered into the diary. At one of their usual Monday meetings, Brooke showed Liz and Sophie the progress she had made on the data base she was creating.

'I've been checking back over the year and coordinated all the payments with the orders. And I went back over all the job cards for the last few years and built up a base of clients with details of where their photos are filed.' She handed them the printed pages.

'That's great,' Liz was really pleased. 'The info we had before was sketchy to say the least and to have it all done in such order for the accountant means a lot.'

'Yes, you've done really well, Brooke. Now we can email all the clients if we want to inform them of any new opportunities. Or special offers. Or maybe invite them for a glass of wine like we did for the book launch.' Sophie was delighted too.

'And I had an idea. Have you ever considered running a photography course? I was thinking I should take a few lessons,' she said with a grin. 'I know a couple of really good photographers.'

'Do you?' Liz and Sophie laughed together.

'Anyway, why don't we run courses?' Brooke suggested.

'That's interesting,' Liz was immediately engaged.

'How would we have time to give courses?' Sophie wasn't so enthusiastic. 'We sometimes work in the evenings.'

'Maybe just one evening a week?' Brooke asked.

Liz and Sophie looked at one another. 'It's not a bad idea,' Liz admitted.

'I'm not too pushed,' Sophie said.

'We can think about it. Thanks Brooke, it's always good to have some new angles on the business.' Liz made a note.

'But there is something else, a problem with one client,' she said, a slight hesitance in her voice.

'What sort of problem?' Liz asked, smiling.

'Was it that soft focus one that I did?' Sophie asked.

'No, it wasn't that. It's another one and because there was only one it stood out so I'd rather we dealt with it now.'

'Is it someone we know?' asked Sophie.

'I didn't notice the name cropping up on a regular basis, just saw one appointment in the diary, but there was no job card, and no bank lodgement to reconcile with it.'

'That's strange.' Liz was puzzled.

'What's the name?' Sophie asked.

'Taylor.'

She paused for a few seconds. 'I don't remember the name. When were they in?' she asked in a rush.

'I rang Mr. Taylor just to check, and he said he comes in every few weeks.'

'People don't come in so frequently, does the name mean anything to you?' Liz looked at Sophie.

She shook her head.

'We'd better get to the bottom of this, the accountant might spot it at the end of the year and we won't remember the details of one client at that point. Maybe we should have a look at the photo files and then we'll know what was done on which date. Would you do that, Sophie? And Brooke, thanks for finding that anomaly. You're certainly doing a good job. I'm so glad you're with us now. I hope you're enjoying it?' Liz smiled at Brooke.

'I love it, Mum. At least I'm not totally dependent on Rory.'

'What's happening with the sale of the house?'

'Lots of people looking. Traipsing in and out.' She shivered. 'I hate it.'

'Any offers?'

'Yes, one, but the agent is holding out as he feels the house is worth more and in the present climate we should get a higher offer.'

'But you could refuse to sell. Why don't you do that. It is your home. Rory must support you and the children.'

'He's changed, Mum. If I refuse he will give us nothing and I can't pay the mortgage and support the kids.'

'But you could take him to court?'

'With his money, he could tie me up in knots. No, I've made up my mind. I don't want the house now. Without Rory it's tainted.'

'But you love it.'

'I know but if I find a smaller place, it will be just mine and the kids.'

Liz put her hand on Brooke's. 'Maybe that would be the best for you, love,' she felt helpless.

'I've made up my mind, Mum. I'm happy with my decision.'

'I admire you.'

'Thanks to both of you for giving me the job, it's been wonderful, and so liberating.'

'I wish I could do more.'

'I want to be independent, it's important to me.' Brooke put her arm around her mother's shoulders.

There was a moment of silence between them.

'I'm happy for you,' Liz glanced at her watch. 'I'm sorry, but I must go.' She picked up her briefcase.

'I'll have to head soon to pick up the kids.' Brooke filed papers away.

'Are you feeling all right?' Liz stared at Sophie.

'Yea.'

'You look very pale.'

'Do I?'

'What have we booked in this afternoon?'

'Three sessions.'

'I can handle them. Why don't you go home early, I won't be long,' Liz suggested.

'I'm grand, Mum, don't worry. I'm probably burning the candle at both ends as usual,' she smiled.

'I hope that's all it is.' Liz turned back at the door. 'I don't want to see you here when I get back, go catch up on some sleep.'

Liz was worried about Sophie, but even more so about Brooke, although she did seem to be dealing with the break-up of her marriage quite well. Such a terrible thing to have happened to her. They had seemed to be so happy. The perfect couple with their two darling children living in a beautiful home. She couldn't imagine how hard it must be and would have given anything to help in some way. She imagined the awful sense of rejection which Brooke must feel. Like she had lost a part of her body. An arm or a leg. Worst of all the feeling that her heart was broken, an integral part of her which couldn't function without Rory.

## Chapter Thirty-five

Scott picked up the post from the floor, and looked through the envelopes. They were mostly bills. Then he pulled out one which had been personally addressed. It had an English postage stamp, and as he stared at the thin sloped letters which had those distinctive gaps between each one, it screamed only one name to him.

He was unable to open the envelope at first, in dread of what he would find inside and walked back into the kitchen. He threw the other envelopes on the table. It was almost twenty-two years since his wife had left. And such a shock, as she never gave him the impression that she wasn't happy. Just left a note telling him that she wanted to live somewhere else.

Finally, he opened the envelope, and took out the folded piece of paper.

*Dear Scott,*
*It's been a long time since I've been in contact with you and I'm sorry about that. I hope the boys are well and you too, and wonder would it be possible to meet you all and catch up. I would like to say how sorry I am for leaving so abruptly back then. It was so selfish of me to do that without warning.*
*I hope that you can forgive me, and I look forward to hearing from you soon.*
*Yours,*
*Ciara.*

He sat down then. Stunned. Unable to get his head around this unexpected development. His heart plunged. How would this affect his relationship with Liz? He had intended to tell Cathal and Ryan about her in the next day or so and was just waiting for the right opportunity.

In the early days after Ciara had left, he would have given anything to receive a letter from her, particularly as their boys had found it so difficult to deal with her disappearance. She was beautiful. He loved her when they first met and had been very hurt when she left. But he was angry too. Obviously she didn't care how he felt. Or her children either. And there had been no contact over the years. That worst of all. Nothing. Birthdays and Christmases passed unmarked as if she had died.

Now she had decided to come back into their lives. Why? He wondered. He looked at the address. It was in Ealing. London.

He replaced the letter in the envelope. To choose the moment when he would give the letter to Cathal and Ryan was going to be difficult. But it had to be soon. The letter was dated and they wouldn't appreciate it if he left it too long. He couldn't tell them that some years before, Ciara's mother Kathleen had told him that her daughter was living in London with another man, but that she didn't know where she was. Her sister, Maura, had never said anything at all. He couldn't tell his sons that Ciara was living with someone else, it would have hurt them too much so he stayed quiet, always dreading the day when they would demand to know everything.

Now he was thrown back into the past. To those early days when he had first met Ciara. All through college he and Liz were an item. But when he had left to go to England for further study, his friend Ethan had stepped into his place and Liz had somehow been persuaded to marry him.

Scott and Liz had been so close over the years. Deeply in love. Bound to each other for life. They would settle down. Marry. Have children. It was their plan. To know that she was married to another man cut through him like a knife and on the rebound he married Ciara when he returned to Ireland. He did love her, but the depth of his feelings in no way compared to his love for Liz.

Cathal and Ryan came over that night. It was a regular thing. Every week. They would talk about work. An opportunity to chat casually about where the company was going, without the hassle of formal meetings. But they never stayed very long and were already in the hall about to open the front door by the time he summoned up the courage.

'Lads?'

They looked at him. 'I've something to show you.' He took the envelope from his pocket. 'This came today and I want you to see it. As you're the eldest, Cathal, I'll give it to you first.' He handed it to him.

He was desperately aware of a tense unnerving silence as Cathal read the letter. He read it through and then handed it to Ryan, pushing his hands into the pockets of his jeans.

'This is from our mother?' Ryan asked.

'Yes.' Scott wasn't sure how to react.

'She wants to see us?' he asked.

Scott nodded.

Ryan looked at Cathal who stood awkwardly, head down. 'When?'

'As you can see she's living in England, we would have to wait until she comes to see us,' Scott said gently.

'I don't know why she wants to see us now. We needed her years ago when we were young,' Ryan said.

'I'm not sure of her circumstances,' Scott admitted.

Ryan glanced at the letter. 'She didn't give us a phone number.'

'Why don't you write to her?'

'I'm going to call and see her, I'll be in London on business next week,' Cathal said, looking at him for the first time, moisture in his eyes.

'To just turn up on the doorstep without warning may be awkward, you don't want to make life difficult for her. She could have a family and they may not know about us. That sort of thing happens,' Scott advised.

'We're her family,' Cathal growled.

'I know, but we must handle this carefully. She has made this approach to us, so we should just respond in the same way and let it take its course.'

'I can't do that,' he said.

'Maybe we should talk to Maura and find out what she knows. Although with the dementia, Kathleen may not remember very much.'

'Gran never told us anything,' Ryan muttered.

'It was your mother's choice.'

Scott was finding it hard. He was as shocked as his two lads. He had often wondered if Ciara came back how he would deal with the situation. Any feelings he had in the beginning had long since disappeared. Now he thought he wouldn't even know her. He recalled their early years together. She was busy with the children and he worked all the hours he could, assuming they were happy. But there was little time for themselves in the daily grind. When he arrived home usually Ciara had already gone to bed and left his dinner warming in the oven. Sex was an occasional hurried coupling usually on a Sunday night. It was his only day off, and he spent it with the boys. Ciara sometimes came with them to the beach or playground or fishing if the weather was pleasant. But more often than not she went to see her mother.

When she left, he had been angry. How could she leave her children? It was impossible to imagine any woman doing such a thing. But as time passed, he realised that he couldn't blame her for leaving him. He hadn't been a very good husband. But he was still hurt by the rejection of her little children who had to struggle hard to come to terms with the loss of their mother as they grew up. They were like two little birds who had fallen out of the nest. He had to gather them up in his arms and try to protect them against a world which preyed on defenceless creatures. Be both mother and father. Soft. Strict. Depending on what was needed. Sometimes they hated him. Sometimes they loved him. But through all that he loved them without question. Terribly hurt when they threw things at him, screamed and shouted, or didn't speak at all.

## Chapter Thirty-six

Sophie went home, feeling sick. Brooke had stumbled on something so unexpected. A sense of dread whirled through her. She had committed a fraud on her mother and sister by keeping the money paid by the Taylors for their photographic sessions.

Why had she done such a thing? If she was honest she had to admit that the need for drugs had twisted her morals. She had battled hard. Had tried for months to stop. To say no. To refuse. To resist. But hadn't got the strength. She was useless. Tears spurted.

Sophie lived in two worlds.

A wonderful life with her family and friends. Enjoying her career with her mother, photography the only thing she ever wanted to do.

And another place. An underground cavern which pulsated and throbbed. Where her head spun. Lost in the unreal world of addiction.

Sudden clouds gathered. Dark on the outer. Threatening. A heavy roll of thunder echoed. Pressure bore down on her. There was a sudden flash of lightning. She rushed to pull down the blind. Fearful. The air was full of menace. She put her hands over her ears. Always terrified of thunder and lightning since she had been a small child. Rushing into the arms of her mother for solace.

Now she ran into the bathroom which had no window, and sat there, frozen, her arms wrapped around herself. Hugging. The thunder drew nearer. She shivered. Another peal echoed. Even closer now. Perspiration soaked her black shirt. Her palms. Her neck. A crash reverberated. Pounded right on top of the building. Piercing pain cut through her head.

She stayed there for a long time. The noise above drifted off. Her breathing eased. She straightened up, reached towards the wash basin, and turned on the water. Bathing her face under the stream until she felt a little better. She pressed into the soft towel which was comforting and went into the kitchen. The sky above was still a mass of grey cloud, the sea a dirty menacing blue, sequinned with a sliver of light which shone on the horizon. But to her relief the storm seemed to have passed over.

Her phone rang. She searched for it and found it in her handbag. It was her mother. Her stomach dropped. She dreaded talking to her.

'Are you all right?' Liz asked.

She could hear the concern in her voice.

'I'm fine.'

'I was worried about you. We've had a storm over here, thunder and lightning. Has it reached Clontarf? I know you hate it.'

'Still like a kid,' Sophie murmured, flopping down on the couch. 'It's gone now, out over the sea.'

'I'm glad.'

'Thanks for ringing.' She was suddenly grateful to her mother.

It was strange for Sophie to be doing nothing. But she couldn't even have opened up her laptop. It would have been too much of an effort. All she could think about now was what she was going to do about the situation with her mother and Brooke. She would lodge the money into the bank account of course, that was definite. But she didn't have enough unfortunately, not now. But hopefully she would manage to get it together. But there was a bigger question. How to absolve herself? Liz had asked her to check the photo file. But she hadn't put the photos she had taken of the Taylors in the office file. She had kept them herself and wondered how to explain that to Liz and Brooke? Would her mother ever forgive her deceit?

# Chapter Thirty-seven

La Modena was busy tonight. The restaurant crowded, a group of people at the bar waiting on tables. Luke checked the orders. Two beetroot and goats cheese. One scallops and black pudding, hake, lamb shank. He called out to the sous chef, his right hand man. One smoked salmon mousse. One asparagus. Steak. Prawns. And so on. he felt better when he was at work. It kept him focused. He caught a glimpse of Daniel through the hatch. He was smiling at the customers. Handing someone a menu.

But the turnover was not enough to achieve a profit. They needed twice the number of customers to cover the basic costs and their accountant had warned them that they were teetering on the edge of insolvency.

'The turnover hasn't improved, we're just about the same as last month,' Luke said when they had returned home.

'We're struggling,' Daniel agreed.

'Having the music hasn't made much difference.'

'People stay on a bit later but they don't always spend enough money to justify our costs.'

'We'll have to look at what we take out of the business ourselves.'

Daniel looked at him sharply, concerned.

'I know we're already cut back to the bone,' admitted Luke.

'Cut back any more and we won't be able to pay the rent on our apartment.'

'All the landlords are raising rents.'

'At least it's fixed at the restaurant.'

'A rent increase would finish us off altogether.'

'Maybe we should put off getting married for a bit.' Luke put into words what had been on his mind for a while now.

'I thought the only obstacle in our way was the fact that you hadn't come out, now you've talked with the family there is no reason for us to cancel our wedding plans.' Daniel seemed very disappointed.

'There's no point in getting married on a shoestring. We'll regret it.'

'But surely the event itself is the only important thing?'

'Of course it is.'

'Then let's get married. The two of us and two friends as witnesses. We'll just have a few jars afterwards to celebrate.'

'It's not the way I want to get married. I want it to be special. Magical.'

'I don't think you want to get married at all,' Daniel blurted.

'I do,' Luke said. 'Of course I do.'

'You're not that enthusiastic.'

'We have financial problems, it affects everything we do.'

'The way I want to do it won't cost a fortune.'

'Us and two witnesses? That's pathetic.'

'Then maybe we should call the whole thing off? You've been dragging your feet ever since we decided to get married. First, you hadn't come out to your family, and now you don't want to spend any money. Make up your mind, Luke, once and for all or I'm out of here.' Fuming, he stood up and marched upstairs to the bedroom, banging the door loudly behind him.

Luke sighed. He regretted upsetting Daniel. He had been very sure that once he had talked to the family about his sexuality he would be even more enthusiastic about getting married. But that hadn't happened. And he realised that perhaps he had been using the excuse of coming out to Liz to avoid making a final decision. Now he wondered if he wanted to get married at all.

He followed him, and stood outside the bedroom door but couldn't go in at first. He knocked. There was no reply. He pushed it open.

Daniel sat hunched at the end of the bed.

Luke put his hand on his shoulder. 'I'm sorry.' He sat beside him.

There were tears on Daniel's cheeks.

'I've hurt you.'

They sat there, silently, for what seemed like ages.

'Daniel, I still love you but maybe I'm not ready for marriage yet,' Luke said slowly.

'I thought we wanted to spend the rest of our lives together?'

'If I'm completely honest I think I was using the fact that I hadn't come out as an excuse.'

'I don't think I can go on if I don't know whether you want the same as me. It seems pointless.' Daniel brushed the tears from his face.

'Maybe it's the pressure of trying to run the restaurant. I feel I can't even buy a newspaper without thinking twice about spending that amount of money.'

'We should save as much as possible so that we can actually get married. I was the one who put the money in the bank.'

Luke laughed. 'Does that make me the waster?'

'No,' Daniel put his arm around him.

'Let's not rush, we'll regret it if we do,' Luke said slowly.

They drew close, and kissed.

'You're all I want,' Daniel sighed.

'We'll have the big bash, some day,' Luke said with a wide grin. 'It will happen.'

## Chapter Thirty-eight

Brooke took the children to the park. The estate agent said he needed at least three hours. She glanced up at the sky. It was cloudy. She felt a few drops of rain. Cian and Jess were playing on the climbing frames, and took no notice, as children seldom do. So when she insisted that they come back to the jeep with her, there were cries of protest. But eventually she managed to persuade them to get down and she strapped them into their seats, realising only then that she hadn't decided exactly where she was going. She couldn't go back home, so where?

She stared along the road ahead, and thought about Peggy. She hadn't mentioned anything about Rory when she brought the kids over recently, and dreaded the thought of discussing what was going on, thinking that the woman would blame her for everything. Maybe Rory had already mentioned what was going on. At least, she hoped that he had. She stopped off to buy some chocolates for her and as she drew up outside the house was glad to see her car in the driveway.

'Brooke, how lovely to see you?' Peggy put her arms around her.

'Granny Peggy?' The two kids ran to her.

She looked down at them, and Brooke could see the glimmer of tears in her eyes. She was such a gentle person, thought Brooke, and would be upset to hear that Rory had left her.

'Where's Ginger?' Cian asked.

'He's inside.'

'And Blackie?' Jess shouted, and they ran through.

'Come on in.' Peggy closed the front door.

'Thanks.'

'It's a bit cold today, and probably going to get worse,' Peggy spoke over her shoulder as she led the way into the kitchen. Brooke handed her the gift bag.

'Thank you so much.' She kissed her, and then opened the fridge door and took out a carton of orange juice. She called the children, and poured two glasses for them.

'I'm sorry I couldn't get over in the last few days it's been hectic.' Brooke waved her hands helplessly. 'The job is quite demanding and I'm not used to being so busy.'

'Don't worry, I'm delighted to see you any time. Is Liz a hard taskmaster?'

'No, not at all. I do my own thing. I know they didn't have a real job for me so they weren't looking for me to do anything specific, except some admin. Anyway they seem delighted with what I've done already. I've set up a data base which should be an advantage for the business down the line.' Brooke couldn't help being pleased with herself.

'I'm really glad for you,' the silver haired woman smiled.

'There is something I should tell you, although maybe Rory has already explained,' Brooke said.

'He made a vague reference to problems between you, but refused to tell me any more than that.' Her eyes were sympathetic.

Brooke was taken aback. The woman didn't know that Rory had left. This was going to be harder than she expected. And was it her place to tell her? Maybe it should be Rory.

'I'm hoping that things will work out.'

'You poor thing.'

Cian and Jess ran into the kitchen and Cian opened the press door. 'I want some chocolate, Granny.'

'So do I,' Jess added.

'No chocolate, Cian,' Brooke said. 'Just give them a plain biscuit, Peggy.'

'How are things really?' Peggy asked later.

154

'We're managing. It'll be all right.'

'I hope so, I'll say a prayer.'

'I must get back,' Brooke checked the time.

'It's been so lovely to see you,' Peggy said, with a smile. 'I can babysit this week if you want, or the kids might stay over, they enjoyed being here that last time.'

'They did.' And probably being spoilt too, Brooke thought. But then they needed a little extra pampering these days. Her little ones sensed what was going on and if they were over here with Peggy then they would forget.

'Let me know if you need me,' Peggy insisted.

'You've been very good to look after them recently, I appreciate that. And I had a lovely night out with Mum and Sophie.'

'I'll look after the darlings any time,' she smiled at the kids.


Rory rang to enquire about the estate agent. Had he said anything to Brooke? That was the only reason he called lately. It was all he was interested in.

'I called to see your mother,' she said.

'What did you tell her?'

'I didn't tell her anything, but you've obviously mentioned that there were problems between us as she said it to me.'

'I don't want her to know the details.'

'That's crazy, she's going to find out. The kids could say something.'

'Don't bring them over to see her again.'

'Rory, she deserves to see her grandchildren and she's looking forward to having them stay overnight with her soon.'

'For God's sakes.'

She could sense his anger building.

'How long do you think you can hide the fact that you're living with another woman?'

He was silent.

'Look, take her into your confidence, she is your mother. Anyway, all she has to do is drive past here and she'll see the estate agent's sign. The fact that you didn't tell her we're selling the house will upset her anyway, not to mention that you're living with someone else. Just come clean.'

He still said nothing.

'Well, I don't want to exclude your mother, so I'm going to tell her. But it would be better coming from you. It won't take you long. And bring flowers or something, she'll appreciate that. Now I'm going around tomorrow and I'll know immediately if you haven't told her. Then I'll explain what's going on.' She waited for a response, but there was none.

## Chapter Thirty-nine

Celine welcomed them into her home. It was Liz's turn to do the driving tonight and stay sober.

'Now we can enjoy ourselves, what's your poison girls?' Celine asked.

'Gin and tonic, thanks.' Leah flopped on to the comfortable couch, and kicked off her shoes.

'Same for me,' Megan added. 'Just to start.'

'I'm the one on the dry,' laughed Liz. 'Should be wearing my chauffeur's cap.'

'I'll get the drinks.' Celine went to the sideboard and poured. 'Right, what's new?' she asked, handing out glasses.

They looked at each other.

'Well, let's see?' Megan mused.

'I'll start us off. I had a phone call the other day from London,' Leah announced.

'Tell us?' They were all very interested.

'Harry could be coming over soon but he hasn't been specific but at least it was contact.'

'Why don't you go over to see him?' Megan asked curiously.

'That might be a bit pushy.'

'Not at all, you could just call and say you're coming over with us, how about that, girls?'

'I wouldn't mind a break.' Celine was enthusiastic.

'We could take in a couple of shows.'

'And have a wander around the shops.'

'Let's have a look at flights, see if we can get a bargain.'

'Maybe I might do that, if he says he can't meet me then so what.' Leah seemed suddenly excited.

'Weather should be nice.'

'I don't think there's anything particular happening which would prevent me from going,' Megan said. 'So, I'm on for it.'

'What day will we go?'

'Friday and come back on Monday?'

'I should manage to take a couple of days off.' Celine sipped her drink.

'What about you, Liz?' Leah looked at her.

'I don't know if I can make it.'

'You're not very enthusiastic.'

'What's happening?'

They quizzed her.

'Scott comes up most weekends.'

'You can't tie yourself up with him completely. That's crazy. What if he drops out of sight suddenly?'

'I don't expect him to do that.'

'Come on, it'll be great, we'll have a ball.'

'I don't think it's quite that,' Megan said, with a coy grin.

'What do you mean?' Liz objected immediately.

'I have a sixth sense.'

'You're going on again about that spiritualist stuff.'

'It's just something I feel.'

'Go on, open up.'

Liz felt suddenly guilty. The girls were her best friends and she certainly didn't want them to think that she wouldn't share things with them.

'All right, I suppose I should have told you. Scott has asked me to marry him.'

'Liz?' Celine screamed.

'And?'

'Well?' Leah demanded.

'I've said yes,' Liz blurted.

'But what about his wife?'

'He's getting a divorce.'

'And she keeps it under her hat, what about that girls? The biggest thing that's happened to our Liz in years and she kept absolutely quiet about it.' Megan fanned herself dramatically.

Liz had to laugh.

'You still love him?' Celine asked.

She nodded.

'Do you really believe him? He's not having you on just to get into your bed?' Leah was always the doubtful one. 'Do you remember my Brian. He was full sure he was going to divorce his wife, using the old *she doesn't understand me* excuse.'

'How long were you with him?' Liz asked, curious. 'I can't remember.'

'It was over five years. And it came to nothing. No moves at all. Just promises which didn't materialise into anything. I wasted all that time on him. Bastard. There's a lot of them around, Liz, and you can't fall into the same trap as me.'

'I know Scott. I trust him.' Liz was quite definite.

'Don't be so negative, Leah,' Celine cautioned.

'I'm the one that's out there looking for a man, I meet these guys all the time. I want to warn Liz of what can happen. She hasn't been around. You don't know what it's like, Liz.'

'I don't, I have to admit that.'

'Then you have to be ultra-cautious.'

Liz didn't know what to say. Was she dashing into this relationship without a thought for herself?

'Leah, stop, give over.' Celine waved at her. 'Enough.'

'Well, on your own head be it, I've warned you.'

'Been in the sack yet?' Megan asked, with a mischievous grin.

'Yea,' Liz smiled.

'And how was it?'

'Amazing. I'd forgotten how good it was,' she laughed. They

jumped up together. Yelling. Screaming. Dancing in a circle.

'Time for champagne.' Celine rushed into the kitchen. 'Just as well I put a bottle into the fridge earlier.' She came back in and handed out glasses. Then popped the cork. They cheered loudly.

'To Scott and Liz.'


Scott came up for the weekend. She was so happy to see him. It was like they were already living together. Such closeness and warmth between them. Liz wanted it to last for ever.

There was something she wanted to say to him, but found it difficult, and eventually it was Sunday morning before she could brace herself to mention it.

'I'm really worried about Sophie,' Liz confessed. 'Remember you thought they were all high on something that night we met them on Grafton Street?'

'It's pretty much par for the course now for a lot of young people,' he said.

'It never dawned on me. I was thinking that it could be an illness,' Liz whispered. 'Sometimes she's sweaty. You can see perspiration shine on her skin. She almost passed out another time. She says she's been to the doctor but he doesn't seem to be doing anything for her.'

'I regretted saying that to you.'

'Why did you anyway?'

'I felt that perhaps they were. Look, forget I ever mentioned it, please Liz, I wouldn't want it to come between us. I'm so sorry.' He put his arm around her.

'Just tell me why you thought they were high?' she insisted.

'Well, there were some physical signs I noticed.'

'What were they?'

'Their pupils were dilated and, as you said, they were all perspiring.'

Liz hated being so ignorant about such things.

'You'll see her today, so tell me what you think. Oh, I'd better check the meat.' She opened the oven and took out the roasting dish. 'Rack of lamb, looks good, just about done.'

'Delicious. You'll have to let me cook for you sometime,' Scott offered.

'You can do it all next time,' she smiled.

He laughed.


To her surprise Sophie arrived first for lunch, opened the door and came into the kitchen. To Liz's delight she looked much better than she had the day before. The others followed on her heels, and they were all introduced again to Scott, and sat down to lunch. Cian and Jess ran around as usual, refusing even to sit at their own small table. Brooke insisted on drawing up two chairs and having them sit with the adults. There they slopped with their dinner, knocked over glasses of orange, grabbed at people with sticky fingers and generally kept them all laughing. Sophie seemed in very good form. Scott was like one of the family. It was a milestone. But as dessert and coffee was served, for Liz the moment of truth drew close.

'That was lovely Mum, I really enjoyed it,' Luke said, and the others joined in.

'Before you all go, there's something I want to tell you,' she said.

They stared at her.

'You only have to look at the two of them to know something is going on,' Sophie said, laughing.

'Scott and I are ...' She almost choked over the words.

'What?' Brooke seemed surprised.

'We're hoping to live together.'

'That's a bit quick, you only met a couple of months ago?'

'Because we lost so many years we're cutting out the preliminaries,' Scott said, smiling.

'I'm sorry I didn't get a chance to tell you all but it's only happened recently.' Liz felt very uncomfortable. The air was tense and full of questions.

'I'm amazed at you, Mum,' Sophie said, astonishment on her face. 'Going to live with someone just like that. Wow.'

'She's an amazing woman,' Scott said.

161

'We know that, and don't need you to tell us,' Brooke snapped angrily.

Liz was surprised by her remark.

'Don't worry, Brooke,' Scott said. 'I just hope that you'll be happy for your mother and me.'

'I have to say I think it's far too soon,' Brooke said abruptly. 'And what is your own situation?'

'I've asked Liz to marry me when I'm free.' Scott took Liz's hand. 'I've been separated from my wife for many years and intend to divorce her as soon as I can.'

No one said anything for a moment.

'I wish you every happiness, Mum,' Luke murmured and kissed her. 'Congratulations, Scott.'

'Thanks Luke.' Scott shook his hand.

Both Brooke and Sophie kissed her, but said nothing more and left shortly afterwards.


'You've a lovely family.' Scott drew her close to him as they sat in the den later.

'I'm not sure if they were that keen on us getting together,' Liz said.

'I suppose it was a bit of a shock for them.'

'They can't imagine their mother having a man in her life, I suppose. I don't know what I expected.'

'They'll come around.'

'I hope so,' Liz wasn't convinced and wondered if they should have been as honest as they were.

'All I want now is to have you to myself, no one else around,' Scott said.

'It reminds me of the old days.' She kissed him.

'I can't believe this is actually happening.'

'It's like a dream.'

'Do you believe that I love you?' he asked softly.

'Yes, and I love you. It's amazing to imagine that we still feel so much for each other after all this time. Where have the years gone?'

## *Chapter Forty*

Sophie prepared the camera equipment and set up the studio for the sessions which had been booked in. She threw herself into the work, making it as creative as possible, and tried to forget about the Taylors. The first group came in and she was glad to give them all her attention. No rush. That took until lunchtime and with Liz and Brooke gone in the afternoon, Sophie was glad to have the place to herself now. It gave her a chance to think.

Then, about three o'clock, she took a call.

'Keith Taylor here. Is Sophie there?'

'Speaking,' she forced her voice to appear normal.

'I'd like to arrange another appointment, we've all enjoyed our sessions with you.'

Sophie took a deep breath. She didn't know what to say to him.

'Let me check the diary.' She gave herself a moment. Her heart thumped as she flicked through the pages. 'We're quite busy, I don't know when I can fit you in.'

'That's unfortunate. Is it not possible to give us an hour or two one evening, like we did before?'

'I'm sorry.'

'I regret this. You have added something special to our experience.'

Sophie took a deep breath. 'I can't do it anymore,' she said.

'You're not busy then, it's something else?'

She could sense the suspicion in his voice. 'Yes.'

'What is it?'

'It has nothing to do with you personally, it's business.' She tried to explain.

'Is there any way you might change your mind?'

'No, I can't.'

He was silent.

If her mother saw the photos, she would be shocked. There was something in them which wasn't in any other photos she had ever taken. A restlessness in those sessions which drew her into their fantasy world, and kept her mesmerized by that strange connection between mother and son, father and daughter. Her own addiction to drugs had twisted her mind. It was only now she realised that she had been confused by the wildness exhibited by them. Fascinated.

'We'll call to the studio,' Keith said.

'No,' she felt under pressure.

'I'm looking at my diary. If you can't give us an appointment in the evening, how would next Saturday be?'

'No.'

'We'll call anyway, you might change your mind and fit us in?'

'I won't.'

'Shall we say about lunch time, one o'clock?'


This was horrendous. She was in a deep hole and couldn't see the sky. She reached upwards. Her hands clawed at the sides. Her nails scratched. A shock wave shuddered through her. She wanted out. Anywhere. Just out.

She rushed into the toilet. Held on to the wash-hand basin. She couldn't get the image of being underground out of her mind. It was like being buried. Her breathing was short. Jerky. Perspiration gathered on her forehead. She felt hot suddenly. And then cold. Very cold. And hot again. She retched. Spewed thin liquid. She hadn't eaten anything this morning and felt weak. The walls of the small room weaved in and out, up and down. The ground under her feet was unsteady. It was as if she was on board ship in a bad storm. She grabbed a towel, held it under the tap, and pressed her face into it, slowly taking deep breaths in an effort to get this under control.

She hated these panic attacks. At first she didn't know what caused them, but she had done some research and discovered that they may be a side effect of her drug taking, or as she was trying to reduce the amount she took, possibly withdrawal symptoms. She wondered about going to her doctor, but couldn't mention what drugs she was using to him, so had to deal with it herself. She must stop. It was imperative before her life was destroyed. She had tried before. Given up for a couple of weeks but had been drawn back into the loop again. Even this week she had reduced the quantity. All her friends took drugs to escape reality. Morning and night. It kept them on an even keel. Able to deal with any situation. And no one noticed.

## Chapter Forty-one

Brooke took the children over to visit their Granny Peggy the following day. She didn't know if Rory had actually told her about their split, but she was determined to tell her if he hadn't done so.

'It's lovely to see you so soon again.' She opened the back door and the children ran out into the garden to play. 'I haven't seen Rory lately, he must be very busy,' Peggy said.

'He is.'

'How are things going between you?' she asked. 'I hope it's all been forgotten now?'

'No, Peggy, it hasn't.'

Her face crumpled. Tears flooded her eyes.

'Rory has left me.'

'What?'

'We're separated now and he's living with another woman.'

'My God.' She dabbed the tears with a tissue.

Brooke put her arm around the older woman's shoulders.

'I can't believe that a son of mine would do such a thing. What happened between you. Why would he leave you and the children?' She was shaken.

'He's in love with her. They work together.'

'It's so unfair on you.'

Brooke shrugged. 'I have to put up with it.'

'But you did nothing to deserve this?'

'He said I was boring.'

'That's such an insult. My husband said that to me too.'

Brooke stared at her, astounded. 'But you were happy, you loved each other?'

'We stayed together for the sake of the family. I couldn't tell anyone that there were a couple of women in his life.'

'How did you manage to live like that?'

'It wasn't easy.'

'Did Rory know?'

'No. It was a secret.'

'How awful for you. Who were the women?'

'I don't know.'

'Bitches. What is it with men that they must have women who make them feel like they're young again, it's little boy stuff.' Brooke was furious.

'At least Rory is only with one woman,' Peggy murmured sympathetically.

'Well, I'm not going to tolerate even one,' Brooke said.

Peggy said nothing.

'It's so hard to think of him with her. I keep imagining them together.'

'I know what that is like,' Peggy agreed.

'I want to kill him sometimes, to get my own back,' Brooke said furiously.

'Never say that.'

'I don't care.'

'Maybe he'll give her up?'

'And pigs might fly.'

'I'll talk to him,' Peggy offered.

'He will probably take the head off you, the way he does me.'

'I'll call him, persuade him to call around.'

'Don't upset yourself. He's determined to live with her. And he wants to sell the house.'

'But where will you go with the children?'

'We will find somewhere else to live.' Brooke felt a certain amount of relief telling Peggy. 'I'm hoping to stay in the area, I have Cian and Jess's names down in schools already.'

'And that's important. When the sale goes through would you like to come and stay here until you find a new apartment or house. I'm on my own and I would love to have you all staying. Then you'll have no problem going into work and I can drop them off at play school and pick them up.'

'That's so nice of you, Peggy, I really appreciate it.'

'Then let's agree then, it will make life easier for you.'

'I hadn't actually decided what I might do, I suppose I felt that I'd go home for a bit.'

'But Liz works, and you can't expect her to be able to help with the children.'

She thought about her Mum and this man who had come into her life. He was part of the problem. If Liz was living with him then Brooke couldn't go home. Anger surged. How could her mother turn away from her family and bring him into their home? The thought of that was almost impossible to bear. She had chosen him over the people she always said she loved most in the world.

'Come and live with me. It would mean so much. And there's plenty of room here for all of you,' Peggy was saying.

'Thank you.'

'Don't thank me, Brooke, just say you will.'

'I don't know what Rory will think.'

'He'll be fine. Don't worry.'

She embraced the older woman. In the back of her mind there was the possibility of seeing Rory when he came to see his mother, however infrequent that happened to be. And it would give the kids a chance to see their Dad too.

Brooke hadn't heard from Rory in the last week and was longing to see him. She would have given anything to relax into his arms like she used to. And find that this nightmare was only that. Why couldn't she be consistent, she thought. Why did she long for him one day, and hate him the next. But to stay angry with him all the time was difficult, and today she was weak. She just didn't have the energy. Just call, Rory just call. Suddenly, it didn't really matter to her what he said.

She had carved out her own niche in the studio by now, and more and more Liz delegated various tasks to her. She noticed a note she had made about that Taylor job which didn't seem to have any proper job card. Sophie was to check it out but there had been no mention of it since. She was surprised, but decided to talk to Sophie. Brooke hated loose ends. When her sister arrived in, it was the first thing she mentioned.

'I was to check that, wasn't I,' she said vaguely.

'I rang the man and he said he's been in a few times. Is it possible that you forgot to make out a job card?'

'I don't remember,' Sophie said.

'It's unusual, it never happened before.'

'Maybe I was having an off day, forgetful.'

'Yea, could be,' Brooke said slowly. 'We all have them, I suppose.'

Sophie didn't say anything.

'Maybe it's been mislaid. But there's the first note you made in the diary. Have a look at that, it might jog your memory.' She pushed it towards Sophie.

She glanced at it in a disinterested fashion.

'Is there something wrong, Sophie?' Brooke asked softly. 'You seem to be under pressure. Are you thinking about Mum and that Scott guy?'

'Not really.'

'Well, I am. Who is he anyway?'

'He's an old boyfriend.'

'Boyfriend at Mum's age, it's ridiculous.'

Sophie shrugged. 'I don't want to talk about it now.' She went into the studio. 'I have to organise for the next clients.'

That was the end of their conversation.

Brooke continued on with her work. There was an awkwardness between the two sisters, and she was very aware of it. It wasn't that unusual but she was puzzled. Perhaps she shouldn't mention the Taylors again, it seemed to upset Sophie, and maybe this thing with Liz was part of it too.

It was later that night when Rory called in.

Brooke was so relieved. At last. Tears flooded her eyes.

'I'm going to accept the offer for the house,' he said.

She was shocked. Caught in a bubble of disbelief. She knew this would happen but now that he had made the decision there was no turning back.

'I've decided to accept the latest offer,' he repeated.

She felt as if she was a child and he had to explain word for word.

'The solicitors will draw up contracts as soon as possible. They're cash buyers and have already sold their own property.'

'How soon?' she asked.

'A couple of months I hope.'

She compressed her lips.

'You'll have to find somewhere else to live. Why don't you move back with your mother?'

'I don't want to do that.'

'Why not?'

'Mum has enough on her plate. Anyway, your mother has asked us to stay.'

'My mother?' He was surprised.

'Yes, she loves the kids and she wants to mind them while I'm at work.'

'I don't want my mother interfering in my life.'

'She's not doing that.'

'She will influence my children.'

'They're her grandchildren.'

'I don't want my kids to have the upbringing I had myself. She tried so hard to push her and my Dad's brand of conservatism down my throat. They almost succeeded until I finally broke through and got out of there. I want my kids to be free thinkers.'

'Don't worry, I will give them what they need. I have been doing that or have you not noticed?'

'But they're going to be brainwashed.'

'Your mother isn't going to do that.'

'I don't want them living with her.' His voice was hard.

'You can't do anything about it.'

'Can't I?' he snarled.

'No.' Anger swept through her. He was trying to bully her.

'I still have responsibility.'

'But you don't accept it. How often have you called to see your children since you left this house? Once or twice?'

'I have a lot to do, constantly on the go, travelling, meetings, conferences, it's tough.'

'That's not good enough. Don't make excuses. I'm just telling you that as you're not around I'm making the decisions for my family, and we're going to live with your mother,' she steeled herself.

'You'll do as I tell you.' He stepped closer to her.

She stood her ground nervously, refusing to be cowed. 'You can't order me around, Rory.'

'You're a stupid bitch.'

'To have stayed with you for so long,' she snapped.

He turned on his heel.

She stood staring at the door for what seemed like ages, tears drifting down her cheeks, and knew it was the end.


'We've had an offer on the house and Rory has accepted it,' Brooke told Peggy.

'I don't know whether I should be glad for you or not,' she said, putting her arm around her and pulling her close. 'Although maybe it's best if you have your own home.'

'Anyway, in the meantime I wondered if we could move a few things over bit by bit.'

'What will you do with all your furniture, you have some lovely pieces?'

'I haven't talked to Rory about that yet. We'll probably split everything down the middle, and I'll put my half into storage until I find somewhere else to live.'

'You don't need to look for anywhere else, Brooke, just move in here with me.'

'I'd like to have my own home, my independence,' Brooke tried to explain.

'I understand,' Peggy said gently.

'And I'm very grateful to you for letting us stay for a while.'

'You're all very welcome. I'm looking forward to it. I'll start organising the bedrooms immediately,' she was excited.

'Don't worry, I'll do all that.'

'You will not. Sure what else have I got to do?'

'I don't want you to be doing too much.' Brooke hugged her.

'I'm glad to do it, I need to make the place nice for my little ones, and you. No matter what happens, you are my only daughter in law.' She returned her embrace.

'Thanks so much, Peggy, I'm really grateful,' Brooke hesitated. 'Has Rory been in to see you?'

'I hardly ever see him these days.'

'That's such a pity.' Brooke was sorry for the woman, but sorry too for her children. She had hoped that by bringing them to stay with Peggy they would get to see their father more often, but now that didn't seem likely. 'Does he phone?'

Peggy shrugged. Her expression morose.

He didn't phone her either or his children. When Brooke met him first, he had been a most loving, gentle man, and she wondered if money had been the cause of the change in his personality. He had become very successful over the last few years, and in that meteoric rise, Brooke and the children were left behind. 'It's no way to treat you. I wish I had realised what was happening, but I suppose I was a bit concerned for myself and the children, I'm sorry.'

'Don't worry, I'm happy you're coming over to stay with me for a while, it's such a comfort. Rory will come around, you'll see, he can't turn against all of us who love him, he could never be that foolish.'

'I wouldn't hold my breath,' Brooke said bitterly.

The next time she met Rory it was like a formal meeting. He came in with his briefcase and took out a bunch of papers and a notepad.

'We'll need to decide what we do with the contents of the house.' She got in first, determined she wasn't going to be bullied by him. 'Who owns what for instance.'

'I own everything.'

'You do not.' Her eyes flashed.

'I bought it all.'

'But we chose all our furniture and art together,' she said.

'I paid for it.'

She was silent, realising that he was right.

'It doesn't matter, I don't want most of it, there are just a few things.' He looked around.

'What things?'

'The paintings, sculpture, glass, and some of the silver.' He opened the pad.

'No, you can't, I love them,' she objected.

He went around the room and noted the details of the paintings which hung on the wall. There were some bronzes on a side table, and exquisite ceramics. He went through the rest of the house, into every room that contained any paintings or pieces of art, making notes as he went. She followed silently. She couldn't believe that this was happening.

'Now, you can have the basic furniture, but I want the antique bureau, the cabinets and other pieces, I'll send a removal firm around to pick them up as soon as I can.'

'You're leaving me with the ordinary stuff, taking all my precious things.' Tears filled her eyes.

'You'll survive.'

'Do you want to look in on Cian and Jess?' she asked.

'It's too late. I'll come over one night and take the paintings and other small items. The removal people will contact you to arrange an appointment to collect the furniture.' He tore off the page on which he had been writing and handed it to her.

Brooke stared around. Her home had begun to disintegrate. She would have liked to move what was left into storage immediately, but that was very expensive and she didn't want to do it until she had to. But she began to pack some other things in the meantime. There would be very little space at Peggy's house, and she and the children would have to get used to living out of a suitcase. But what to take? That was the big question. The kids would want every toy they possessed, and she could see a lot of arguments ahead. She went upstairs and checked on them. Poor things. Their lives would change radically when they left the only home they had known in their short lives. She adjusted the duvets and kissed the little heads gently. Her babies. How she loved them.

But as she went downstairs, she realised that this fixation about *things* was crazy. That's all they were. The paintings and other bits and pieces which they had collected were only canvas, paint, wood. Whatever. If Rory took them all, so what? They weren't going to make any difference to her life if she didn't see them around the house every day. All that mattered were her two darlings. Her heart was suddenly lighter, and for the first time she felt that she could tackle this challenge.

## Chapter Forty-two

Scott, and his two sons continued to work together. Neither of them made any further reference to Ciara's letter. Cathal was in London this week and Scott wondered whether he might call to see Ciara as he had said he would. It was like a secret between them. Something which couldn't be divulged. It stretched back into the past beyond remembering. The identity of a wife and mother was lost in shadow when she had chosen to suddenly disappear out of their lives. Now a road stretched ahead of them, a light shining in the distance. For Scott, there was a sense of dread. For his two sons he couldn't tell how it was. But surely there had to be hope in their hearts. Hope that they would find their mother after all this time?

But Scott was fearful for Cathal and how he would handle meeting Ciara. He stared at a group of photos on a low table. His own parents. The boys when they were young. And Ciara too. On her own. At the seaside with the boys. Her arms around the two of them. Her fair hair blowing in the breeze. From her letter he sensed that she was looking for forgiveness. Could he extend that to her. In a broad sweeping way. Without any recrimination. Had he got that much goodness inside him? He didn't know.

He had taken a photocopy of the letter and now looked at it again. It was strange to be writing letters. That last one to Liz and now to Ciara. Snail mail. And he, like everyone else, only used email or text instead of that age old time-consuming method of communication which had almost gone out of fashion. He remembered when he was a child at school carving out the letters of the alphabet with painstaking care on headline copy. Each letter had to be exactly the same size. He was left-handed and been forced to use his right hand by his mother who knew what he faced down the line. With the result, his hand-writing was never good, and he received much admonition from various teachers. When they were in college, Liz always teased him about that. Thinking of her suddenly reminded that he should phone her. But he hesitated. How could he tell her about the letter from Ciara over the phone. He should have told her the truth at the weekend. It was such awful timing. Moreover, would she understand that Ciara had suddenly made contact without any influence from him. And believe that he had no feelings for this woman and hadn't had for many years. He felt sick, and sent a text, saying he was held up in a meeting. It was a lie and the first time he had ever done that. He felt a huge wave of guilt sweep through him.

Now he had to reply to Ciara. What to say? He didn't know if the lads had already done so but he had to write regardless. He began.

*Dear Ciara,*
*I was surprised to hear from you after all this time. Cathal and Ryan*
*are well. I have given them your letter and I will leave it up to them*
*to make contact with you.*
*Scott.*

It was very brief. Even cold, he thought. But he had nothing to say to her now. Then, before he had a chance to put the letter in an envelope, Cathal called.

'I'm in Ealing, Dad.'

Scott's heart almost stopped. 'Where exactly?'

'Outside the house.'

'What are you going to do?' he asked, worried. His main fear was that Ciara's current partner or perhaps one of her children, if she had any, would open that door. 'Perhaps you should write first. Arrange to meet somewhere. I've just written a letter,' he said.

'No, I don't want to do that. I'm here now. I'm going to knock on that door. I must. I'll call you later.'

Scott sat down, and put the phone on the arm of the chair. He stared at it and waited. Nothing happened. He went through a nervous evening, not even bothering to eat. Over two hours passed. Then suddenly the phone rang. He grabbed it and the number came up. It was Cathal.

'I met her, Dad, and she was asking how you are, and Ryan, and wants to meet you soon,' he sounded excited.

A feeling of dismay swept through Scott.

'I invited her over.'

'What about her family?' he asked. In his mind, the image of Ciara was graphic. 'Does she have a partner, children?'

'She said she's on her own now.'

He said nothing.

'I don't think she has much money so I said I'd arrange the flight. It was amazing to meet her, Dad,' his voice was full of emotion. 'I can't wait to tell Ryan.'

'When is she coming over?'

'The weekend after next.'

## Chapter Forty-three

Sophie dreaded going into the studio on Saturday hoping the Taylors wouldn't turn up, but as the last of the early sessions finished, they arrived.

'Sophie, how nice to see you,' the mother was effusive, as were the daughter and son.

'Thanks for fitting us in.' Keith's piercing eyes cut through her.

'I'm sorry. I've already told you that I can't take photographs of you,' she said.

'It's a simple request, and I'm sure you enjoyed the experience,' he said, smiling. 'Don't say you didn't.'

'We'll set ourselves up. We've brought our own costumes and props as usual,' the mother said and disappeared into the studio.

'I said no,' she was becoming angry with him now.

'Sophie, don't be difficult.' His long thin fingers touched her arm. 'This won't pay in the end.'

'You can't force me to take photographs of you. Are you mad?'

'You've already taken some, and they are unusual you must admit. Do you want to show them to anyone? Your mother, your sister?'

'I will if I have to.'

'Now, I'm sure you wouldn't want that, they might be a little perturbed.'

'I don't care whether they are or not.'

'Hurry up, or the other people will be in here on top of us.' The mother looked around the studio door, a red velvet wrap around her shoulders.

'Lock the front door, you know how fond we are of our privacy.'

She had no option but to comply and turned the lock, feeling distinctly manipulated by this man.

When she went into the studio the mother, son and daughter were already in pose, and to her surprise, they were wearing even less than usual. The daughter's flowing see-through blue gown revealing a great deal of her pale body underneath.

The father positioned himself in the tableau and pulled off his shirt. 'Get on with it,' he said, curt.

She was faced with no choice and set up the camera.

'Give us the moves, Sophie.'

She took a few shots, and in a very desultory manner suggested they might move this way or that. But there was no spark in her voice, or manner.

'You're not very communicative, not at all your usual self,' he said.

'I'm sorry, but I told you I don't want to take photos of you,' she snapped.

'Your attitude will reflect in your work,' he sniffed.

She ignored his remark and continued shooting. Quickly. She didn't care what position they took and was so anxious to get through the session she hardly looked at them.

'And you're not taking much care with the shots.'

'You've been happy up to now.' She couldn't prevent herself making the comment.

'And we thought that would continue.' He brought his wife over to the chaise longue, placed his daughter lying in a languid position on the floor, while his son stood behind.

'That's it,' Sophie said.

'What do you mean?'

'It's time.'

'But we're not finished,' his wife retorted.

'You are now.'

'Really, Sophie, you leave a lot to be desired.'

'I don't want to see you again.'

'But I thought we had something going between us.' Keith came close. 'We value your assistance. Very much so.'

'I don't like taking photographs of you. It's too ...' she couldn't quite explain how she felt.

'Too?' he repeated.

'Volatile.'

'Interesting word.' He pursed his lips.

'I might remind you that I had to squeeze you in without an appointment.'

The doorbell rang. 'My next clients have arrived,' she said. 'You'd better get changed quickly. I'll need the studio.' Sophie walked into Reception and unlocked the front door.

'Sorry, we're a little late.' The woman was immediately apologetic.

'Don't worry, come along in and take a seat. I won't be long.'

She went back into the studio. The Taylors were dressed in their outdoor clothes. She stood waiting to escort them out.

'I won't say thanks,' Keith said, handing her an envelope.

'There's no need,' she stepped back, refusing to accept it.

'What do you mean?'

'I don't want any money.'

'I always pay you.' He pushed the envelope into her hand.

'Forget about it.' She gave it back. 'I won't be printing these photos so you needn't bother paying. And I don't want to see you here again, any of you.'

'You're an ignorant bitch,' he snarled. His hand twisted into a fist, and he raised it until it was right in front of her face.

'Are you threatening me?'

He grimaced.

'Mr. Taylor, I'll call the Gardai if you don't leave immediately.'

'What's going on here?'

Sophie turned around sharply, surprised to see Liz standing in the doorway.

Keith Taylor hustled his family out of the room, pushing past Liz into Reception. 'We won't be back, and I wouldn't bother hanging around here if I were you,' he yelled to the other couple.

They looked at each other.

Sophie closed the door after them. 'I'm so sorry, he's just a difficult client.'

There was a question in the woman's eyes.

'I'm sure you always get a few odd balls who drive you mad, just ignore them,' the man said, laughing.

Liz and Sophie both joined in, but Sophie definitely didn't feel like laughing.

'Why was that man so aggressive?' Liz asked later.

Sophie didn't know what to say and was reluctant to tell her mother who they were.

'Is that the same Taylor we were talking about recently. The one Brooke found in the diary?' Liz asked.

Sophie shook her head.

'He was threatening you, so much so you said you would call the Gardai. Why don't we do that anyway? We can't let him away with it. What sort of photos were you taking?'

'Just ordinary.'

'Let me see them.' Liz was firm.

'There's no need,' Sophie said. 'These people dress up, they're actors and need the photos for their portfolios.'

'But you said you didn't know anyone called Taylor?'

# Chapter forty-four

Sophie was making another effort to reduce the level of drugs she was using, and managed to get through Sunday on a smaller dose. She knew that she should spend the evening doing her usual routine. Cleaning the apartment, catching up with personal admin, emails, etc. But she couldn't concentrate and found herself pacing up and down in an erratic fashion, unable to do anything for longer than a couple of minutes. All the time her mind was drawn towards her handbag where she kept her stock of tablets. It was as if she was receiving subliminal messages. A longing swept through her. It was hard to resist. She made coffee. Strong. Sweet. And drank two mugs in quick succession.

With a sudden burst of energy, she took out the vacuum cleaner. Dusted. Changed the bedlinen. Scrubbed pots. Tiles. Units. All the time trying to get away from the insidious thought of taking another tablet. Wiping down the counter, she noticed her hands shaking. She stopped. Held her hand up. It was steady. But within a minute the tremor returned and grew stronger. She had no control over it. Her phone rang. She couldn't answer it. She held her hands tight. But it made no difference.

She lay on the couch and closed her eyes. This was withdrawal. And the worst it had ever been. How would she manage to succeed in coming off the drugs? Tears filled her eyes. A wave of shame came over her. It was something she couldn't tell the people who meant most to her in the world. Her mother, sister and brother. Yet Luke had come out to all the family. He had managed to climb over that hurdle and he admitted that it had been very difficult for him.

She stood up. A terrible craving gnawed at her insides. The tablets were just over there in her handbag. She began to walk towards it convincing herself that if she just took one the symptoms would disappear. She picked the bag up. The tremor in her hand made it hard to open the zip of the inside pocket. She couldn't quite grasp it.

She swore out loud, irritated.

Tears began again.

Her heart was racing. She couldn't breathe properly. The zip wouldn't open. Frustrated she realised it was the wrong one. She tried another. Where had she put them? She upended the large Gucci handbag. A stream of possessions cascaded out over the coffee table and on to the floor. Keys. Wallet. Perfume. Notebook. Make-up. And all the other bits and pieces she normally carried in her handbag. She bent down, searching among the stuff. Then went back to the pockets in the bag. Easier now to access them. But there was no logic in her search. She opened pocket after pocket, but repeated the same ones more than once.

'Where are they?' she shouted out loud, and threw the bag across the room where the handle clanged against the glass pane of the large window. She bent down on her knees and searched among the various items on the coffee table and floor. But she couldn't find what she was looking for and began to fling other things after the bag. Then she lifted a make-up case and to her great relief found the box under it. She took one immediately and even the taking of it helped her to feel a little better, although the effect of the drug didn't kick in until later and gradually the craving eased.

But these days the symptoms didn't reduce completely. The nervous agitation continued from time to time. The tremors in her hands. The palpitations. It was more and more difficult to conceal. She was tired too yet found it hard to sleep. And then didn't hear the alarm clock and was late for work more than once recently.

She tried to cover up. Finding excuses. But now she had to deal with Brooke as well as her mother.

'You're not looking well. You don't seem right. Some days you look as if you've put on weight, and then a week later it seems to have fallen off again. And you're not sleeping, I know by the look of you.'

'The pattern has changed. Some nights I sleep like a log, other nights I wake on and off,' Sophie said.

'You'll have to change your lifestyle,' she said firmly.

'Yes mother.'

'I don't think Mum realises how bad you are.'

'Don't be going on about it.'

'You have to look after yourself, your health is everything. Have you been to the doctor?'

'I have. He says there is nothing wrong and I should just get more sleep. Now, are we going to do any work this morning?'

'I've already started,' Brooke said.

'What time did Mum say she'd be in?'

'Later, she has an appointment.'

'We usually have our meeting on a Monday.'

'Well, she's not here.'

Sophie was irritable and was just about to snap at Brooke again when something made her hold her tongue. There was no point in alienating her sister, they had to work together. She went into the studio and busied herself with her cameras preparing for the session which was booked in for twelve.


It was a family who wanted a series of graduation photographs with their daughter. By the time they arrived, Sophie was in better shape. They made it a very easy hour or so and by now she was happy enough with the results. Later Sophie brought the photos up on the computer and went through them. Liz walked past, stopped and looked at the screen over her shoulder.

'Nice family,' she said.

Sophie had an immediate urge to close down the computer but couldn't with Liz there.

'There are some nice shots, you're very good at isolating the essential detail, but there are a few shaky ones too,' she said. 'Better not show them.'

'Are you criticising my work?' Sophie flashed angrily.

'I'm sorry.' Liz straightened up.

'You're always doing that lately, what is it with you?' She turned around to glare at her mother.

'I've apologised,' Liz said.

Sophie stood up abruptly and went outside into Reception.

'What's going on?' Brooke asked.

'Nothing,' retorted Sophie.

'I thought I heard raised voices.'

'That's your imagination.'

'Didn't seem to be.'

'Can't you mind your own business. Not in here a wet day and already you're trying to rule the roost,' Sophie muttered.

Brooke made a face and bent her head down to continue with her work.

Sophie went out the front door. She was furious with her mother. How dare she made a comment about her work. She walked up the street, darting between people who were making their way towards her, every one of them in a hurry it seemed. It was a chilly day and she was cold, only wearing a light black suit, her usual work uniform. She clasped her arms around herself, but the wind was strong and gusty, and tore at her clothes. As she went, she calmed down a little. Realising that she shouldn't have shouted at Liz who was one of the most easy-going people in the world. Brooke probably deserved it, she usually did, sticking her nose in where it didn't belong.

It began to rain. But she continued on regardless. Her long dark hair twisted and sharp raindrops beat against her face. She felt the better of the long walk, her anger diminishing as she hurried along. Her photos hadn't been good, she had seen that immediately and just should have accepted what Liz said. And she knew exactly why her work wasn't up to scratch. It was the tremor in her hands. What was she going to do about that? Her work was everything to her. If she didn't get that tremor under control, then her career would collapse and the one thing she loved above all else would be gone. She couldn't bear the thought of that. Tears moistened her eyes and she could barely see where she was going. She stopped then, realising how ridiculous this was, and turned back.

She pushed open the door of the studio, feeling foolish now.

Brooke was just about to leave. 'Sorry, I don't know why I said that to you earlier.' She hugged her. 'Forgive me please?'

Brooke nodded.

'I'll call you later, I've to talk to Mum.'

# Chapter Forty-five

'You're soaked,' Liz exclaimed.

'It doesn't matter.'

'Take off that jacket, there's a fleece of mine in the press.' She found it and stood waiting while Sophie took off her wet things. 'Here's a towel, dry your hair. I'll turn on the heater to warm you up.' Liz went into the back and poured coffee from the percolator. She waited for Sophie to say something. She didn't want to be the first one to refer to what had happened earlier.

Sophie went over to the computer. 'I'll delete some of these. They're not good. I hope the clients won't notice that there are a few missing,' she said.

'I'm sure they won't,' Liz said gently. She was still worried about Sophie and wanted to coax her to explain what was happening to her. 'Will you have a look at some of these photos I took yesterday,' Liz asked, 'I'd value your opinion.'

'I don't know why, my own work isn't exactly up to scratch,' Sophie muttered.

'What do you think?' Liz brought them up on the computer.

'That's a big gathering.'

'A sixtieth wedding anniversary.'

'You've captured the happiness, it's touching.'

'It was lovely to meet them all, and it makes what we do worthwhile.' Liz watched Sophie's expression. Her eyes were red-rimmed. Was it possible that Scott was right. Her heart pounded. It couldn't be. No. I don't believe it. She sensed a quivering within her daughter and could see that Sophie was trying desperately to hold her hands together to hide it.

'Sophie, what's wrong?' she asked gently.

'Nothing,' she snapped.

'There is, I know you,' Liz insisted.

'You don't understand where I'm at, Mum.'

'Let me in, tell me about it and I'll help you. I promise I won't judge you,' Liz said.

'I must check my emails.' Sophie pulled her phone from her pocket and read a text. 'Oh God, the baby's due tomorrow, I'd forgotten.'

Liz said no more.

Sophie pressed her face into her hands. 'I hope I'll be able to photograph the birth.'

'You will, love. Do you want me to come with you?' Liz asked.

'No, I'll manage, thanks.'

Someone came in then and there was no further opportunity to talk.

'Why don't you relax for the weekend?' Liz asked when they closed up for the night. 'I'll cover tomorrow just in case the baby arrives.' She tapped in the alarm code. They left together and went around to the garage where they parked their cars. 'Thanks Mum, I might if you're sure you can manage?'

'Of course I can,' Liz reassured. 'And I hope you feel better tomorrow.'

Driving home, Liz was so concerned for Sophie she decided to detour to her apartment in Clontarf, stopping off to do a quick shop on way. Standing at the checkout she texted Scott to tell him she would be late and where to find the key.

She pressed in the code number on the panel by the gates of Sophie's apartment complex.

'Yes?'

Liz heard her voice on the intercom. 'It's me.'

She waited until the gates slowly opened and drove around the building, parked and went in. Sophie met her at the door, and Liz put her arms around her. Sophie burst into tears.

'Let's go in,' Liz whispered.

'Mum, I don't know what I'm going to do.' She clung to her.

'Come on, you'll be all right.' She sat her down on the couch and dried the tears on her cheeks with a tissue.

'You don't understand.'

'Tell me.'

'I've done terrible things.'

'Now, I'm sure that isn't true,' Liz said, smiling.

'I have, I stole money.'

'From whom?' Liz was astonished.

'From you.'

'How did that happen, I'm not aware of it.'

'Remember Brooke discovered an anomaly in the books, the Taylor order, and then you met them in the studio.'

'That horrible man?'

'I took his money and kept it.' She clasped her hands tightly. 'I feel so ashamed.'

'Did you need the money for something?' Liz couldn't believe what she was hearing.

Sophie nodded. Her head down.

'What did you need it for?' Liz asked.

She didn't reply. Just covered her eyes with her hand.

'Sophie love, tell me why you wanted it, I don't care about the money, that doesn't matter. It's just why you needed it. What is so important?'

'My friends and I ...' Sophie whispered brokenly.

Liz's heart sank as she remembered what Scott had said.

'We take Ecstasy or other drugs.'

'Is it just when you're out for an evening?' Liz prompted gently.

'No, I take them all the time, I can't get through the day, that's what's wrong, and I try to get off them but I can't, I just can't, Mum.'

Liz couldn't say anything. Her heart hammered inside and tears flooded her eyes. She hugged Sophie.

After a while, she got herself under control. 'We won't talk about it now, I'll make something to eat.' Gently she took her arms from around Sophie and let her sink into the cushions. She busied herself in the kitchen and heated the chicken dish she had bought.

'Try some of this, love, you'll feel better.'

'I'm not hungry.'

'Just a little, please?' Liz handed her the plate and a fork, and began to eat herself.

Sophie ate a little but then put down the plate, and just sipped a glass of water.

'You look tired, would you go to bed early?'

She nodded, and pushed herself up.

'I'll be here with you tonight,' Liz said.

'Thanks Mum.'

After Sophie had gone to bed, Liz cleared away the dishes and called Scott, explaining that she had to stay. He offered to come over to keep her company but reluctantly she refused. She needed to be there for Sophie.

She slept fitfully. Waking a few times during the night and going to look in on Sophie. But she seemed to sleep well and didn't even move when Liz pushed open the door. In the morning, she left her a note and went to open up the studio. She didn't want to wake her too early and held off until about eleven before she rang. 'Sophie?'

'Yes, Mum.'

'How are you?'

'I'm all right, and thanks for being here last night.'

'Can we talk again, I'd like to. Have you heard anything from the woman who's having the baby?'

'Not yet, they'll only call me when the labour is fairly advanced and then I have to drop everything.'

'You should stay at home and take it easy, you could be up all night,' Liz spoke gently.

'I will, thanks Mum.'

'Take care of yourself.'


'It's as you said, she takes drugs all the time. I can't believe it,' Liz was upset when she arrived home.

'We'll have to help her.' Scott pressed her lips softly with his.

'She's in a terrible state,' she whispered.

'It's a social thing, people become addicted and use drugs to keep going from day to day. Then they can't live without it.'

She was shocked. 'How is it that I've never noticed?'

'When people use daily and can afford to buy what they need to stay on an even keel, it's just part of their lives.'

'I'll have to do something for her, but what?'

'It's very difficult to force people to admit to addiction. They have to face it themselves and there has to be a very strong reason for them to do that. I have a friend who is an addiction counsellor, maybe Sophie might go to see someone like that?'

'I'll mention it or maybe you might talk to her as well?' Liz sighed and leaned closer to Scott.

'Of course I will. Although she may not want anyone else to be aware of it.'

'How do you know so much about drugs?'

'I worked with young people involved in sport with a friend, Ryan was a very good footballer and still is.'

'It's great to have you here,' she murmured. 'I can't believe how my life has changed in such a short time.'

He kissed her.

She responded. Her body craved his touch. His smile drew her into him. That smile she had known for so long. From that first day in the library when, timid, hesitant, she had accepted a chair beside him.

She couldn't believe how much she adored this man. Such happiness to have found him again. His hands cupped her face. His lips found hers. They moved off the couch on to the rug in front of the fire. Their clothes were stripped off urgently and flung aside. She lay against him and could feel the drumming of his heart.

'You're so beautiful,' he whispered.

She explored those intimate little places that were Scott. She clung to him. Like he was a raft in a storm. Their movements in unity. As their passion heightened, everything else was forgotten. He reached for the innermost being of Liz. She gave of herself and touched those same depths in him.

## Chapter Forty-six

Paula's baby didn't arrive until the following week. Sophie almost missed the call from the midwife, and it was only when the session with her clients was finished that she rang back.

'This is Paula's midwife, she's already in labour and I hope you can come over soon. I don't think it will be too long.'

Sophie's heart dropped. 'Yes, of course, I'll just have to arrange for someone to cover here.'

'There mightn't be time.'

'I'll be there as soon as I can,' she promised, and called Liz. 'The baby's coming and I have to go over to take the photographs, how long before you'll be here?'

'I'm on my way.'

'Thanks be to God, I'll have to go now.'

'Don't worry. And best of luck.'

She gathered her cameras and put them into the car. Then she opened her bag and was about to take a tablet. She needed it. She told herself. Needed to be in control. Thinking that her work wouldn't be up to scratch if she didn't take something, and that she could have some sort of episode or panic attack without its support. Then she wouldn't be able to complete her assignment. And she couldn't come back later if anything happened, this baby would only be born once. There were no second chances. She took it.

Husband, Barry, ushered her into the living room, where Paula lay on a pile of cushions. She waved to Sophie. 'Thanks for coming over, you mightn't have to wait too ...' she stopped speaking suddenly in mid-sentence as a contraction made itself felt. The midwife was urging her to breathe and not to push as each contraction happened. To Sophie's horror they were quite close which meant that baby would arrive soon. She looked around, surprised to see their two other children sitting in front of the television watching a cartoon. Music played in the background although she didn't recognise the tune. It was all very bizarre.

She went back into the hall and with shaking hands she chose the particular cameras which she would use. She was terrified and aware that if she didn't get a hold of herself then any photos she took would be all out of focus. She urged herself to get back into the room or it would be all over before she had a chance to take a shot. She grabbed her handbag, pulled out a small box and swallowed another tablet. Then she was aware of Barry standing in the doorway.

'Can I help?' he asked.

'No thanks, I'm ready now.'

'Barry?' There was a call from inside the room.

He disappeared. Sophie followed.

Things had advanced since she left. The midwife knelt in front of Paula and it looked as if the baby was about to be delivered. Barry held his wife's hand and Sophie went to the other side where the two children stood beside their mother. She began to take photos. Paula was amazingly calm, not at all as Sophie had imagined. She was obviously in some pain but managed to hide it.

Sophie took the first photographs and video. Shots of their faces. All of them so different. Excitement in the eyes of the children, and anxiety in Barry's. She could feel each contraction herself, and winced every time. She moved down behind the midwife. This was difficult. The head of the baby had already appeared. She gasped. Caught up in the whole thing.

'Push Paula, push, just a few more, you're nearly there,' the midwife encouraged.

She groaned now.

Sophie wanted to scream. A crazy thought sped through her mind. She was never going to go through this herself. Not for anything.

She took photos at a fast pace now. Every second recorded. Click. Click. Click. The video ran at the same time.

'We're nearly there, Paula, just one more push.' The midwife worked with her.

'Oh God ...' Paula gave one last shout as the baby whooshed out. A tiny little body glistening with birthing juices.

'There he is, a beautiful little boy.' The midwife cleared his airways and he cried. That new born sound. Then she lifted him on to Paula.

They all surrounded her, gazing enthralled at the little child which she held in her arms, including Sophie who still snapped. Barry held Paula and the baby close, and he was in tears as were the children too. Even Sophie was filled with a most tremendous rush of emotion.

They were so happy. She took photos of the family as they gathered together. It was a most amazing scene. She couldn't see them being like this if the baby had been born in a hospital. She was so glad to be part of it, finishing up when Paula decided to take a rest and the midwife had left.

Sophie sat into her car, but couldn't even turn on the engine at first. The birth of the baby was both shocking in its intensity and beautiful too. She was deeply affected by the experience. Eventually, she managed to get going and went home. It was after nine now, although she had had no perception of time during the birth of the baby. But now she wanted to see the photos and video. To go through it all again.

She uploaded them on to the computer and sat staring at the screen. Once again, seeing that tiny little baby come into the world swept her into a state of utter bewilderment. She felt that child was hers too. She loved him. She wanted him.

## Chapter Forty-seven

'I've been thinking some more about Mum and Scott,' Brooke said. 'How come we've never heard of him before?'

'She only met him again a while ago, didn't you hear what they said?' Sophie asked.

'Is it true that they met in college?'

'Why would she say otherwise?'

'Maybe she's seeing him for much longer and kept it a secret.'

'So what?'

'You don't seem to be so concerned about it, Sophie. Or Luke either, he hasn't even bothered mentioning it.'

'The only thing I'm worried about is that he could try to take advantage, she's vulnerable,' Sophie added.

'Well, I don't even like him,' Brooke was adamant. 'What is Mum thinking of at her age? My husband walked out on me, you're still looking for a man, and there she is picking up a guy just like that.'

'I think you're jealous?' Sophie said with a laugh.

'I am not, I'm concerned for her. Why is she getting married?'

'Why not?'

'And all that about the divorce, it's such a line, I don't believe a word of it. And where is his wife now? She's probably living in Cork and knows nothing about the other women in his life.'

'I don't know, Brooke.'

'And if he does divorce his wife and they do get married, is he going to move into our house?' Brooke asked.

'It's not our house.'

'It is too. It's our inheritance. Look how Rory is insisting on selling our house.'

'You could refuse,' Sophie suggested.

'And then what? I'll be left to pay the mortgage and have to chase Rory in court for every cent.'

'Why don't you divorce him, then let the judge decide how everything is divided between you?'

Brooke stared at her. 'Divorce?'

'Yes. It's probably what you will do eventually.'

'Maybe.'

'Are you hoping to get back with him?'

'No, never. He has abandoned us. Just like Mum will.'

'She won't do that. All this thing with Rory is affecting your judgement, Brooke.'

'I'm thinking how this man might affect all our lives. Have you thought about the business?' She wrote that word down on a notepad, and added *house* below.

'No.'

'If anything happens to Mum then he inherits our house.'

'Don't say that,' Sophie exploded.

'And he will probably get a portion of her estate which includes the business. He could put us out. All of our work would be for nothing.'

'Mum's work and my work, Brooke, I own half the business I'll have you know,' Sophie corrected.

Brooke felt ticked off. 'Ok, I'm not really part of the business, I didn't mean it that way.'

'I don't know what we can do anyway, Mum's a very independent woman.'

'We'll have to tell her how we feel.'

'And expect her to give him up?' Sophie seemed astonished.

'She probably doesn't see how it will affect us. We're her family. Her children. And she has left everything to us in her Will, she told me that. If he is her husband then we may get nothing particularly if he's living in the house. And if we want our share, then he might just sit

197

there and refuse to sell. I've heard of that happening before, it causes terrible problems in families. And even if they don't get married then after a certain length of time he's still entitled to something'

'I'm more concerned for Mum,' Sophie said. 'She's obviously very keen on him.'

'But what if this Scott is a chancer, you know, he might just want to use her. Get his foot in the door. He could break her heart,' Brooke said. 'And another thing, our mother is getting married, can you imagine what people are going to say?'

'So what? Are you living in the last century, Brooke? You're over the top, calm down. Wait until they tell us what they're going to do exactly.'

'We have to make our point before they decide. Force them to think about us. And then there are Cian and Jess to be considered as well.' Brooke found it very hard to get her head around the whole thing.

'What do you want to do?' Sophie asked.

'We should talk to Mum as soon as we can.'

'What are we going to say to her? It's none of our business.'

'It is our business,' snapped Brooke.

'I don't feel as strongly as you about it. While I am worried about her, if he turns out to be a nice guy why should we deny her happiness? Dad died a long time ago.' Sophie pointed out.

'We have to warn her. I can't help the way I feel.'

'Just hold back for now.'

'We can't, before we know it they'll be living together. We must tell her how we feel.'

'I suppose we could talk with her,' Sophie said.

'I can't do it myself, you must support me,' Brooke insisted.

'We'll just play it by ear. Now, let's change the subject. When are you moving?'

'I'm gradually bringing some of my stuff over to Peggy's house. Mum said I could come and live with her, but I decided to stay with Peggy so that the kids might see more of Rory if he happened to call to see his mother. Then I was thinking I'd come home if I got fed up, now

I can't change my mind at all as Scott is living there.'

Brooke was furious. Since Scott had come into her mother's life, Liz's brown eyes glistened brighter. Her smiles held secrets. There was a luminous aura about her. She was somewhere else. And it seemed to Brooke that she had lost her mother. Left behind like a small child in a crowded street, pulled, pushed, terror stricken as she ran this way and that, frantically searching for Liz.

Now there was only incoherence in her mind. The edges sharp and brittle. She was disconnected from her life. The beautiful life she had treasured. She didn't know what lay ahead, the future shrouded in mystery.

Brooke collected Cian and Jess from school. At home she had begun to fill boxes with some of her belongings, and they began to build up in the dining room, all neatly labelled.

Rory came around later to collect the items he wanted. It was unusual for him to come early in the evening, particularly when the children were still up.

'You've already started packing?' he asked, wandering across the room to look out into the garden where the children played.

'Yes.'

Cian and Jess came in.

Brooke watched with a smile. It was so good for them to see him.

'Come and play with my train set, I've a new carriage.' Cian pulled at his trousers.

'Who bought that for you?'

'Granny Peggy.'

'And she bought me a new book.' Jess pushed it towards him.

'She's very good.'

'Please read me a story, Daddy?' Jess asked.

'Not today.'

'Look at my train,' Cian cried.

'I want to take those paintings.' He went back into the living room and began to lift them down from the wall.

She didn't say anything.

He went in and out to the jeep carrying them, and then examined the boxes in the dining-room. 'I don't want any of that stuff, you can keep it. But have you packed up the John Rocha glassware?'

'Yes, there it is over there.' She pointed.

'I'll take that.' He lifted the box and took it out.

She steeled herself. Reminded that *things* didn't matter.

'The silver cutlery?'

'It's still in its own box.'

'I'll take these decanters too. You can have the Waterford, it's old hat now.'

'Daddy, can I go with you in the jeep?' Cian ran over and clung to him.

'I want to go too.' Jess followed.

'Get off me kids, I'm trying to lift this stuff.'

'What stuff?' Cian demanded.

'This glass.'

'Why?'

'Why?' Jess usually repeated everything Cian said.

'What is it?'

'What is it?' she giggled.

'Stop that,' Rory snapped.

Brooke could see he was becoming irritated.

'Stop that,' Cian repeated what Rory said.

'Kids,' Brooke shouted. 'It's no time for games.'

'It's no time for games,' Jess giggled.

Rory put the decanters up on the top of the sideboard.

'I'll get a box for them,' Brooke said, and went into the utility. She returned and handed it to him. 'Wrap some newspaper around them to keep them safe.'

'They'll be all right,' he said, and put them into the box.

'I'll carry it for you,' Jess offered. She stretched a small hand up.

'It's OK.' He lifted it.

'I'll carry the other one,' Cian said and ran to pick it up.

'No Cian, that's too heavy.'

'It isn't.' He put his little arms around it.

'Don't, it will break.'

'No it won't.'

'Cian, let Daddy lift it.' She went over to him.

'I want to help him.'

'I don't want your help,' Rory yelled.

'No, Cian.' Brooke unclasped his little hands from around the box.

Cian's lips trembled. Tears filled his eyes.

'It's all right love.' Brooke kissed him.

'Take the kids out of my way, will you. Get out.' He waved at them.

Brooke took their hands and they followed her into the playroom. She put her arms around the two of them, listening to the sounds made by Rory as he carried out the boxes, and closed the front door.

## *Chapter Forty-eight*

'It's great to see you,' Liz hugged Celine, and then Leah and Megan in turn. 'Come on in.' She welcomed them.

They sat down in the living room.

'Love your house, it's so comfortable,' Megan said.

'Drinks girls? Wine, gin and tonic, what would you like?'

She brought in the drinks and finger food. They sat around and chatted.

'How do your three feel about Scott?' Celine asked.

'I'm sure they're thinking I'm going to run off into the sunset with a strange man and really live to regret it.'

'Do they object?'

'Brooke didn't seem to be too keen on the day we told her.'

'Hope they will be mature enough to understand.'

'Kids can't even imagine that their mothers or fathers have normal needs. That they would be bothered making love. You probably couldn't even mention the word *sex* in their hearing. They'd collapse.'

'Mine would be the same. If I announced I was getting married again, they would all freak out,' Celine grimaced.

'Why is it that kids can't imagine their parents even wanting a partner in their lives?'

'Liz is leading the way, so we'll all be following her example.'

'If I can find a man,' Celine said, laughing.

'One of these days it will happen, don't worry,' Megan reassured.

'It was lovely to meet Scott at the book launch, he's still a good looking hunk, always was,' Leah said, sipping her glass of wine.

'I had imagined a big overweight guy,' Megan giggled.

'I can't believe that you've finally nailed a man.'

'That sounds like I've gone through dozens of them.'

'She was just waiting for the right one to come along.'

'And no dust gathering under her feet either.' Celine raised her glass.

'Family can sometimes take you by surprise,' Megan said slowly.

'I've certainly been taken aback by Brooke's reaction,' Liz admitted.

'It's something you can't predict,' Celine said. 'So maybe it might be better if some handsome hunk doesn't propose to me.'

'If you meet a gorgeous guy you go ahead and enjoy him,' Leah said. 'That's what I would do.'

'Top up?' Liz asked, holding the bottle.

'Yea, go ahead.'

'Well, tell us, what's Scott like these days? He seemed so nice the other night,' Celine asked, with a coy grin.

'He hasn't changed much.'

'Good in bed?' Megan quipped.

'On the floor.' Liz nodded her head towards the fireplace, and burst out laughing.

'You didn't even make it to the bed?'

'Not always,' Liz giggled.

'I'm envious,' Leah sighed.

'I tell you, girls, it's something else to have a man who wants me. It's like being in a dream, and I expect to wake up any moment and discover that's all it is.'

'We're really glad for you.'

'And he's asked you to marry him already? Fast worker.'

'I know, I wasn't sure whether I was mad to say yes, but I did anyway, it seemed so natural.'

'Do you remember what Niamh said?' Megan asked.

'Niamh?' Liz asked.

'The medium.'

'Oh, that woman.' Liz was dismissive.

'Ethan was supposed to say that you should take a chance on life, something like that,' Leah said.

Liz nodded. 'I didn't believe it.'

'I've had a couple of sessions with Niamh, and she's told me things which have actually happened.'

'I couldn't accept that Ethan was talking to me.'

'Why not?'

'It seemed ridiculous.'

'But if you think of what she said, isn't it exactly what you've done. Taken a chance. To agree to marry someone you only know a short time is taking a hell a chance, do you not think so?'

'I suppose.'

'For someone as conservative as our Liz,' they screamed with laughter.

'So, what's the plan?'

'No plan yet until he has his divorce.'

'You must have some idea. Are you going to live in Cork, or is he coming up here?'

'Both of us have businesses so that's going to be a difficult one. But we can always commute.'

'That's not easy.'

'I don't care about the details, all that counts is that he loves me and I love him. We'll be together.'

'I wish I could meet some old boyfriend,' Celine shifted the cushions on the couch and repositioned herself.

'How about your English guy, Leah?'

'Haven't heard from him in a while. We only met that one time.'

'He'll probably be in touch when he's over again.'

'Next time maybe he might bring along the friend who was with him that night in Ashford Castle and we can make it a foursome,' Celine asked.

'Liz's phone rang. 'Excuse me, girls.' She picked it up, surprised to see Scott's number come up. 'It's Scott, do you mind if I take it? know it's breaking the rules but …'

'Go ahead,' Megan said. 'We couldn't refuse you.'

'Look at the light in her eyes,' Leah said, with a wide grin.

Liz took Scott's call.

'Are you busy tonight?' he asked.

'Just having a glass of wine with the girls.'

'I'm sorry for interrupting you.'

'What are you doing?'

He hesitated. 'I'm actually in Dublin, that's why I called.'

'Where are you?'

He didn't answer.

'Scott?' Immediately, she looked out the window and laughed. 'Don't drive away, I can see your car.'

'I'll come back later.'

'Sorry, girls, he's outside.' She looked at them.

'Give me a call when they've gone home.'

'Tell him to come in,' Celine said.

She beckoned him. He climbed out of the car and walked up the drive.

Opening the door, she put her arms around him, and kissed him.

'I just had to come up to see you and left the office as soon as I could,' he smiled down at her.

'You know you're always welcome.'

'Young love,' someone said from behind, and there was a loud cheer from the girls who had gathered in the doorway.

Scott went towards them, hand outstretched.

'Can I get you something to eat, you probably haven't had any dinner?' Liz asked.

'Cup of coffee would be fine. I'll make it myself, you sit down.'

'I'll get it, won't be a minute.'

Liz went into the kitchen, heated quiche and garlic bread, put some salad on the side, brought it in and set it on a small table beside him.

'You shouldn't have gone to so much trouble, but thanks, this is great,' he smiled at her.

The girls were chatting, and Scott was the centre of their attention.

He had brought two bottles of wine and he opened the red. They raised their glasses and made a toast.

'To Liz and Scott.'

'Let's take a photo,' someone suggested, and with much laughter, they sat in various poses and snapped themselves.

It was late when the girls finally left. Scott and Liz waved them off, closed the front door and went inside, arms around each other.

'Let's talk,' he said and they sat down.

'Is something wrong? I wondered if there was a reason why you came up tonight, I wasn't expecting you.'

'Well, there is a reason. Although I don't need one to come and see you. But I couldn't have told you this over the phone.'

She stared at him, suddenly worried. 'It sounds serious.'

'It's not really serious in that sense. It could even be advantageous.'

'What are you on about?'

'Ciara has come back.'

Liz didn't sleep well that night. Her mind twisted and turned as she thought about Ciara, jealous of the time Scott would spend with her. Regardless of what he said about her, it was hard for Liz not to imagine that this woman wouldn't cause a rift between them. When he left early the following morning, she drove into work. May as well beat the traffic, she decided. Then went into a nearby café and had breakfast there as she read the newspaper.

She rang him from the office.

'I'm on the road, almost there. But I miss you already.'

'Miss you too.'

'I'll be up as soon as I can, love you.'

'How are you feeling, Sophie?' Liz enquired softly, when she arrived.

'Not too bad.'

'You were saying on Friday that...' She hesitated for a few seconds. It was the first time she had said anything to Sophie about her upset the previous week, and Sophie had said nothing either. 'Can I help in any way?' she whispered.

'I don't know whether anyone can help.' Sophie bent her head.

'Scott has a friend who's an addiction counsellor.'

'You told him?' she stared at her mother, her expression aghast.

'He guessed, that night we met you on Grafton Street with your friends.'

'How could he guess?'

'He's had some experience.'

'I don't believe it.'

'Here's his card, give him a call and talk to him.' Liz gave her Scott's card. 'You must get help, and his friend will be discreet. It would be much better if you had an introduction. Otherwise you'll be just walking in off the street and they won't know you at all, please do it for me?' Liz begged.

Sophie stared at the card. 'I'll think about it.'


Later, they sat together in the kitchen.

'Mum, there's something we wanted to ask you,' Brooke said.

'What is it?' Liz asked.

'Are you really going to marry Scott?'

'He's asked me,' she smiled.

'Do you want to?'

'Of course I do.'

'Why?'

'What a question?' Liz raised her eyebrows. 'Why do two people usually decide to get married?'

'You love him?'

'Of course.'

'Has he told you he loves you?'

Liz frowned. 'You're interrogating me, why?'

'We want to know what's at the back of it. We need to protect you from him.'

'Protect me?'

'If I announced I wanted to get married to some guy you had never heard of before, wouldn't you want to interrogate me?'

'Well, I'd hope I wouldn't interfere too much, you're an adult.'

'But you would say something?'

'I might.'

'Well, I'm your daughter, and it's my duty to say that this man is a complete stranger and totally unsuitable for you. Both Sophie and I feel the same. You can't suddenly settle down with him.'

The doorbell rang, and someone pushed it open.

'We can't talk about this now. Come around to me this evening,' Liz said.


Liz was nervous as she waited for the girls to arrive, and dreaded to hear the sound of the doorbell, which when it happened made her heart begin to thump. She had thought that they mightn't really understand why she wanted to get married, but Brooke's attitude had been so strident she was shocked.

'Mum, it's us,' Sophie appeared in the kitchen. She kissed her.

Brooke did the same.

'Is Peggy watching the kids?'

'Yea, she came over.'

They chatted about nothing in particular. Liz wondered who was going to broach the subject of Scott. In the end she did it herself.

'You were talking today about Scott.'

'Can you understand, Mum, how concerned we are for you?' Brooke asked softly.

'I'm a big girl.'

'But we don't want him taking advantage of you. What are his intentions?'

'That sounds like something my mother would have said to me,' Liz laughed.

'Is Scott going to move in here with you,' Brooke asked.

'He comes up at weekends and sometimes during the week too.'

'But how can you take such a risk. Can you be sure that he'll treat you properly. Will he ever get a divorce, or keep stringing you on for years?'

'I've known Scott since I was seventeen, I trust him with my life.'

'But you have to understand where we're coming from,' Brooke insisted. 'We love you and have to look out for you. This man comes into your life, a person we've never heard of before and the whole family dynamic will change. You're vulnerable.'

'I don't feel vulnerable,' Liz responded vehemently.

'But you are.'

'In what way?'

'A woman on her own. Men are very devious, you don't know his reasons for hooking up with you.'

'I wouldn't call him devious. I'm no amazing catch. If I was your age then I can understand where you might be coming from, but I'm a middle-aged woman. For God's sakes, girls.'

'Look, Mum,' Sophie intervened. 'We just care about you and we want you to take your time, and not jump into this without a thought. You know what my experience has been. There are all sorts out there.'

'But we're not young any more, and Scott and I want to make the most of our lives, I don't want to hang around counting time.'

'Just do it for us, please?' Brooke begged.

'I'm not sure whether I can do that or not, girls, I really don't like being pushed into a corner like this. I've made my own decisions since Ethan died, and it's a bit hard to find myself being questioned in this way.'

'But it's because we care about you, don't you understand that?' Brooke asked. 'Look at me and Rory. I thought I knew him and then suddenly he's gone and I'm left high and dry. Now you're going off with a man and I can't bear it, Mum, it's too much.' She burst into tears.

'Brooke, I understand how hard it is for you but I must make my own decisions about my life.'

'I'm devastated and you're over the moon. I'm completely lost with nowhere to go.'

'Brooke, pull yourself together,' Sophie said.

'You don't know how it is for me.'

'Of course I do, and I'm worried about you,' Liz insisted.

'You haven't a clue. I look around me and I see nothing. Some of my friends have deserted me. I don't receive invitations, I'm *persona non grata*. No one wants to know me. Now my mother turns her back on me too, it's unbearable.'

'I haven't turned my back on you, and never would, Brooke, please don't think that,' Liz reassured.

'It's the way I feel.'

Liz was very upset. She couldn't persuade Brooke to see things from her point of view. The girls left shortly afterwards, and if anything, things were even worse between them. Brooke seemed to hate Scott. Sophie was less vehement and actually said little, but Liz could still sense her disquiet. She had always been there for them since they were children. They took her for granted. And then, without any warning, her attention wasn't on them any longer. It was on a man they didn't know.

She felt sorry for them, and could understand their panic at finding themselves in this position. They wanted her to be always there in the house in Howth, growing older every year, white haired, eyes clouded, skin lined, until finally she would reach a stage when there would be no enjoyment in anything any longer. Only loneliness. Then the family would move her into a nursing home, and finally, helplessly, she would drift out of life. She shivered at the thought of that scenario.

## Chapter Forty-nine

Scott and Ryan sat at a table in the restaurant. Cathal had gone to collect Ciara from her mother's house. They were already late.

'How do you feel, Dad?' Ryan asked.

'Nervous.' Scott was conscious that his breathing was rapid. He could hear it, and clenched his hands in an effort to gain control. A coldness swept through him. Life was catching up. Dragging at him from behind to stop his wild rush in the opposite direction. I don't want to see her, he thought, and would have given anything to be with Liz at this moment.

'I don't know how I'm supposed to feel, I never expected to meet my mother again,' Ryan admitted.

'Do you remember her?'

'I know what she looks like from the photographs, but I can't imagine what sort of person she was.'

'She was a very beautiful woman, and still is, I'm sure,' Scott said.

'Did she really love us?' His voice was very unsure.

'Oh yes, Ciara loved you very much.' Scott didn't feel he could go into detail about why Ciara had left them. He knew now there was another man in the picture, but didn't want to say this to his sons and couldn't bear the thought that they would feel even more rejected.

Each time the door opened Scott looked around expecting to see them, but it was always someone else. Time dragged.

'Here they are,' Ryan said hoarsely.

Scott forced a smile on his face when Cathal, his partner Gillian and Ciara walked through the tables towards them.

'Dad?' Cathal smiled broadly.

He stood up. Ciara looked flamboyant, wearing a slinky red dress, and high stilettos. She was heavier than he remembered. Her blonde hair was shoulder length, and in much the same style as it was when she left. She was heavily made up. Ciara had aged, no more than he had himself, but still looked attractive.

'Scott, how are you?' She came towards him.

'I'm fine,' he put out his hand, but she pressed close to him and kissed him full on the lips. He was shocked, thinking it was like she had returned after only a day or two away. He stepped back from her, immediately drawing his youngest son into the circle. 'This is Ryan.'

'My baby.' She threw her arms around him.

He didn't say anything, caught up in her embrace.

'Let me look at you.' She stared at him. 'You've grown so tall and handsome I can't believe it.'

He looked distinctly uncomfortable.

The waiter pulled out chairs.

Ciara moved between Scott and Ryan, an arm around each of them. 'I have to say it's wonderful to see all of you,' she smiled broadly.

Gillian, Cathal's partner, stood behind, and Scott realised that he hadn't welcomed her. 'Thank you for coming along tonight, Gillian.' He kissed her cheek. She smiled.

'Scott, you're looking well too,' Ciara said in a teasing fashion. 'I thought I'd be meeting an old man but you've held your good looks.' She turned to Cathal and Ryan. 'All my men look great.'

Ciara had caught Scott unawares. Memories of the early years tumbled into his mind. He decided to dive in and ask that question which was never far from his mind. He didn't know how much Cathal had found out when he met his mother in London and he hadn't wanted to ask him. Whatever lay in the past must come directly from her. 'Ciara, what have you been doing in recent years?'

'This and that.' She waved a manicured hand, red nail polish gleamed.

'Mum worked in television,' Cathal said.

'For a time, although I wasn't on camera. I've done a lot of things.'

He noticed she still held a little of her Irish accent, but it was only the slightest trace on an occasional word.

Cathal talked a lot about their lives. Ryan was unusually quiet. Gillian was lost in this torrent of reminiscence. Scott listened sceptically. It was a strange evening and he thought it would never end. But he was anxious to talk to Ciara on her own. To ask her to give him reasons why she had left. He wanted that above all else. But there was no opportunity to ask the big questions. The why and the wherefore. A mother had left her husband and two sons one day without explanation. A brief note left on the dressing table. Propped up against the mirror, staring at him when he walked in, wondering where she was. The two boys were in the playroom unaware that their mother had gone.

He had asked them gently when they had last seen her, but couldn't find out exactly how long they had been alone. He had raged at first. Wanting to chase after her but couldn't leave the boys who were complaining about hunger by then. Her car was still in the driveway. Her keys were on the kitchen table, and there too was her wedding ring.

Now she had returned to claim her sons something tightened inside Scott and a terrible thought occurred to him. Would he lose them altogether?

'It's been a wonderful evening. To meet my two boys again has been fantastic,' Ciara said as they left the restaurant.

In the morning, he rang her. 'I want to talk to you, Ciara,' he said. 'I'll call over.'

'No, I'll get a taxi and go to you. I'm longing to see my old home again.'

'It would be better away from the house.' He didn't want her here.

'It would mean a lot to me to see it again,' she said.

'All right,' he agreed reluctantly.

'It's lovely to be back.' She wandered down the hall and into the sitting room. 'And it hasn't changed that much. I like the colour scheme, it has a nice minimalist feel to it. Pale grey. 'Oh, you still have some of the old photos.' She picked one up. 'I wasn't bad looking in those days,' she said, with a grin. 'Happy families.'

He was annoyed at the inference.

'Sit down, Ciara.'

'Give me a minute, I want the guided tour.' She crossed the room to where he stood and slid her arm through his.

'There's nothing much to see,' he said, moving out into the hall forcing her to let go of him.

'Is the kitchen the same as ever?'

'No, it was done up a few years ago.'

They went in.

'Very swish altogether. It's strange to be here after all these years.' She stared around her.

'There's only one thing I want and that is to know why you walked out on us,' Scott demanded, trying to control his pent up anger.

'You can't understand how I was then.'

'Tell me. Give me an explanation. How could a mother leave her children, two little boys, it's impossible to understand. One thing to leave me, but entirely different to walk away from your own flesh and blood.'

'I don't know why,' she murmured.

'That's ridiculous.' He was scathing. 'Tell me why? Why?' He leaned closer to her.

'Don't hit me, please?' She flinched and moved away

He was suddenly aware that she seemed afraid of him and was shocked at that. 'I'm not going to start hitting you now, I never did before. I just want you to tell me why you wrote that note and left. That's all. Simple.'

She didn't reply.

'I heard from your mother many years later that you went away with another man.'

'That was a mistake.'

'But it's true?'

She nodded.

'Who was he? Someone I knew?'

'No.'

'Where did you meet him?'

'Through one of my friends.'

He was astounded.

'He was over here on holiday from London.'

'Did I ever know him? Was he an acquaintance of someone in the family? What was his name?' He rattled off questions.

'That doesn't matter.'

'But you had an affair?'

She nodded.

'And then you went over to him?'

'Yea.'

'You're despicable.' The thought that he had probably come face to face with the man made him furious. Bastard. He wanted to know everything that went on inside Ciara's head.

He thought of his two sons. They were no longer the Cathal and Ryan he knew or thought he knew up to the day Ciara's letter had arrived. They had a mother now. A biological mother. There was a completeness about their lives. A roundness. Like those photos on the mantle. And they would never want to lose Ciara again no matter what he thought. They were part of her. He could lose his sons. That possibility spread its unwelcome way in his head like a high tide creeping up a river threatening destruction.

'I want you back Scott. I want our lives to be the same again,' she whispered.

'You're crazy,' he said.

She leaned closer. 'But I'm your wife.'

'It's a long time since you were my wife.'

'We could be a married couple again. It was always good between us.'

'Never, Ciara, never,' he said angrily, but regretted his outburst immediately.

## Chapter Fifty

'What do you mean, Sophie, weaning yourself off?' Robyn stared at her in amazement.

'The tablets we take are not good for us. You must realise that. We're drug addicts. If I try and reduce the amount I take I feel really bad.'

'But you won't enjoy yourself, we never have hangovers, we feel perfect the following day. Who wants to go back to that?'

'I'd prefer to have a few beers and take my chances,' Sophie insisted.

'You're mad,' Lucy said.

'I'm going to try and get off the drugs altogether. It affects my work and I can't let that continue.'

'Surely your photos would be much better?' Robyn asked.

'They're terrible.'

'You're not going to be much fun anymore.' Lucy took a box from her bag. 'Can't I tempt you?'

'No, please don't, I've only taken two instead of the usual four and I'm doing well. I just want to try and keep going day by day.'

'How long have you been reducing the amount?'

'I've been trying to get off them for ages.'

'Well, I suppose we should admire your efforts but we think it' crazy, don't we Lucy? We've never felt so good,' she grinned at Sophie

'Come on, girl, let's party, enough of that stuff about cutting back. Lucy grabbed her arm.

They walked along Leeson Street to a nightclub.

'Once you get down here, you'll change your mind. I picked u some interesting stuff, apparently it's powerful,' Robyn whispered.

'You don't know what it's doing to you,' Sophie said, worried. 'Some of the chemicals in these things can have all sorts of weird affects.'

'Look, we're not junkies on the street having to steal for the gear. It's just recreational with us. Instead of drinking too much we take a few tablets. Alcohol has a much more powerful affect and we'd be useless for anything the following day. And you have to admit, sex is something else,' Lucy and Robyn laughed out loud as they walked to the gate.

'Just in time, girls,' the security man said and stood back to let them down the steps into the club.

The place was crowded. The music pounded. Lights flashed. They pushed towards the bar and ordered beer. When finally they were served they found somewhere to put their glasses, coats and bags and immediately began to dance. Sophie didn't recognise the tune, it was just a drum beat and the crowd waved their arms in the air and chanted. She watched the faces around her, particularly Robyn and Lucy, and tried to join in with enthusiasm but couldn't lose that feeling of being somewhere she didn't want to be.

A familiar smiling face came close. It was Josh. He said something but she couldn't hear. He moved close. His hands closed around her. His lips touched hers. Pressed. Sucked. Wetly. An instant aversion to him swept through her. She tried to pull away but was surrounded by bodies and it was difficult. She raised her arms in the air and threw back her head moving from side to side just to get away from his embrace.

She pointed in the direction of where they had left their beers, managing to turn and force her way through the dancing crowd. She passed the girls and reached for her beer, swallowing the liquid which by now had warmed and wasn't quite so refreshing.

'I haven't seen you in ages, how've you been?' Josh asked.

'Fine,' she yelled.

'Beer?' he waved his glass.

She shook her head. 'Water please?'

He looked at her, puzzled.

'Water,' she said again. 'I'm thirsty.'

He disappeared.

The girls came back.

'Was that Josh?' Robyn asked.

She nodded.

A couple of other guys they knew joined them. They offered some E's and both Robyn and Lucy accepted. Sophie refused.

'Sophie, why can't you join in?' Robyn seemed annoyed.

'I don't want to.'

'You're miserable, what's wrong?'

'Nothing. What does it matter to anyone else if I don't take drugs. Why should you care?' She was upset now.

'But we've been friends for years and have always done everything together.'

'I am your friend, but I just don't want to take drugs any more. Can't I do that without losing my friends?' There were sudden tears in Sophie's eyes.

'Of course you can.' Robyn hugged her.

Sophie felt a little better.

'Let's dance,' Lucy shouted.

They pushed on to the floor. Josh had never come back with the water but she didn't care if he came back at all. She threw herself into the dance, and let the music take over.

Normally after a night out at the weekend, Sophie would sleep soundly until almost lunchtime, now she woke up early immediately feeling the need to take a tablet. She checked how many she had left and counted out the days. She would run out of them in another couple of weeks if she only took two a day. And if she could manage on one they would last even longer, but really she knew that she shouldn't take any at all. But it was hard. She stared at them. The urge to take one was almost impossible to resist. She felt cold and hot at the same time, and her hand inched towards them. She tried to stop. But couldn't. Just one. Her mind said. Just one.

Paula called the following week, and said she was delighted with the photos and video of the birth of her baby. Then she asked her if she would do another baby photo session for Kirsty, a friend of hers. Sophie was surprised, but had found the experience of being there at the birth of Paula's baby so beautiful that she immediately said yes. Called Kirsty, and arranged to be there for her too. But was immediately reminded that her drug habit didn't fit with the purity of new birth and it made her even more determined to quit, however she was going to manage it.

That evening, after she had checked her emails, and replied to a few, she filled the bath and lit some candles. The atmosphere in the bathroom glowed soft and shadows drifted. She soaked. Closed her eyes. Feeling relaxed for the first time that day.

She wondered about Liz and Scott. What if he left her after building her up with words of love and marriage? How would she cope? Maybe she might have a nervous breakdown? Sophie was worried about her mother, but was reminded then of the business card that Liz had given her. Would she call Scott as she had suggested? Did she want to get help from him of all people?

## Chapter Fifty-one

Brooke packed up more of the kids' toys when they were in bed. As she didn't want to clutter up Peggy's house, she had already given some of them to the charity shop. The kids grew tired of everything and once they had their favourites probably wouldn't even notice the disappearance of some of them. The house was becoming empty. And a cold hollow feeling permeated the rooms. She had booked a small storage unit and rented a van. On Sunday, Luke and Sophie had helped with the removal of the furniture to the unit.

The doorbell rang.

Brooke's heart jumped. It could be Rory. She hurried down the hall and opened it.

'How are you, love?' Liz came in, her arms outstretched.

Brooke allowed herself to be embraced for a few seconds, but then stepped back. Antipathy towards her mother rose inside and she found it hard to hide it.

'Oh my God, your house is so empty.' Liz wandered down the hall and stood staring into the living room.

'Nothing much left. I've stored most of the furniture.'

'When did you do that?' Liz asked.

'Last weekend.'

'Why didn't you tell me, Scott and I would have come around and given a hand.'

Brooke shrugged.

'How are Jess and Cian, are they well?' Liz asked.

'They're fine. They don't understand what's happening. Would you

220

like a coffee or something?'

'No thanks, I just called around to have a quick chat. I'm sorry to miss the children but I was held up at the studio.'

'Was it busy this afternoon?'

'Yea, quite a few sessions. We miss you when you go home. We could do with you all day,' Liz smiled. 'When it's busy it's great to have someone there.'

Brooke nodded. She felt awkward.

'We need to talk,' Liz said gently. 'I want to know exactly how you feel about Scott. Can you tell me?'

'It's difficult,' Brooke muttered.

'We have to clear this up, I don't want a person whom I love so much to hate me.'

'I don't hate you,' Brooke gasped. 'Hate?'

'It almost feels like that.'

'You're my mother. I love you more than anything, but now you have rejected me for this man, the same way Rory dumped me for another woman, and I can't bear that.' There were tears in her eyes. 'It's too much.' She bent her head into her hands.

'Brooke, I love you too and I'll always be there for you,' Liz assured.

'You can't be. That's impossible. All your attention will be on Scott, he'll take up your time.'

'I'll still be working. We'll see each other every day.'

'But you'll probably be in Cork with him, and you'll forget about us.'

'I don't know where I'm going to be, we've made no decisions, and don't forget both of us have businesses so we'll probably commute. When we're in Dublin we'll come over, Scott loves kids.'

'I don't want him around. He's a stranger, no way,' Brooke snapped.

Liz stared, her eyes wide. 'I'm surprised at you.'

There were a lot of things on Brooke's mind and now that she had Liz to herself she wanted to explain exactly how she felt. 'You don't know him. You haven't seen him in thirty years. What does that say?'

'I don't understand you.'

'Where has he been all that time.'

'Living life like the rest of us. He has two sons. He worked hard.'

'Supposedly.' Brooke let her venom boil over. 'And where is his wife? Still at home maybe? And how many other women have there been?'

'I can't imagine how you could possibly accuse Scott of that.' Liz was angry now. 'You have no proof.'

'You never know. Have you checked him out?'

'Brooke?'

'You should get a private detective, he could have a record.'

'I don't get this, Brooke, where is all this coming from?' Liz's hands twisted nervously, and there were tears in her eyes.

'You have responsibilities to your family.'

'What are you talking about?'

'You know what I mean,' Brooke said. 'He'll come into this family and what will happen to our inheritance? Our home?'

'I can't believe you're worried about the house? You think that Scott will inherit if I die, God forbid. I know I'll pass on at some stage but I hope I'll have a good innings. There will be a lot of changes by then and you'll all have moved on. Who gets the house will be irrelevant.'

'It happens in families, you know that.'

'And this is why you don't want me to marry Scott?'

Brooke suddenly realised that she had taken a step too far. She hadn't meant this to explode into something quite so big. She thought just a suggestion of disapproval would force Liz to withdraw from this relationship and things would settle back to normal.

'I'm blown away, Brooke, I never thought you could be so selfish.' Liz picked up her bag and left.


Brooke went into the studio as usual the following morning. Liz was out and Sophie busy with clients. She opened up the computer, working on the accounts for the month. She hadn't slept well and during the night, had wandered in and out of the twins' rooms watching them sleep. She had to protect their future. As it was she was homeless. Although she would have money from the sale of the house, that wouldn't be enough to replace her home. Her twins were her life. Two little children, twin eggs. Always so close together. Jess imitating Cian, reluctant to leave him out of her sight. Brooke felt rejected. By Rory. By her mother. And there was no support from Luke or Sophie either.

'You're looking a bit rough today,' her sister came in.

'I didn't sleep much.'

'Kids kept you up?'

'Yea, they sense stuff is going on. All the packing. The empty house. Rory taking the stuff he wants. And some of their toys are missing so they keep looking for things I've already given away.'

'They have so much they'll soon forget,' Sophie murmured, concentrating on the screen of her laptop where she scrolled through photos she had taken at the last session.

'I thought that too, but they're surprising me.'

'Cute as foxes.'

The door opened and Liz arrived.

'Hi,' she said briefly, and went straight into the back room.

'Mum?' Sophie stared after her, then stood up and followed.

'Hey, are you all right,' she asked. 'You're looking as bad as Brooke, what's going on around here?'

'I'm tired.'

Sophie walked back out to Reception. 'Mum doesn't seem well either, have you both picked up some sort of bug?'

'I told you, the kids kept me awake.'

'I hope I don't catch whatever it is.'

'It isn't anything, let me concentrate on this, I have to get finished before I go,' Brooke snapped.

Sophie went in to Liz again. 'Mum you're really looking under the weather, maybe you should go home and rest.'

'I'm fine, I've a lot to do.'

The day continued. The tension palpable. Brooke was still upset. Her mother had walked out on her. How had she forced such a situation?

This morning, she could see that Liz was very annoyed with her. Her head bent low. No glance in her direction. Her whole demeanour downcast.

Brooke pressed her fingers into her temples as if to ease the noise which whined through her head. But it was to no avail. All she could think of was that her mother had changed. All her attention was on this man who caught her hand and drew her away.

## Chapter Fifty-two

Sophie was worried about Liz whose features were so pinched it seemed a heavy weight had descended upon her. She wondered had something happened between her and Scott? Had his professions of love suddenly fallen on hard ground. Was he like one of those men she had met herself. Men who wanted all they could get from a woman and then dumped her, making their merry way from one flower to another like a bee sucking nectar.

'Are you upset about what we said to you, Mum?' she ventured later, when things had quietened down somewhat.

'Yes, of course, what do you think?' Liz continued to stare at the screen.

'Does Scott know?'

'He doesn't know how strongly you both feel,' she said. 'It's very upsetting to know that you and Brooke dislike him so much.'

'I'm sorry, we're just worried about you. You know we love you.'

'I do,' Liz sighed. 'How are you today?'

'I'm all right, thanks.'

'Did you call Scott about his friend?'

'Not yet.'

At home, Sophie sorted through her desk which was in a mess. Suddenly, she came across Scott's card and stared at it for a moment. Then she put it aside and continued what she was doing. Finished, she wondered why she couldn't escape from this monster which lurked inside her. As the evening wore on, she found her eyes straying to the

225

card more than once. Eventually, she picked it up again. Took a deep breath and pressed in the digits. It rang out. Once. Twice.

He answered. She recognised his voice.

'Scott?'

'Yes?'

'It's Sophie.'

He seemed pleased to hear from her.

She hesitated, unsure what to say next. After a few seconds, she took the plunge. 'Mum gave me your card and she mentioned you know someone who might be able to help me.'

'Yes, I do, he's a good friend of mine.'

'Could you give me his name and number?' she asked, a nervous shiver sweeping through her.

'Certainly. His name is Gary Weldon.'

She jotted that down, and then he called out the telephone number, and the details of the clinic.

'This is his private mobile?'

'Yes, but that's no problem. Would you like me to mention that you might call?'

'I'd appreciate that.'

'I'll phone him straight away.'

'Thanks for offering.'

'When you go to meet him, I could come along and introduce you?'

'That would be too much.' She was surprised.

'Not at all. Just let me know when you have arranged the appointment.'

'Thanks, Scott. Oh, I haven't mentioned it to Mum yet.'

'I won't say anything.'


Now she had to make another call, and that proved to be even harder. The circle of people who knew about her problem was widening and she was afraid of that.

Her home cast its arms around her. She felt comforted. Everything here she had chosen herself. It was hers, and hers alone. The two bedroomed apartment was spacious and decorated in natural colours. She loved it.

But financially, it was very difficult. The mortgage had to be paid. Utilities. Food. Her social life must be financed. And worst of all, her drug habit. Her credit card debit balance grew larger by the day, and now the Taylor money wasn't there any longer it would be even more difficult to manage.

She wandered around from room to room. Touched the soft purple velvet throw on the bed. Trailed her fingers along the smooth surface of the wardrobes. In the gleaming white bathroom, she stared at herself in the full length mirror. Surprised that she hadn't changed in any way. Her long dark hair shone. Her eyes were bright. The physical torment wasn't apparent now. But once she came off the drugs totally, it would certainly show. How long until she was clean, she wondered. Weeks? Months? And was she dirty now. Filthy. Gross. Was that how people would describe her? Did she want that for her whole life?

She went back into the living room and picked up the piece of paper on which she had written Gary's number.

## *Chapter Fifty-three*

Liz felt physically ill since talking with Brooke. While they had met today at work they hadn't really communicated. Eyes slid past each other and they hadn't spoken unless it was absolutely necessary. Her stomach was tense. A band of pain across her forehead. But Scott was coming up tonight and she was looking forward to seeing him. To her relief they hadn't planned to go out, so at least she wouldn't have to put on a face like she had all day which was such an effort.

Scott kissed her and she leaned into him. It was so good to feel his arms curl around her, and the tension which had built up drifted away. But with that, she immediately began to cry and held on to him.

'Hey?' he asked softly, and pulled slightly away from her, looking into her face quizzically. 'What's wrong, my love. You're looking very pale, are you ill?'

She shook her head.

'Why these tears?' His finger traced the moisture which had drifted down her face. 'Is it about Ciara?'

'Well, partly.'

He held her close to him again for a moment saying nothing more. There was a dread in her heart that she was going to lose him. How quickly things had changed.

She lay in his arms. He stroked her hair. She closed her eyes.

'I'm sorry,' she murmured. 'I suppose I'm jealous.'

'There's no reason to be jealous,' he said quietly. 'She is no threat to us. The fact that she's turned up now might be good from a divorce point of view.'

'You shouldn't have to drive up all this way and find me in such a state.'

'I want you in whatever state you are. I love you, Liz. Every part of you. Do you believe that?' He put his finger under her chin and tipped her face up to him.

'Of course I do,' she managed a smile.

'That's better.' He kissed her.

She responded. Needing him so badly. She curled into his embrace, and held tight. They made love. He was even more sensitive towards her tonight. They moved closer. Skin against skin. His hands held her like a delicate butterfly, and her need for him reached heights she hadn't known before, like a crescendo in a piece of music which swept them along until they gave of each other, letting go slowly in a wild teasing rhythm.

'I love you so much, Scott, I don't know what I'd do without you.'

'You won't have to.' He pulled the throw on the couch around them.

Liz reached closer. Wanting to hold even more of him. But the fear of loss returned with a vengeance and cut through her.

'I can feel you tremble,' he said. 'Your heart is beating. Are you still worried about Ciara?' he coaxed.

'And other things.'

'What other things?'

She looked into his eyes. So much warmth there. She felt swallowed up by his gaze.

'Sorry, maybe I shouldn't push you,' he said.

'No, I must tell you,' she replied, holding his hand. 'Brooke doesn't want me to have a relationship with you and Sophie is worried too.'

'And Luke?'

'He doesn't seem to be so concerned.'

'What is their reason?'

'They don't want a stranger coming into the family, and you might run off on me because I'm so vulnerable.' She was furious even thinking about it. 'Then I had an awful row with Brooke, she was even talking about the house and their inheritance.'

'I had expected it might happen, money is always a very contentious issue.'

'Anyway, the bottom line is that she doesn't want us to get married or even live together.'

'Maybe she'll come around?'

'I don't know, she was adamant.'

'I'm sorry, my love.'

'I simply don't know how to deal with her,' She leaned against him.

'Do you want me to talk to her?'

'No, I don't think that would do any good. I'm going to have to get through to her somehow. We can't continue like this. We're barely speaking. I feel she hates me.'

'I'm sure she doesn't, you've always had a good relationship with your kids.'

'I have and I love them so much, but she has this feeling of rejection which is all wound up with Rory.'

'It's a bad time for her.'

'I wish I could help, but I don't want to interfere.' She had an image in her mind of putting a hand out to Brooke. Clasping her soft palm, their fingers interlaced. This connection took her back down a road into the past. It was like she was in a dream. Her children were young. Full of joy. Dancing their way to the beach during long summer days. Dragging her with them. Buckets. Spades. Togs. Towels. But all she could see was their exited running figures as they charged into the blue sea, screaming, waving arms, clothes already wet before they even had a chance to change into their togs.

Now she had happiness within her grasp, and her children didn't really understand. They wanted to keep her. *You're ours.* They shouted. *We won't let you go.*

'Liz?' Scott squeezed her hand and brought her back.

'Sorry, I drifted off.'

'What were you thinking?' he asked.

'Remembering what it was like when the kids were young.'

'It's hard to go against them,' he said slowly. 'I feel the same way, particularly about Cathal.'

'Do they understand that you want to have another life?'

'I haven't told them about you yet, but I intend to do that the next opportunity I get. They're caught up with Ciara at the moment, although that's mostly Cathal.'

She was disappointed, and somehow had assumed that he had told his family also. 'Do we put our own feelings before our love for our children?' she asked him.

'That's a huge question.'

'It could be considered very selfish by our families, and people we know. I haven't even mentioned you to my sister who is my closest relative. I don't know what she's going to say.'

'We're like sixteen year olds,' he said with a wry smile.

'It would be easier if we only had to deal with our parents.'

'I don't know, remember my mother and father were pretty much against anything I wanted to do, I was just lucky to get away from home to go to college.'

'Mine weren't too bad.'

'Your parents were really nice. I was very fond of them. I had so many lovely dinners in your house. Your mother was a great cook.'

'It was a pity you lived in Cork, I didn't see very much of your parents.'

'Pity about a lot of things …' he murmured.

## Chapter Fifty-four

Sophie and Scott met in the foyer of the clinic.

'I'm nervous,' she admitted. 'What sort of person is Gary?'

'Friendly, easy going. I got to know him years ago when I was involved in youth sports. He's very good at what he does.'

'I don't know what I'm going to say to him.'

'You don't have to worry, here he is.' Scott stood up.

Sophie looked around to see a stocky, well-built man approach.

'How's it going, Scott? I presume this must be Sophie?' He pushed out his hand towards her.

'Sophie, this is Gary.'

He had a firm handshake and she felt reassured.

They chatted, Gary quizzing Sophie about her interest in photography. But she had little to contribute and felt so tense she could hardly utter a word.

'Right?' Gary smiled at her. 'Let's go.'

She grabbed her bag.

'Are you coming with us?' he asked Scott.

'I just came along to introduce you two.'

'You might need company,' Gary said to Sophie. 'We recommend that you bring someone.'

Sophie was confused.

'Perhaps you would prefer to ask your Mum?' Scott suggested.

'No, I'd prefer if you would …?' Sophie felt that if she was going to do this at all then this was the day. If she changed her mind now, she might never do it.

'I'd be delighted.'

The clinic was in a beautiful old Georgian house set in magnificent gardens. The first thought in Sophie's head was that it would probably cost an arm and a leg, and prayed that her VHI insurance would cover it. They took the lift upstairs.

Gary led the way into his office, and they sat down.

'First things first, Sophie. I'll need a few details so would you please complete these forms here. Then there will be a meeting with our assessment team who will consider your case and decide what treatment would be best for you.'

'How long will it take?' she asked.

'A couple of hours.'

'I hate filling in forms,' she said to Scott with a rueful smile.

'So do I.'

'I'm sorry about delaying you. Had you something else to do?' she asked him.

'I had an appointment earlier, and I'll be heading back to Cork when we're finished here.'

'You don't have to stay.'

'I want to. As Gary said, you may need company. But I'll just sit in the background. Just tell me if you want me to get involved in any way.'

'All I'm worried about is the cost. Have you any idea?'

'I'm sure your health insurance will cover it.'

'I hope so.' She gritted her teeth and continued to complete those inane questions in the form. Suddenly, she would have given anything to tear it up and leave. Just leave. 'They want to know so many things, pain in the ass,' she groaned.

'Can I help?' he sat beside her.

'I don't want to tell anyone what I had for my breakfast.' She put her hand over the form.

'Sorry,' he moved away again. 'I didn't see anything.'

'I don't know why I did that, all I wrote down was coffee.'

'That's all?'

'Yea, I'm not a breakfast person.'

'I'm not much better. Unless your mother is cooking.'

'Yea, she does a mean breakfast.'

'I agree.'

'You do love her?' Sophie asked suddenly.

He smiled. 'Yea. Always did.'

'You won't mess her up?' she asked suspiciously.

'No, Sophie, I've no intention of doing anything like that. All I want is for us to be together for the rest of our lives. If we can get married that will make it pretty special, but even if we just live together I'll be happy.'

She said nothing and bent her head to finish off the last page of the form.


Gary returned, and took them both into a conference room where a group of people were gathered around a large table. This was the most difficult part of it for Sophie. Now she had to bare herself in front of a bunch of strangers. Her stomach was sick.

He introduced Sophie and Scott to the group. They were pleasant and she felt a little better. Then the questions began. This was even worse than the information needed on the form. They wanted to know everything. Her lifestyle. Her friends. The drugs she used. How often. What it was like when she tried to cut down. She found it hard to describe the panic attacks. Those nights when she simply didn't remember anything. The sickness. The fainting. And most of all the feeling of not being in control.

'We'll have to discuss your case, Sophie, and decide the best form of treatment. You will be assigned a specialist addiction team and they will work with you in a holistic way with the mind, body and spirit, whether outpatient or residential,' Gary said. 'And there will be one to one counselling and group sessions.'

'I don't think I want residential, how long would that take?' Sophie

234

asked, suddenly worried.

'We run a five week programme.'

'I'd be stuck here for that length of time?' She stared around her.

He nodded.

'I know it's beautiful but I don't want to stay.' Her voice trembled and sudden tears filled her eyes. She looked at Scott.

'Are you all right, Sophie?' he asked.

She nodded.

'I think we have enough information for now, so we will meet again when a decision has been reached,' Gary smiled and ushered them out of the room.

'Do you feel like going somewhere for lunch?' Scott asked.

'No thanks. I couldn't eat. That was tough, I feel I've been through the wringer. Do you think I'll be able for it?' Sophie asked him.

'You will of course. But I know it's hard.'

'Thanks for introducing me to Gary, and for being there, I really appreciate it.'

'Any time, Sophie. Are you going back to work now?'

'Maybe later.'

'Relax for the afternoon,' he advised.

'Perhaps I will.'

'Let me know what happens,' he said.

Sophie went home, unable to face anyone. She didn't know what to do. Had she even got a choice, she wondered. This seemed to be the only option open to her. She just wasn't able to reduce the amount of drugs she took on a daily basis. The drugs had too much of a hold on her and she couldn't escape from the terrible cycle which dominated her life.

# Chapter Fifty-five

Cathal came into Scott's office. 'Mum is arriving in a couple of days, she's settled up her affairs in London,' he said.

Scott stared at him, a sense of shock coursing through him. He couldn't say anything, other than to think it was very soon.

'So, what do you think?' Cathal asked.

'I'm glad for you and Ryan.'

'Mum's hoping to stay at home, there's not a lot of room in Gran's. And you know the way Gran is at the moment with the dementia, Mum mightn't be able to deal with it,' Cathal said.

'She can't stay with me,' Scott immediately objected.

'Why not?'

'I won't have Ciara staying, that's all there is to it. Why don't you invite your mother to stay with you, or Ryan?'

'That wouldn't suit us, Gillian works shift, we couldn't have someone else there.'

'What about Ryan?'

'It's a bit awkward as well.'

'Then you had better suggest she stays with her mother. Maura needs help looking after your Gran anyway.'

'I can't tell her what to do,' Cathal said.

'Give me her phone number and I'll talk to her,' Scott offered.

Cathal stared at his phone. 'I'll text it to you.'

Scott called Ciara. He didn't know what he was going to say, but whatever, it had to be said.

She answered the phone.

'Ciara, it's Scott.'

'How are you?' She seemed pleased.

'I've been talking to Cathal, he tells me that you're coming over in a few days.'

'Yes, I'm so excited.'

'Where are you going to stay.'

'I'm looking forward to coming home.'

'You can't stay here,' he said, bluntly. 'You must find somewhere else.'

'But I really want to stay at home, it will be like old times.'

'No Ciara.'

She did stay with her mother, and he made no contact for the first few days. Then unexpectedly, she arrived over to see him one night. He was glad to see her in one way, anxious to talk to her about a divorce.

'You didn't come over to see me, I was disappointed,' she complained.

'I was busy,' he said.

'You haven't changed.'

'I'm probably always busy, although now Cathal and Ryan run the business and it's not as bad as it used to be.'

'Why do you think I left you?'

'I don't know.'

'You didn't take any notice of me.'

'I'm sorry about that. How is your mother?' He changed the subject, and brought her into the living room. She sat down.

'She knew me the first day, and after that it varied, today she didn't know me at all.'

'I'm sure Maura was glad to see you.'

'She's hoping I'll start looking after Mam.'

'She has had to carry the burden since your mother became ill.'

'I'm not a nurse, and I've no intention of going into that field at this stage of my life.'

'What are your plans?' he asked.

'I want to live here with you, Scott,' she said.

'You can't live here, Ciara. It would be better if you rented somewhere.'

'I've heard rents are very high.'

'That's right.'

'I don't see why I should rent at an exorbitant rate when there's a house here with only one person living in it, particularly as I own half of it.'

Scott stared at Ciara. Suddenly it became obvious to him why she was here. He knew she was entitled to something, but didn't want to discuss it now. He would have to meet his solicitor and find out the situation in these particular circumstances.

'Why did you come back, Ciara?' he asked her.

'I wanted to be with my family again. I still love you, don't you realise that?'

'I don't believe you.'

'You've no idea how many years I've spent longing for you.' She reached across the table and covered his hand with hers.

'What about the man in your life? The man you went to London with?'

'I never loved him in the same way as I did you.'

He only vaguely remembered those early days after she had left. His own personal loss overshadowed by the terrible loss of a mother experienced by his boys.

'How long were you with him?'

'A couple of years.'

'And after that?'

'There were others, but I've never been happy since I left you,' Ciara said, in a soft babyish whisper. She came around to his side of the table and put her arms around him.

He stood up and moved away from her clinging embrace. 'Ciara, there is no future between us. What was in the past will be left there.'

'I don't know how you can say that.' Tears glimmered in her eyes.

'I'll help you. Give you some money.' He made the suggestion in a vague hope that it might be enough.

'If I'm living here you can support me as your wife,' she retorted.

'We can't live together.' He was adamant.

'How can you say that to me?'

The door opened. Cathal came in. 'Mum, I went over to Gran's and Maura told me you'd come over here.'

'How are you, love?' Ciara kissed him.

'Fine, Mum.' He hugged her. Only then glancing in Scott's direction and nodding.

'I'm so glad you've arrived now, your Dad and I have been talking but he's not being very nice to me.' There were tears in her eyes again.

Cathal raised his eyebrows quizzically.

'I don't think we need to talk about it now,' Scott murmured. He didn't want to involve his son.

'But I want Cathal here,' she put her arm around him.

'Well, if you wish,' he agreed.

'So, where were we?' Ciara asked.

There was a pause. Scott felt uncomfortable and said nothing.

'Basically, he doesn't want me to live here,' she said.

'But Mum loves you,' Cathal said.

'I may as well tell you that I want a divorce,' Scott said.

'I can't believe you would treat Mum like that. She's come back after all this time and you immediately ask her to give you a divorce?' his son gasped.

'We've been apart for over twenty years, there's no way we could live together again.'

'But you could at least try.'

'There, that's exactly what I want but he won't give us a chance,' Ciara said.

'I think that's so unfair,' Cathal said.

'We don't love each other anymore,' Scott stated.

'I still love you.' Ciara moved towards him, her hand outstretched.

'But I don't love you.' He had to be blunt.

239

'I can't believe this,' Cathal exploded.

'I'll tell you what I want. Firstly, a divorce. And secondly, I'll give you a financial settlement which will be worked out by our legal people,' Scott said.

'It's so bloody cold.' His son scowled.

Scott could feel the hostility which emanated from Cathal.

'I don't want to divorce,' Ciara cried.

'You have to give something as well as me,' he sighed. Having his son here complicated the situation.

'What do you think, Cathal?' Ciara stared at her son.

'I want you to be happy, Mum.'

Scott was at a loss. It was a crazy situation. A nightmare. And he was caught in this quagmire, unable to free himself from its sticky grasp.

## Chapter Fifty-six

Sophie received the call from Kirsty's husband, Paul, late in the evening and he asked her to come over some time in the next couple of hours to photograph the birth of their baby.

For a moment she did nothing. Just stared into space as her teeth gripped her lower lip, cutting through the soft skin until she felt blood in her mouth. She hadn't taken anything today, but would have to take something now to help her get through this. And it could be a long night. She took an Ecstasy immediately, and set about organising her cameras and other equipment she would need.

She drove to the house, all the time praying for a miracle. She was tempted to take another tablet but resisted. To be high would possibly be worse than the way she was at the moment. At least she knew what she was doing and the one tablet had satisfied the craving temporarily. She gripped the steering wheel, determined to get control over this. Whatever she had to do, this was a watershed. Photography was everything to her and presently it was going down the tubes. How many times had she said that before, she asked herself, speaking out loud. Too many. The answer came quickly.

She pulled up outside, took her cameras and rang the front door bell. Footsteps echoed on a hardwood floor and the door burst open to reveal three children of varying ages.

'I'm here to take photos,' Sophie said.

Their father, Paul, appeared. 'Thanks for coming Sophie, although nothing's happening just yet.'

He helped her carry in the equipment.

'Mum's swimming in the pool.' The youngest girl danced along beside her.

Sophie smiled down at her.

'Will you take our photo?' she asked.

'Sure I will.'

'We're in the living room.' Paul led the way through.

Kirsty was sitting in a blue plastic pool and smiled as soon as she saw her.

Sophie was amazed to see how calm everyone was.

Paul explained how the birthing pool actually worked. It was positioned in the middle of the floor on a large plastic sheet, and there were various hoses and other bits and pieces attached. 'We must have hot and cold water, and be careful about the temperature obviously.'

There was a little cry from Kirsty as she experienced a contraction. Paul immediately rushed over. But after a moment, it passed. 'It's amazing, the pain isn't so bad in a pool. And the warm water is relaxing,' she smiled.

There was another contraction, and Sophie could see her tense up until it passed.

Paul looked at his watch. 'The midwife should be here any moment.'

The woman did arrive quite soon after that and took charge. She attended to Kirsty, and Sophie chose her underwater camera. Thinking that this was going to happen as quickly as it had the last time.

But it didn't. The contractions slowed down. And Sophie was relieved. She changed the camera, took a few photos and glanced at the screen. They looked all right. She flexed her hand and held it tight. There was no tremor.

Paul brought the children in for a photograph. They gathered around the pool close to their mother. Sophie snapped. Getting into the swing of things.

'What do we look like?' The elder boy peered at the screen. 'That's me and Mum.' He pointed.

Time dragged and Sophie began to feel nervous again. But then suddenly it happened. Kirsty cried out a little. The midwife encouraged her to breathe. Paul held her from behind. Sophie moved around to get various shots, so engrossed in what she was doing she had forgotten how bad she felt earlier.

'Nearly here now. Push Kirsty. Push,' the midwife encouraged.

Kirsty groaned.

Sophie stared through the lens amazed when she saw the head of the baby begin to inch out between Kirsty's legs. Then she knelt on the floor and dipped the camera in the water hoping to get as close as possible.

'Nearly here.'

She held her breath as the baby fully appeared into the water. She took still shots and video in the few seconds before the baby was swept up by the midwife and placed on Kirsty.

'It's a girl,' she said, smiling.

Paul kissed Kirsty. 'You were wonderful, my love. She's beautiful.'

'Look, look, the baby's here,' the children cried out, excited.

The little girl stood close to her mother and put her hand on the baby's head.

'Let's wrap her up.' The midwife put a white towel around the baby.

Tears moistened Sophie's eyes. She blinked, and continued to shoot, hoping the photo and video would show the mystical beauty of the arrival of new life into the world.

## Chapter Fifty-seven

Scott tried to choose the right time to tell Cathal and Ryan about Liz but found it difficult until one evening Ryan was playing a football match and he went along to support the team. Afterwards, they went for a drink and he took the opportunity.

'Have you talked to your mother?'

'I called in at lunch time yesterday for a sandwich,' Cathal told him.

'I have the gym, training and matches, it's difficult,' Ryan said.

'You haven't been around to see her at all, Ryan,' Cathal accused.

'I don't feel the same as you, Cathal.'

'You're right about that.'

'I don't remember her.'

'She's still your mother.'

'She's too forceful, hard to take. I can't switch on feelings just to suit her. She did abandon us, and it was a terrible thing to do.'

Scott listened, surprised. It was the first time Ryan had expressed how he felt about Ciara.

'She had her reasons,' insisted Cathal.

'What could possibly make her walk away from two small children who were utterly dependant on her?'

'She was unhappy.'

'And she left us unhappy,' Ryan said. 'I had nightmares for years. Weird inexplicable dreams about being lost, and searching for something which I couldn't find.'

'You should have said,' Scott was perturbed.

'What could anyone do about it?' Ryan snapped.

'I'm sorry about that.'

'We all have stuff like that, I have the odd nightmare too.' Cathal shrugged.

'Since Ciara came back, so have the nightmares,' Ryan said.

'That's just a coincidence,' Cathal shrugged it off.

'Lads, we all have different responses to Ciara's return after so many years. It's been a shock.'

'I don't understand you Dad or Ryan either. You should both be over the moon to have Mum back in the family.'

'I'm glad that she's home, but for me it's too late,' Scott said.

'I feel the same way.' Ryan nodded.

'Mum will be very disappointed to hear that from you Dad, she still likes you.' Cathal swallowed his pint.

'There is something I should tell you anyway, I don't want to hide anything,' he paused. 'I've met someone,' he said awkwardly.

'You've met someone?' Ryan stared at him.

'A woman?' Cathal exploded.

'Yes, a woman,' he nodded, unable to hide the wide grin on his face. 'It's hardly a man.'

'You never told us.'

'It only happened recently.'

'So that's why you didn't want our mother to come back?' Cathal accused.

'I never wanted to get back with Ciara. If she had returned a year after leaving, I couldn't have forgiven her for leaving you. To say she didn't want to live with me any longer was one thing, to abandon you was something else entirely. Even to go out of the house for hours and leave you alone was unforgiveable.'

'Who is this woman?' Cathal demanded.

'Her name is Liz, and we knew each other at college. We met again just a short while ago.' He felt like he was the son and was explaining to his father.

'I suppose there have been other women over the years and we never knew a thing about it,' he was angry.

'I've met women, I'll admit that, but there have been no relationships as such, I wasn't interested, you were everything to me. There was no time anyway, I had to keep the business going so that I could give you both a good lifestyle.'

'What is she like?' Ryan asked.

'She's a lovely woman, a photographer, you'd like her.'

'So that's why you've been away for a few weekends lately?' Cathal asked suspiciously.

'Liz lives in Dublin and yes I did go up.' He was reluctant to say any more. Why should he give his sons chapter and verse about where he had spent the weekends?

'Did you tell Mum?' Cathal asked.

'No, I haven't.'

'Don't you think you should?'

Scott was in a quandary and just didn't know what to do. He hated himself for being unable to handle Ciara. But then he was caught between his sons and didn't want them hurt in the ensuing battle. He thought about the amount of money he had available, and wondered how much Ciara actually wanted. But more importantly, he wanted a divorce. If he gave her the money first she might just disappear again and he would be back where he was before she returned. Now he had a reason for the divorce. A very good reason. Up to this it hadn't bothered him too much. But since he had met Liz again everything had changed.

He talked to Ciara, determined to keep his cool this time.

'What do you really want?' he asked gently.

Her eyes met his, but he could see nothing in their depths that gave any indication of how she might respond.

'What do you mean?' she snapped. 'You know I want you.'

'But I'm not available. I may as well tell you there is a woman in my life now.'

'Who is she?' she snapped.

'A woman I knew many years ago, we just met up a few months

ago.'

'But I'm your wife. She can't push her way into our lives and take you away.'

'Ciara, don't be ridiculous.'

'Are you going to marry her?'

'We hope to, eventually.'

'Over my dead body,' she said, vehemently. 'Are you bringing her in here?'

'No.'

'Don't even think about it. This is my house, well, half my house.' She wagged her finger at him. 'And something else, where is my wedding ring?'

He stared at her, shocked.

'Have you got it?'

He couldn't speak for a few seconds.

'Don't tell me that you can't remember where you put it? Or that you threw it away?'

He felt a sense of panic. He knew where it was but wondered what she would do if he did give it back to her.

'I'm waiting, Scott.' She folded her arms.

'I'll get it.' He went upstairs. Opened the dressing table drawer, stretched his hand into the back of it, and took out a box. For a few seconds he stood there, but then he went back down.

'You found it?'

'It's in this box.' He handed it to her.

She opened it, and took out a smaller black ring box. 'My ring, how beautiful.' She picked it up. 'Put it on my finger?' She held it out to him. He noticed that she wore no rings but that there was a slight indentation on the third finger of her left hand.

'No Ciara.'

He went up to Dublin the following night, and took Liz in his arms the moment she opened the door. 'It's so good to see you.' He kissed her, feeling such a sense of relief.

'Come on in, my love.'

'How are things?' he asked, kissing her again.

'Not great, Brooke and I are still at loggerheads.'

'And I'm being driven around the twist by Ciara.'

She stared at him. 'What's happened?'

'She's still on about getting back together again. Pick up our marriage where we left off as if nothing had happened. Can you imagine? And she insisted I find her wedding ring which she left behind when she decided to run off with that guy. She's wearing it now.'

'And how do you feel about that?'

'I don't care whether she wears it or not, I haven't the slightest interest in living with her again. You're the only one I love, Liz.'

'How will you persuade her that you don't want to be with her?'

'I've told her it's never going to happen.'

'What about your sons?'

'Cathal is very annoyed with me. He wants us to get back together too.'

'Did you mention me?' Liz asked.

'Yes, but it didn't go down well either particularly with him. Ryan doesn't feel the same way about Ciara, or you either.'

'It's such a mess. Brooke and me, you and Ciara and your sons, I'm so tired of it all.' She lay her head back on the couch and closed her eyes.

'I'll sort it out, don't worry,' Scott was suddenly concerned. 'I will, I promise.'

'But how can you persuade her to give you a divorce?'

'I've every intention.'

'What if she just walked into the house and refused to leave?'

'She won't go that far,' he said. 'She wants money and I want a divorce so we'll have to do a deal in the end, she knows that well and is just playing games.'

'It's too much, Scott, I can't take any more of it.'

'What do you mean?'

'Let's take a break, I need to clear my head. And you'll have mor time to sort out things with Ciara. Everything has changed. I can't be involved with you if she's in the background, it's impossible,' Liz said.

'We can't let her upset what we have, Liz. Please don't let her away with it.' He took her hand.

'I must relax for a while, I can't live in this way. Brooke and I have such a bad relationship now. The silences. The avoidance. I don't see Jess and Cian much either. She's even missed coming to lunch on Sundays. It's awful. I can't do it any longer. I just can't.' Tears filled her eyes.

He put his arm around her and held her close.

'I still love you, Scott, but let's see how things pan out down the line.'

He drove home later. It was the first time he hadn't stayed with Liz in recent times and it cut right through him. If he was to lose her, then he would lose everything he valued. His whole life.

## Chapter Fifty-eight

'What's going on with you, Liz?' Leah asked.

'What do you mean?' She was immediately on the defensive.

'There's something, you don't seem yourself, the sparkle is gone. Wouldn't you say, girls?' Megan said.

She felt embarrassed.

'Someone has a secret.'

Eyebrows were raised. Smiles were knowing. Teasing.

She thought of Scott. For months he had been the only thing on her mind. Now she was going to go back to her life before she met him again. When she had been very busy. Working hard. And happy too. But given no other choice, was it mere contentment with her lot, she wondered. Now, having found love again with Scott, could she endure that life again?

The girls laughed.

'Something's going on, and it's there, right there on your guilty face.'

They topped up their glasses of wine. The mood grew more raucous. There was more teasing. And all directed at Liz.

'We'll wheedle it out of her.'

'Ok, I'll tell you.'

They were quiet.

'I'm not seeing Scott for a while. There are problems with his wife.

'What sort of problems?' Celine asked.

'She has come back.'

'But it's been over twenty years since she left,' Megan gasped.

'Scott is very worried about it. She wants to get back with him.'

'After all this time?'

'But she also wants her half of the house.'

'Is she entitled?'

'She has some rights, but it might have to be sorted out in court.'

'But why have you split?'

'It's a combination of things I suppose. With Brooke's disapproval and all of this I feel I just can't take it at the moment. Until he sorts it out with Ciara I don't want to be involved with him. And maybe she might be more amenable to an arrangement with him if I'm not around.'

'Do you trust him?' Leah asked.

'Of course I trust him,' she said, vehement.

'Maybe it's something that's been going on for a while, and he had kept it a secret,' Megan ventured.

'At the outset he told me that he had a wife who had left over twenty years ago, so he wasn't trying to hide it.'

'And then she turns up. Very odd,' Celine seemed puzzled.

'It's not that I don't believe him, girls, it's just I can't be involved in it. What if she came up here?'

'What would be the point?'

'She knows about me.'

'What are your girls going to say?'

'They'll say they warned me and I took no notice, particularly Brooke,' she grimaced.

'But you still love him?'

'Of course I do.'

'Well you just have to believe in him.'

'I'm trying to do that.'

'We'll support you.' They hugged her.

Liz was so grateful to her friends. They had always been there for her over the years and she loved them dearly. But she couldn't bear being separated from Scott. Each day she decided that she would have to see him, hear his voice, touch him. But as the hours passed the sensible side of her personality persuaded that there was no point. She couldn't deal with it. It was impossible to imagine a wife returning after all that time. It would be like Ethan coming back from the dead and expecting to pick up where he left off. She felt guilty even saying such a thing.

Her head was spinning. She was a woman who had had no man in her life for fifteen years. Who lived like a nun. Who had forgotten how to reach into a man's heart. Who was afraid of changing direction. In these last years she had followed her own path. It was straight, without any deviation, and she faced it courageously each day. Her children grew up and did their own thing and she didn't need to hold their hands any longer, shield them from fearful monsters or dry their tears.

Now for Liz to be at such a crossroads caused chaos in her heart.

## Chapter Fifty-nine

Scott wondered whether there was any way of raising money for Ciara rather than sell the house. Because of the recession the amount of cash and shares in his portfolio had diminished drastically. Fortunately, property values had increased lately, so the only way he could see out of the situation was to sell. He would have to persuade her to give him a divorce. That was what he wanted. To be free and unencumbered. And be in a position to marry Liz.

In the meantime, he would have to find somewhere to live. Although if Liz agreed to live with him then everything would change and he could base himself in Dublin. If she didn't, there was the house in Rosscarbery but it was a long commute to work. Still, if it was the only alternative then he would have to take it. He sighed, and wondered what Cathal and Ryan would say.

'I know you're hurt about my attitude to your mother,' he said. They didn't respond to him and the silence was palpable. 'And I'm sorry about that. But I've come to a decision,' Scott said.

'What is it?' Cathal demanded.

'I'm going to sell the house and Ciara will receive fifty per cent.'

'But she wants to live in the house, it's her home,' Cathal said. Ryan was silent.

'She also wants money,' Scott said.

'She doesn't need that much. You could give her something every month just to keep her going,' Cathal suggested.

'She wants half the house,' Scott stated.

'She's emotionally attached to it.'

'That may be, but the only way she could remain on would be if she bought me out, and I don't think she'd get a mortgage.'

'It sounds fair,' Ryan spoke for the first time.

'I have to live too.'

'You've plenty stashed away,' Cathal accused.

'I haven't enough money to give her half the value of the house.'

'You could get another mortgage.'

'I probably could.'

'Then why don't you do that?'

'I want to have a new life and I can't do that without money. I can't give everything I have to Ciara, however much she wants it.'

'You make her sound so unfeeling and she's anything but that.'

'You should talk to her.'

'I talk to her all the time, she's my mother.'

'What does she say to you exactly?' Scott was curious.

'She wants to live in her old home, that's all, and have a few euro,' Cathal glared at him.

'It's not as simple as that.'

'How do you know?'

'She had a partner, and I think he could still be around.'

'She's entitled.'

'I agree with that. But if I walk away and leave her the house, what's to prevent that man joining her here?'

'No way,' Ryan exploded.

'And what if she sold the house as soon as I've left?'

'She'd never do that.'

'Look lads, I hate this situation. It's come between us and we were never like this with each other. So I'm looking for the best possible way out of it. I want to sort it quickly so that we can get back to normal. I still love you two, you're my life, and never forget that,' he appealed to them.

Ryan looked embarrassed.

'I've already asked Mum what happened between you,' Cathal said.

'And what did she say?'

'You forced her to leave and wouldn't let her take us,' he accused.

'That isn't true, I've shown you her note.'

'You could have written that yourself. Forged her handwriting.'

'Then why didn't she come back for you. Get on to social services, go to court to force me to give her custody?'

'You threatened her.'

'With what?' Scott was astounded.

'A legal case for desertion. She had no money and couldn't have fought you in court.'

'Ridiculous. It was only in recent years that her mother told me she had gone to live with another man in London, I never even knew where she was living until I received her letter a few weeks ago.'

'I don't believe you.'

'You know I love you both very much and was glad to raise you myself, but I would have been happier if you had your mother in your life. We could have come to an arrangement if she had made contact with us.'

'She doesn't tell it like that. And now she wants to be part of the family again, and you won't let her.'

'I don't mind her coming back to live in Cork, and I'm glad that you have been reunited. But for myself personally, I can't have her dropping in here whenever she feels like it. I have my own life,' Scott said, hating this argument with Cathal.

'Such a thing to say, she's your wife, our mother.'

'You can't blame everything on Dad,' Ryan said unexpectedly. 'He has to take a share of it.'

'What about the other man you were talking about? Where is he now?' Ryan asked.

'I don't know.'

'People make mistakes. We all do,' Cathal said.

Scott's mind was in a frenzy. His relationship with his sons, particularly Cathal, seemed to have changed, and he was the one at fault.

'Anyway, you probably just want to get rid of Mum so that you can have that other one,' Cathal accused. 'Tell the truth.'

'Don't speak about Liz like that,' he said sharply. 'Have some respect.'

For once, his eldest son had the grace to remain silent.

## Chapter Sixty

Sophie received an email from Gary in which he asked her to come into the clinic for a meeting. She called Scott. Not really even sure why. But needing to talk to someone who seemed to understand where she was at.

'Would you like me to come with you?' he asked.

She hesitated for a few seconds. Knowing full well that Liz would be very annoyed that she had put Scott under such pressure. 'I don't want to ask you to come up especially.'

'It's no problem, I can do some business in Dublin,' he said immediately.

Sophie was grateful to Scott. 'It's so good to have company. I don't know what Gary is going to suggest. The residential care is more expensive than the outpatient, but either way the VHI won't cover it. I only have limited cover.'

'Sophie, let's see what the actual cost is, and,' he hesitated. 'I hope you don't take this as too forward, but I'd like to help with the financial side of it. We can always sort it out at a later date.'

'No, Scott, I couldn't possibly let you do that, I'm going to get a credit union loan.'

'Sophie, I'd like to do this. And Gary will probably give me a better deal anyway, I know him a long time. So, please?' he smiled.

'Well, if he'd do that all the better but you must tell me what it is and I'll arrange the finance. It will be worth it to me, my life has been so awful lately. But one thing I know, Mum won't want you to do this.'

'Just say you had some savings.'

'There's no way she'll believe that. She knows every cent I have is used for drugs, and I may as well come clean with you.' She told him about the Taylors. 'So you see what I'm like. I have no morals at all.'

'I don't believe that.' He shook his head.

'It's true.'

'Anyway, I won't mention it to Liz. But I may as well come clean also.' His eyes met hers. She could see a sadness in their depths.

'About what?'

'I don't know if Liz told you about my wife having left me years ago.'

'She mentioned it.'

'There's been a new development. She has actually come back from London.'

'What?' Sophie's eyes were round with astonishment.

'When I told Liz recently, she said she couldn't cope with it, so, we've split, any plans we had have been shelved.' He looked beyond her into the distance.

There was a silence between them for a moment.

Sophie spoke first. 'Mum never said anything. While I knew she was very upset about Brooke, I assumed her bad mood was because of that, now it seems she had more to contend with.'

'If she didn't tell you, then I presume she doesn't want you to know, so say nothing.'

'You weren't up for the last couple of weekends and when I asked why, she just said you were busy.'

Sophie and Scott were met by Gary and the team, and she didn't feel quite so intimidated by them as she had on that first day.

'Sophie, we have completed a report on your case in the meantime.' Gary glanced down at his laptop screen. 'Our final conclusion is that we all feel that you would be best served by a short residential stay. You have tried to come off the drugs yourself but didn't succeed for various reasons and if you take an outpatient course, possibly the same thing may happen.'

'Will I have to stay here?' she gasped, her heart sinking. Now she had another problem. How would she tell everyone where she was going. And why. It was going to be very difficult.

'How are you feeling?' Scott was concerned.

'Sick at the thought of it.'

'It's going to be hard, but they'll help you through the various stages.'

'I hope.'

'It will be worth it if you can come off the drugs. I'm sorry, I know that doesn't mean a lot, but if there's anything I can do, just let me know.'

'You've done so much already, I'll be forever in your debt.'

'Just remember I'm here.'

She decided to use her mother's Sunday lunch as the best time to tell Brooke and Luke. But Brooke hadn't been there for the past couple of weeks and she rang her to see if she was coming.

'No, I don't want to,' Brooke said.

'Come on, it's not the same without you, and I know Mum is upset that she doesn't see the children. It's not fair on her.'

'It's bad enough to have to talk to her during the week, but at least I can get away from it on Saturday and Sunday.'

'Brooke, you can't talk about Mum like that,' Sophie said. 'What's got into you?'

'She's not bothered about us.'

'How could you say that?' Sophie was astonished.

Brooke was silent.

'Come on Sunday will you? Please? I want you there,' Sophie cajoled.

Brooke was quiet for a moment. 'All right, I will.'

'I'm so happy to see you, love, I've missed you and the children.'

Liz was delighted to see them, and there was an air of celebration as they sat down to lunch. But for Sophie it wasn't like that. She dreaded telling her family that she was going into rehab and they were almost finished lunch when at last she decided to speak.

'I've something to tell you.' They looked at her. 'This is difficult,' she said slowly.

'Go on, Sophie, don't worry.' Liz put a hand on her shoulder.

'What is this?' Brooke asked, impatient.

'For a long time now I've been using drugs,' Sophie's voice was only a whisper. 'And I'm going into a drug rehab clinic for treatment, so I'll be disappearing for a few weeks,' she said lamely.

Liz hugged her.

'I can't believe it, you're a drug addict?' Brooke was horrified.

Sophie nodded.

'I admire you for trying to deal with it like that, it's not easy,' Luke was sympathetic.

'Have you ever taken drugs?' Brooke asked him.

'I've tried some from time to time, I don't know anyone who hasn't.'

'God, I must be living on the moon. None of my friends have ever used drugs as far as I know,' Brooke exploded. 'But Sophie, you don't look like a drug addict, you look normal, the same as any of us.'

'Normal? I suppose I manage to hide the effects of what I'm doing to myself most of the time. Although you've seen how bad I can look, don't you remember?'

'We all look like that occasionally, it doesn't mean we're addicted to drugs.'

'You've shown great courage in telling us Sophie, and we're all behind you. We'll help in any way we can,' Liz said.

'Sure we will, anything,' Luke agreed immediately.

'Of course,' Brooke whispered, tears in her eyes.

Sophie felt a weight lift off her shoulders. Liz already knew so it was no surprise to her. And telling Brooke and Luke eased the stress and having to endure alone whatever lay ahead.

'I hope it's going to be all right for you, my love,' Liz walked into the clinic foyer with her.

'I'll be OK Mum, don't worry,' Sophie assured.

'Call if you need me, will you please?' Liz asked.

'I will, although it's not encouraged in the first few days of detox.'

'You can leave if you want, can't you?'

'Of course, it's not a prison.'

'If you can't do whatever they want, just walk out and come home. We can look at other ways of dealing with it,' she said.

'Thanks, but I'm going to try, I must, you've no idea what it's like to be addicted to something as vile as drugs.'

Liz nodded, sudden tears in her eyes. She embraced Sophie and held her tight.

'Don't cry, Mum.'

She held her even tighter.

Someone stood in the doorway.

'Sophie?' Gary approached.

She introduced him to her mother.

'She'll be fine, Mrs. Nicholson,' he said.

'I know, I'm sure.'

'We'll let you know how Sophie is doing,' he promised.

'Would you, please?'

'But it will be in about a week, after the detox.'

The first day Sophie spent in the medical centre. The thought that she had walked into this place without a tablet was terrifying. She had no back-up. No possibility of support. As the hours passed, her need for something, anything, began to set in. But the staff were there for her. Administering drugs which would counteract the affects of withdrawal. They encouraged her to rest. Sedation eased those symptoms with which she had become so familiar.

She slept heavily that night and the following day. When she awoke for brief periods, she wasn't even sure where she was. Floating in and out of inexplicable dreams. Liz was there. She came and went. Reached out for her. Held her close. But someone struck her mother. Slapped. Thumped. Sophie cried out. Cried. And cried.

It went on like that. They tended to her. Gently. With care. She thanked them. They smiled. Reassured. But she was unable to understand what was happening to her. Time meant nothing. Days meandered into nights. All was dim. Grey. Nothing. Interrupted only by the nightmares.

## Chapter Sixty-one

Luke unlocked the door of the restaurant and walked through. He sighed. It was tough going. The night before he and Daniel had a meeting with their accountant who warned that if things didn't improve soon, then they would not have enough money to continue and the company would be insolvent.

He found it difficult to be enthusiastic about anything. 'I know we have problems, but my sister Sophie is in a bad state.'

'What do you mean?'

'She's in rehab.'

'What?' Daniel was astonished.

'Drugs.'

'I never would have thought, not Sophie.'

'Anyway, I have to get involved in her treatment. Although I don't know how I'll be able to help.'

'You have to give it your best, she's your sister.'

For Luke and Daniel, their dream had collapsed, and while they had struggled, all their money had gone into it and disappeared. They had considered trying to borrow more money, but the accountant told them that there was no way the bank would lend them another cent. And that they would be crazy to throw good money after bad. He advised them to go into liquidation.

'We can try and sell the lease when it comes up for renewal in a few months. Things have improved generally although we're not feeling it, and someone might be glad to buy it. But at least we don't have to sign another contract and can close down if we want.'

'Then let's make the decision. Will we put it on the market?'

'We haven't any other choice. Although we've reduced our own salaries and expenses to a minimum, we might have to come to an arrangement with our suppliers. If we liquidate, the bank will be the main loser.' Luke looked at the figures on the screen.

'What about the staff?' Daniel asked.

'None of them are here for very long, there's been quite a turnover, so we're lucky that we probably don't need to pay much redundancy. We can check that with the accountant.'

'I feel sorry for them, I hate letting anyone go.'

'So do I.'

'The first year of any business is tough, and it's very hard to break even. We probably needed more capital when we started up.'

'And the basic cost of our food is expensive. We sell organic, and we can source everything on our menu, but that is rare. So perhaps we are aiming too high?'

'Maybe, but we can't lower our standards now and start selling cheap stuff, I just wouldn't be bothered.'

'Fish and chips, burgers, pizza?' Daniel asked, with a grin.

'No way, I'd prefer to work for someone else instead.'

'There are jobs out there anyway, at least we know that. We've found it hard to get good staff.'

'What about London?'

'Not a bad idea.'

'We've a few contacts. We've worked there before.'

'We could build up our finances again, and open another place.'

'I've every intention of doing that as soon as we can.'

'In the meantime, if we could get into a Michelin starred restaurant it would stand to us.'

'But first we have to sell here.'

'If we only had enough to keep going another year, I'm sure we'd turn it around. We have a good following of people who love our food and we just have to capitalise on that.'

'Right, let's try and get as much publicity as we can, it might help,' Daniel was enthusiastic.

'I hate to throw in the towel. So upwards and onwards.'

## Chapter Sixty-two

Liz was desperately worried about Sophie. She went through this week with her daughter, living every second, every moment, of what must be hell for her. She couldn't imagine exactly what it was like to endure detox and waited anxiously for a call from the clinic to say that she could visit. Keeping the phone with her all the time, and checking it constantly.

She would have given anything to put her arms around Scott, and feel his love encircle her. But there was a lump in her throat, and her stomach felt like someone had thumped her. She was tempted to phone, but wouldn't have known what to say to him. Was Ciara still there? Had he been persuaded to take her back? She felt sick at the thought.

It was Saturday when she received the call from the clinic, but couldn't leave the studio, appointments stacked up right through the day. It was after six when she finally managed to lock up and drive to Ballsbridge.

A nurse took her to the room. She knocked. Liz could hear Sophie's voice, and almost couldn't stop herself rushing in that door. But she waited as the nurse went ahead of her, telling her to follow.

'Mum?'

'Sophie?' she cried. Going over to where she sat in an armchair, she curled her arms around her, drawing close. Her face in Sophie's soft dark hair, tears spilling over. Then she knelt on the floor and stared into her daughter's face. She was pale. Her eyes shadowed. So tired. She looked as if she hadn't slept for days. Liz kissed her. 'How are you?'

'Worn out,' Sophie murmured.

'It must have been terrible for you,' Liz whispered.

'They gave me other drugs to ease the withdrawal, but I was anxious all the time. Terrified really.'

'You should have called me.'

'It was like being in another world. Awake. Asleep. Dreaming. This is the first day I feel like myself.'

'I thought I'd never get in to you.'

'You wouldn't have wanted to see me in that state.'

'The worst is over now?' Liz asked hopefully.

'I don't know.'

'I only wish I could do something for you.'

'I suppose this is something I have to do for myself otherwise I'll never succeed in getting off the drugs.'

'I'll help, in any way.'

'I know you will, thanks Mum.'

Liz hugged her again and stood up. 'What is the plan for next week?' She sat on the other chair beside Sophie.

'I'm not sure,' she hesitated, and took Liz's hand in hers.

'You seem very tired, love, why don't you get back into bed?'

'I will.' She didn't seem to be able to get up out of the chair.

Liz took her arm and helped her. 'Take care, I'll be in tomorrow.'

'Thanks Mum.'

Liz kissed her. 'Have a good night's rest.' She stood at the door and found it hard not to cry. But not wanting to upset Sophie, she forced a smile and left.


At the Nurses Station outside, she asked to talk to someone who was familiar with Sophie's case. She was taken into an adjacent room.

'Thanks for looking after Sophie,' she felt a word of appreciation wouldn't do any harm. 'How is she really?'

'She's doing quite well,' the nurse said.

'The week took a lot out of her, she's exhausted.'

'That's understandable, but we're hoping that she'll improve over the next few days, and then she'll go on to the next stage.'

'Can we visit her?'

'Yes, we like the family to be involved. So we'll be in touch with you.'

'That's good,' Liz said, feeling very relieved.

She went in on Sunday again and spent some time with Sophie. They just sat together, hardly speaking. The television was on but neither took much notice. Liz read the newspapers, and Sophie dozed on and off. She wasn't sure if she helped Sophie by being there but hoped she would feel more reassured.

During the following week, Brooke, Luke and herself had a meeting with the counsellor who had been appointed to Sophie's case, and they were all asked to complete questionnaires about their own lives.

'They want to know everything. Imagine, have I used drugs?' Brooke complained. 'And what is my intake of alcohol every week?'

Luke was equally frustrated. 'Stop Brooke, I have to admit that I have used drugs. At least you can put in *no*, one simple word and you're done. I have to give so much detail you wouldn't believe,' he grumbled. 'How am I going to answer these questions. When? What? How much? God ...'

Liz had been shocked when Luke admitted he had tried drugs, and prayed that he wouldn't go down the same road as Sophie. But she hadn't said anything to him. Now she stared at her own questionnaire. Finding the questions extremely intrusive. But at least, like Brooke she could answer *no* to those about drug usage. But the alcohol intake was difficult. She tried to think. How many units? Was it a bottle a week, or more? Probably. She decided. When she was out with the girls, they definitely drank a lot. And when she was with Scott? She was disinclined to even think about him. She wasn't an alcoholic at any rate. So just put in her best guess.

The counsellor returned and picked up their questionnaires, informing them that they could join in with a family group therapy session twice a week at which Sophie would attend as well.

## Chapter Sixty-three

Scott went to see his solicitor, Sean. They had been friends for years and he felt relaxed as he explained about the situation with Ciara.

'What is her motivation?' Sean asked.

'I'm pretty sure it's just money. She wants her portion of the house, although she's also talking about picking up where we left off.'

'You're lucky she came back. Since you asked me to check on the situation regarding a divorce, I talked to a barrister friend of mine about divorcing someone who has been out of the country for many years. As you didn't have her address you would have had to make an effort to locate her. That could have taken quite a while.'

'Her sister Maura might have had the address, although she never gave it to me.'

'If you can get her to agree to an arrangement, that's the best thing. It's straightforward then.'

'There's the old house in Rosscarbery. Would she be entitled to that?'

'Did she ever live there?'

'No, my father was alive at the time, and he died after she left. You might remember I bought my brother's share. The house isn't worth much anyway.'

'Unless she goes into court looking for as much as she can get from your assets, that house may not come into play. Did she ever contribute to the household expenses when you were together?'

'Not really. She didn't work and we had a joint account. She bought whatever she wanted and that was fine with me. Regardless of that, I want to begin divorce proceedings,' Scott insisted.

'You need to have an agreement before that. No point in starting without.'

'I'm putting the house up for sale, so that I can give her half the value. That should be enough for her to agree to a divorce.'

'You mightn't have to go that far, if you go to court the judge will assess her entitlement. It may not be as much as you think.'

'I'm not taking that risk, all I want is the divorce.'

Scott was glad of Sean's advice. Even sharing a problem with someone he knew helped.

Later he called Gary to enquire about Sophie.

'Doing all right. Out of detox at least.'

'Will she make it?' Scott was worried.

'That's up to herself. It's a long haul.'

'Have the family been in to see her?'

'They're involved in group therapy sessions. It's helpful for everyone.'

'Do you think I should go up to see her?' he asked.

'No, I wouldn't recommend that, it's just the family.'

'I understand. If you think it's appropriate give her my regards.'

'It's a pity you've broken up with Liz. I like her, she's nice,' Gary said.

'Yea,' he paused for a few seconds, but said no more.

He couldn't get Liz out of his head. She was there all the time. And he was so aware of her loss. His days and nights empty. Without plans to see her. No excitement. No looking forward to that moment when he would hold her close to him. Or waking in the morning and looking into her eyes. And hearing her say how much she loved him. That most of all. His heart was crushed.

## Chapter Sixty-four

Liz held her handbag tightly, her hands shaking. This was the fourth family group session in which they had participated at the clinic and it didn't get any easier. The clinic saw drug abuse as a problem for the individual and the family too. Their aim to help the person who is addicted find a holistic approach to healing using the *twelve steps* to recovery. As time went on, more and more Liz had taken on the responsibility for Sophie's problems. What had she done which had caused her daughter to use drugs at the tender age of fifteen? How was it that she had not noticed it? What sort of mother was she? She blamed herself. There were tears in her eyes, and she dabbed the moisture with a tissue, but it was ineffective. She felt embarrassed.

Brooke sat beside her but said nothing. Luke was very quiet also. She knew both of them were extremely nervous, but didn't know how to comfort them. While she worked with Brooke every day, their relationship was still conflicted. Although she had kept her own problems to herself and hadn't told them she wasn't seeing Scott any longer.

The counsellor, Denise, ushered them into the room. Chairs were arranged in a semicircle. As soon as Sophie came in, Liz stood up immediately, rushed to her and embraced. She didn't care about the other woman. 'How are you, my love?'

'I'm fine, Mum,' she smiled.

Liz was relieved to see that she looked a lot better than when they had last met.

Denise began the conversation. Each session she asked them to talk about some aspect of their lives. What was important to all of them. And today, she asked Liz what was the most traumatic event in her life. Denise sat listening as she explained how she had lost Ethan. Brooke and Luke spoke about that time as well.

Liz had never heard them speak about their father before. The conversation drifted. Events were remembered. Life at home. Schooldays. Holidays. For her, she recalled that time with the medium. And Ethan supposedly speaking through her.

'It was my fault,' Sophie spoke for the first time.

Liz was puzzled.

They listened.

'That's why Dad took it out on you, Mum. I could hear him shouting at you through the wall of my bedroom. And I saw him hit you too. I know it was because of me. I always made him angry.' Sophie burst into tears.

Liz was distraught when she arrived home, sobbing as she stumbled down the hall and into the kitchen. She flung herself into a chair, bent forward and held her head in her hands. What did Sophie mean? She tried to remember her words. Something about *hearing through the wall*, and *took it out on you*. Her body trembled. Pain echoed. Bruised ribs, shoulders, thighs, black, blue. Hidden from the world.

She went to bed straight away. Longing to sleep. To cast out the thoughts which whirled around her mind, hoping, praying that what she had heard from Sophie had been in her imagination. But sleep evaded her and she lay staring into the darkness. Desperately aware of the emptiness of the bed beside her. Scott. She whispered his name. Longing to feel his arms around her, holding her close in his warm embrace. Then a terrible thought swept through her. Would she ever know him again?

## Chapter Sixty-five

Rory was to call this evening. He had phoned Brooke earlier. It was unusual. These days he just burst his way in whenever it suited him, and most of the time caught her unawares. Now she changed into a black dress. Plain. Long-sleeved. Re-did her make-up and blow-dried her hair. She was determined to look as good as she could. Insanely jealous of the woman in Rory's office who had trapped him.

The children were already in bed, and she paced up and down the living room. Her footsteps echoed eerily in the almost empty space. She squirted perfume on her wrists and behind her ears. And waited impatiently.

He arrived about ten. Now she sat on the couch in front of the television, but didn't turn around when she heard his footsteps. He stood in front of her.

'Sorry it's so late,' he apologised.

She shrugged.

'Brooke?'

She looked at him, but said nothing.

'I've changed my mind about selling the house,' he said.

She straightened up, completely taken aback. She couldn't even get her mind around it. Her mouth opened, but no words came out.

'I've been offered a job in San Francisco. I'm moving there.' He pushed his hands into his trouser pockets.

'What about her?' she whispered.

'It didn't work out.'

A sense of relief whirled through her, and an extraordinary happiness took the place of the depression which dogged her these days.

He sat beside her. 'There's an apartment with the job so that's why I've decided not to sell the house.'

'We can still pull out of the sale?'

'Yes. Contracts have not been exchanged yet. And I thought perhaps I could come home for a couple of months or so until I leave and maybe you and the children might join me in San Francisco when I'm settled?'

'You've treated me in a vile way, why should I take you back?'

'Because I love you.'

'Are you for real?' She lost her patience with him.

'Please let me come home.'

'This isn't your home any longer. Does it look like a home? This is an empty house. It's got nothing in it. No love. No warmth. Our marriage is over.' Brooke found strength deep within herself, something she never expected.

'But I want you back, Brooke. And we won't be selling the house now.'

'If it's not sold then I'm going to live here.'

'You can have it for now, we can always sell it in the future if you come over to San Francisco.'

She was silent. Hating him.

'Brooke, can I stay here tonight? Then I'll be able to see the kids in the morning.'

'You can't. You chose to move out so you can stay out,' she glared at him.

Disappointment flashed across his face. 'Can I see the kids now?'

'It's far too late to disturb them,' she snapped.

'Just to look at them?'

'Not tonight.' She struggled to control herself. She wasn't going to give in to him.

'I'll come back in the morning.'

'They're at play school tomorrow.'

'I'll come around and take them,' he offered.

'There's no need, I'll do it. But you can see them later in the day.' She couldn't prevent the children seeing him. It wasn't fair on them.

What made her so aggressive these days? She wondered, and then thought of how she was with her mother and her boyfriend. But she knew she could never accept Scott into the family. And she should have been that way with Rory too, instead of being all sweetness and light. That was probably why he had walked on her. That was why he left her for another woman. I won't let anyone bully me again, she vowed.

## Chapter Sixty-six

Scott drove home and pulled into the driveway. He had played a round of golf this evening and felt the better of it. He hadn't seen Ciara since the weekend and dreaded another confrontation. He had to force her to agree to a divorce, but couldn't imagine how he would manage that. He lifted his golf bag out of the boot and took it into the garage. It was only then he noticed a taxi drawing up outside. He turned and watched Ciara walk towards him.

'Hi Scott,' she said softly.

'Ciara?'

'It's good to see you, I've missed you.' She drew closer, smiling.

He didn't reply.

He put his suggestion about selling the house to her immediately. 'That amount of money would provide you with a reasonable income and make your life very comfortable. You could do whatever you want. Buy a new home. Travel. Anything.'

'All I want is you, Scott, you mean so much to me.' She reached out to him.

He noticed that she was wearing the wedding ring he had returned to her recently.

'Ciara, please, you know there is someone else in my life.'

'Can't you see how close we are, if you just take one step towards me then it will happen like magic and we'll be back where we were.' She lowered her voice to a beguiling whisper. 'Dump that bitch and we can get together again, you never could resist me,' she coaxed, leaning

276

closer to him.

He moved away. 'Forget it, Ciara. We're finished.'

'This isn't working out as I expected. I had such hopes that you would welcome me home.' Her mood changed suddenly and a look of extreme dissatisfaction flashed across her face.

'The lads are over the moon to have you back. To know you at last means so much to them.'

'But what use is that to me if they're not around?'

'They work hard running the company.'

'They should be prepared to spend more time with me, I'm their mother.'

'I'll say it to them.'

'It's not the same if you have to do that. They should want to look after me. Take me out to lunch and dinner. Away for weekends. But all I'm doing is pottering around picking up after Mam. All she does is say things over and over. She drives me mad.'

He felt sorry for her mother. She wasn't the worst, and over the years he knew that she had missed her daughter. 'It was a pity you didn't come home earlier to see her, before she deteriorated.'

She shrugged.

'Look Ciara, let's decide to sell the house and split the proceeds between us.'

She stared around the room. 'I hate the thought of someone else owning my house.'

'It doesn't appeal to me either.'

'Then we won't sell, let me come back,' she coaxed.

'It will be better if you make a fresh start, I'm no good for you any longer,' he said slowly.

She opened her handbag, took out a notepad and pen. Flicking past the first few pages which were full of notes until she came to a blank one. She clicked the point of the pen and pressed it on the first line. 'Then let's get down to business,' her lips pursed.

'If we sell the house then I want a divorce, and I'd prefer if you didn't put up any objections. We should discuss the details with our solicitors.'

'Can't we decide here today? Why do we need solicitors? They only cost money.'

'It's the best way. Then we know where we stand.'

'I want my fair share of money so that I can be independent,' she demanded. As she spoke she scribbled on the notepad. A mess of unintelligible scrawls.

'Your solicitor will discuss the details with mine.'

'How long will that take?'

'It will take some time, but I won't agree to sell the house until we divorce,' he said firmly.

'But I can't wait for months, I need money now,' she demanded.

'I understand that.'

'How much do you think I'm going to get?' she asked.

'It should probably be about two hundred thousand or so but we can't be sure until the house actually sells.'

'Is that all?' Her face crumpled.

'We could get more but that depends on the market. I'll talk to the estate agent.'

'I need a drink,' she snapped.

He poured a whiskey and handed her the glass.

'And I want the money before the divorce.' She gulped.

'It will go together, Ciara.'

'But the divorce will probably take ages.'

'I often wondered why you didn't make contact about that before now. Did you never want to get married again?'

'I did anyway.'

'Got married?' He was surprised.

'Yea, I never said anything to my husband about you.'

'But that was bigamy.'

'So what?'

'You could have been charged, given a prison sentence.'

'Who was going to tell?' she smirked.

'You're still with him?'

'Of course I am. And he misses me, can't wait for me to come home. So you see I'm not dependant on you,' she said sharply.

'Someone could still report you.'

'Who'd be bothered?' she laughed.

'I think the sooner we get divorced the better, Ciara. Then you can regularise your own marriage. Didn't you ever worry about the bigamy issue?'

'No.'

'You should have, it might affect inheritance,' he said.

She looked at him, and he could see that she was suddenly worried. 'Inheritance?'

'Your husband's estate.'

'You mean if he died?'

'I'm not a hundred percent sure, but it could be risky.'

'Are you certain?'

'No, I'm not …but there could be a question mark over it.'

'Maybe I should go back,' she said.

'I'd prefer if you didn't leave until we have the divorce arranged,' he said, suddenly worried. 'Although I thought you were staying here permanently?'

'If you and I had got together again I might have, but because of what you're saying I think it would be better to be at home, but I still want my share of the money,' she reminded, and took another gulp of whiskey.

'Cathal and Ryan won't be happy about that.'

'They'll get used to it.'

Scott felt for his sons, particularly Cathal.

## Chapter Sixty-seven

Liz lay in the rumple of pillows and duvet, her cap of dark hair in stark contrast. The sun streamed through the window, casting mullioned lines across the white bedcover. She wound her arms around the pillow and thought of Scott. But there was confusion in her mind. She was at a crossroads and didn't know which way to choose. He was there at each turn. Waiting. But with a shadow behind him. Threatening.

Liz climbed out of bed and caught sight of her naked body in the full length mirror, a memory of other marks reminded again of what Sophie had said the day before. How had she pushed those incidents into the back of her mind for so long? She had forgotten them completely. What did that say of her? One so closed. So narrow. Who had left her darling Sophie carry the burden alone. A young girl who shouldn't have been exposed to something like that. She wondered how much she understood. Were those phrases she uttered yesterday real to her. Or only vague nonsensical nightmares. Part of a dream scene.

Brooke rushed into the office.

'Mum, Rory's taking up a job in San Francisco.'

'Are you going with him?' Liz looked at her, surprised. It was the first time Brooke had even smiled at her recently.

'No way. But he's changed his mind about selling the house,' she said excitedly.

'Is he giving it to you?'

'No, but now I can continue to live at home. So that gives me some leeway.'

'When is he going?'

'In a couple of months.'

'What about the woman?'

'Gone,' Brooke said, with a delighted grin.

'I'm so happy for you, love.' Liz put her arms around her.

'Thanks Mum.'

'Do you think you will get together again?'

Brooke shook her head. 'I don't trust him anymore. It would be impossible.'

'Do whatever you want, and just be happy.'

'Mum, I'm going to save as much money as I can so that if and when he decides he wants to sell the house then I'll be in a position to get my own place. In the meantime, I don't have to stay with Peggy, it's such a relief, you wouldn't believe.'

'I can imagine,' Liz said. So glad that Brooke seemed happy for the first time in months. 'But I'm sure Peggy will be disappointed.'

'She will probably, but I'll have her over more often to make up. Now to work.' Brooke sat down at her desk.

'You know that client named Taylor, was it ever sorted out?' she asked a little later, waving a sheet of paper.

Liz's mind raced. She looked up, but said nothing.

'What happened there?' Brooke asked.

'Apparently Sophie put it down under another name by mistake and never changed it.'

'What was the name?'

'Couldn't tell you, but we won't bother her now. Forget about it,' Liz said, hoping that Brooke would let it go.

'All right,' she agreed, tore up the sheet of paper and binned it.

Liz couldn't believe that she was reconciled to some extent with Brooke. Such a relief that she could talk with her daughter the way she used to. Without any animosity. Even though Brooke had not apologised about her attitude towards Scott, Liz decided to say nothing more.

Since that last family therapy session Liz had felt very unsettled. Memories of her life with Ethan had dominated her thoughts. And now questions pushed their way into her head. How had Sophie been affected by what happened? Those incidents between herself and Ethan must have been horrific for her. An innocent young girl who couldn't possibly understand why such violence erupted between her parents. She had never made any reference to episodes between them when she was young, and now Liz wondered if Brooke or Luke had been affected as well by what had gone on at home before Ethan died.

She met the girls, so glad to share her problems with them.

'How can you cope with it all?' Celine exclaimed. 'If I had that much on my plate I'd lose it altogether.'

'I feel like that most of the time,' Liz admitted.

'Any word from Scott?' Leah asked, crossing her legs, black mini skirt riding up.

'No.'

'What does that mean?'

'It means he's taking me at my word, but it's hard, I miss him so much.'

'The whole thing about his wife is tricky, will he ever get rid of her do you think?' Celine asked.

'I don't know. But I can't be involved with him while she's still around. And then there's Brooke, we're getting on a bit better, so maybe it's just as well he's gone.'

The girls looked at each other.

'How's Sophie?' Megan asked.

'She seems to be managing all right, but it's terribly hard. I can't imagine how she is surviving without drugs.'

'Withdrawal is terrible. You have nightmares, imagine all sorts of weird things.' Leah shivered.

'Don't say that, I can't bear to think of it. But at least she's over the worst now and will be discharged from the clinic tomorrow.'

'Give her our love,' Celine said, and the others nodded. 'Is there anything we can do?'

'Just be there for me, I'd appreciate it. I know I said that it's just as well Scott is out of my life, but it's such a struggle to wake up each day and face its length without hearing from him. I don't know how I've reached this point.' Her voice quivered.

'It's very hard,' Celine whispered.

The others were quiet and said nothing.

'Enough about me, let's talk about something else, girls,' Liz said, feeling that if she didn't put it all out of her head, she'd go mad.

Sophie was waiting in the foyer of the clinic when Liz arrived. She hugged her tight. 'How are you feeling?'

'All right.'

'I'm so happy you're leaving this place,' Liz said, as they walked to the car.

'I feel the same way. Hope I'll never come back.'

'You won't, I'm certain of that.'

They sat into the car.

'Will you come back home with me for a day or two?' Liz asked tentatively as she drove out through the gates, hoping that she would agree.

Sophie nodded. 'Thanks.'

'You can get back into the swing of things gradually. There's no hurry about work.'

'How have you been managing?' Sophie asked.

'Fine. I do calls in the morning when Brooke is there. And then the sessions in the afternoon.'

'What if someone comes in at that point?'

'I put a notice on the door. People usually call back later. I don't think we've lost any business,' she said, with a grin.

At home, they sat on the patio. Liz didn't know what to say to Sophie. Hating this awkwardness which had reared up between them. Finally, she had to force herself to ask how the weeks had gone.

'It wasn't too bad.' Sophie stared out into the garden.

'Will you keep up the programme?' Liz asked.

'I'll have to.' She seemed distant.

'Once a week?'

'It's like AA. Same idea. To keep you on the straight and narrow.'

'You're strong, I'm certain you'll make it.'

'There's something I should mention,' Sophie said.

Liz looked at her, suddenly worried.

'When I contacted Scott, he offered to introduce me to Gary, and came with me on the first couple of appointments.'

'I'm glad.'

'And he insisted on paying the fee at the clinic, and wouldn't even tell me how much it was going to be, although he was hoping that Gary would give him a good deal.'

Liz couldn't believe her ears. 'I thought you were borrowing the money, but anyway I'm going to share the cost with you, I just didn't want to mention that yet.'

'I'll be paying him back as soon as I organise it, he just wanted me to go in as quickly as possible.'

'Why didn't you tell me that?'

'We decided to keep it to ourselves. So, say nothing to him,' Sophie said. 'Promise?'

'All right.'

They sat staring out at the sea. 'It's a lovely day, would you like to take a walk?' Liz asked.

They wandered along by the edge of the surf on the beach near the house. It was warm, with only a light breeze. The sun shone brightly. It was one of those late summer days, and the beach was crowded with people. Children played on the sand, swam in the sea, and were obviously having a great time.

'Reminds me of the days when you were kids and we spent so much time here,' Liz said, smiling.

'I loved it then. I miss it.'

'We should come down more often, but there just aren't enough hours in the day.'

'We're too busy.'

'I'll have to wait until I retire.'

'You'll never retire,' Sophie laughed.

'Probably won't,' Liz agreed.

'I couldn't even imagine a day without going into the studio and taking a few photographs.'

'Me neither. We're cut from the same cloth,' Liz said.

'It's nice to think of that,' Sophie smiled. 'I love you, Mum.'

'And I love you.' Liz put her arm around Sophie. They were quiet for a moment, but then Liz decided that now was the perfect time to talk. There may not be another opportunity.

'I hope this will not upset you, but you said something about your Dad and me at one of the family sessions and I wanted to find out how you feel about it now,' Liz said.

'I don't know where that came from. But I suppose the therapy unearths things which people don't want to face.'

'Can you tell me about it?'

'I feel bad about even mentioning such a thing, but Denise said that I must talk about it. For your sake as well as mine. She was going to ask you to come in and we would meet with her at the clinic, but I didn't want that, you've been through enough as it is.'

'I wouldn't mind, if you want me to do that.'

'No, I've decided I'd prefer to talk to you away from there because it's something which I've never told you.' Sophie looked at her, worry etched on her face.

'I have to admit that I was very upset when I got home that night, and since then I've done a lot of thinking about those days.' Liz stared out to sea, her hair whipped up in the wind which had strengthened.

'The same as me. If you'd asked me a few weeks ago about my childhood, I don't think I'd remember everything, particularly what happened between Dad and you.'

'Can you remember now?'

'Some of it.'

'Tell me,' Liz encouraged.

'But it's difficult for you.'

'I've been through a few weeks of it, I can take it now.'

Sophie was quiet for a few seconds, then she tightened her grip on Liz's arm.

'One night I was coming back from the bathroom and I saw Dad hit you and then he pushed you inside the bedroom and banged the door.'

Liz listened.

'Other nights I could hear him shouting at you, and I'd cover my head with the pillow. I was terrified.'

'My poor love.' Liz kissed her cheek.

'But it must have been a thousand times worse for you. How often did it happen?'

'I've gone through it over and over, but I know it only began a couple of years before he died. He had a strange aggression and he would boil over with anger. I know he never hit me in front of you, and as it was always late at night, I used to pray that none of you heard him.'

'My room was beside yours.'

There were tears in their eyes, and both of them were very emotional.

'I had actually decided to leave Ethan and then he had a stroke and died suddenly.'

'I used to wish he was dead,' whispered Sophie. 'And I thought he died because of me.'

'No, it had nothing to do with you,' Liz reassured. 'Never think that.'

'I felt so guilty.'

'You did nothing wrong, Sophie.' She hugged her close. 'If anything I should have left him sooner and it's my fault that I never actually walked out the door. I suppose I didn't want to uproot all of you from your home and friends. So I held on, hoping that he would change.' They neared the end of the beach, and then turned back.

'It must have been so hard for you,' Sophie said.

'I was an adult and should have known that you were affected. I feel guilty.'

'Denise said there's no point apportioning blame, we have to forgive, put it out of our heads and move on.'

'That's good advice. Do you think you can do that, my love?'

'All I can do is try.'

'Believe me, your Dad did love you, but he just had difficulty expressing it.'

'Thanks Mum, it's been good to talk, I feel better,' Sophie said. 'I feel like jumping into the sea and screaming.' She waved her arms and ran into the surf.

'You'll get soaked,' Liz burst out laughing.

'I'm going back to get my togs, I think there's some at home, will you come down with me and have a swim?' Sophie asked.

'Yea, sure, love to.'


Sophie had gone home after a few days, and insisted on coming back to work. Since she had been in the clinic, Liz had done a lot of thinking about the past. So upset by what Sophie remembered about Ethan and herself, she felt clearing out the attic would maybe be a first step in the healing process, something she had considered when she took down the old suitcase after Christmas.

She climbed the ladder which led up into the attic and stood staring into the shadows. There was a musty smell in her nostrils. A dry wave of nostalgia wafted around her. She switched on the light and stepped up. As the crowded attic was revealed, she realised that there was a life up here. Years. Decades. Her life. Her children's lives. Ethan's life too. All those things which meant so much at one time had been put away, and forgotten. She had allocated this evening to do the job, and hoped that there would be no interruptions. She wanted to have this time to herself.


She walked to the back of the attic and began there. Vaguely remembering that some of the boxes had a note of the contents, but this first box had nothing written on it. She pulled it out then and opened it. A whirl of excitement swept through her. Here were some of her college notes and books. She picked up the first one. It was a collection of poetry by Wordsworth and other poets. A page sprang open and she remembered how she particularly liked that poem. She read the words aloud smiling at the recollection.

The next box was filled with baby clothes. She pressed a little pink matinee jacket against her cheek and closed her eyes. She could smell that new baby smell from the wool. She wondered how that scent could have lasted over the years. It was astonishing.

The evening wore on. She was caught in a time warp. A child again when she found some of her own toys in a bag. That soft doll with the yellow pigtails which she had been given as a birthday present when she was very young brought tears to her eyes. She hugged her. So glad to hold her now, knowing that she would never throw her out.

This was difficult. Much more so than she had expected. She moved to the other side of the attic. Hoping that the contents of those boxes proved to be utilities which could be thrown away without a thought. The first few were exactly that. Old delph. Cutlery. And curtains which her parents had given her in those first days of her marriage. Ethan and she had been delighted with anything then. But now their final resting place would be the charity shop.

She spent some time then hauling down the boxes, and stacking them in the hall. Old bits of furniture were manoeuvred down. Lamps. Used bedlinen. Books. Tennis rackets. Brooke's violin. Luke's football boots, small, medium and large. So now she resorted to throwing things down into the hall, hesitating as she was about to fling the violin down. Maybe Brooke would like to keep it for Jess or Cian? She sighed and stared around. Should she ask her kids if they wanted any of this stuff? Maybe they wouldn't be too happy if she dumped everything. She looked down through the opening and could see the pile below. How would she persuade them to come and make decisions? That would be difficult. She might ask, cajole, but knew very well that her voice would land on deaf ears. They would make promises to look at what she had brought down, but she knew it could take quite a long time for that to happen.

Then, unexpectedly, she had an idea.

Later, she called Brooke.

'What do you think if all of us were to sleep under the same roof for one night?'

'Who?'

'Me, you, Sophie and Luke.'

'Why?'

'I was clearing out the attic, and I thought it would be nice to go through some of the stuff up there on one night together.'

'I'm sure whatever is up in the attic is rubbish, you can throw it out. I'm not interested in any of it.'

'Perhaps the others might like to hold on to some things, just as keepsakes perhaps?' She didn't get the response she expected from Brooke.

'Maybe. See what they think.'

'I'll ask.'

Liz began to have second thoughts. At the office she had a chance to mention it to Sophie. To her surprise, she was much more enthusiastic.

'I wouldn't mind. It sounds cool. A night of nostalgia. What does Luke think?'

'I haven't broached it yet. Although as the restaurant is not open on a Sunday night, I thought it would suit. How's that for you?'

'It's fine.'

'I'll do dinner, all your favourite dishes when you were kids.'

'Bread and butter pudding? And custard?' Sophie asked.

'Of course. And treacle tart for Luke.'

'He'll love that. Bet he hasn't tasted it in years. What was Brooke's favourite?'

'Pavlova.'

'I like that as well. I'm looking forward to it already.'

Liz was suddenly glad that at least one of her children was interested. 'I'll have to ask Luke.'

'What did Brooke think?'

'She wasn't that keen.'

'I'll persuade her.'

To her surprise, Luke agreed immediately. 'That would be great, Mum, and going through the stuff should be fun, and we can sleep in our old rooms. How did you think of it?'

'Just occurred to me.'

'Next Sunday?'

'Yes.'

'I'm looking forward to it.' He sounded so happy, she couldn't believe it.

Liz spent the weekend working on the house. She was excited by the prospect of having her three children here with her for the first time in years. They had all left to do their own thing as soon as they could. Anxious for their own independence, and wanting to leave their clinging mother behind too, no doubt. So she cleaned, hoovered and dusted. Sorted out the bedrooms. Changed beds. And cooked. That most of all, anxious to put up a lovely dinner on Sunday night with all their favourite dishes. Then she went back up into the attic. Anxious to find as much as she could now that they were coming. And she was rewarded. It was an emotional rollercoaster for her.

## Chapter Sixty-eight

Scott went to see Ciara. He was welcomed in by her sister Maura. He chatted with them for a while, but Ciara's mother, Kathleen didn't know him today and made no response.

'What brings you over?' Ciara asked.

'I just wanted to talk. Did you receive some documents in the post over the last few days?' Scott asked, hoping that she had.

'They're over there on the sideboard.' Maura picked up a large brown envelope. She handed it to Ciara.

'Did you open it?' he asked.

'Of course I did.'

'Let's go into the sitting room,' he suggested.

She followed him.

'Have you had a look at the documents?'

'No.'

'Why not?'

'I didn't feel like it,' she said.

'Take out the documents, please.' He tried to keep his patience. 'I haven't got a lot of time.'

She pulled out the sheaf of papers inside. 'What are these?'

'They're the divorce documents.'

'What about the sale of the house?' she demanded.

'I've only just put it on the market.'

'When will it happen. When will I get my money?'

'As soon as the divorce has gone through. I'll let you know how things are progressing.' He put the documents down on a low coffee table. 'You have to sign these.' He took a pen from his pocket and handed it to her. 'They've been sent by your own solicitor who will represent you, his name is Rushe. I'll cover the cost of that.'

She took it from him and signed where the solicitor had indicated.

'I'll send the documents in to him,' Scott said, with an inward sigh of relief. It was the first step on the way.

She nodded. Finished, she pushed the documents towards him.

'That's fine.' He put them back in the envelope.

'You've got me now,' she muttered.

'It will be the best thing for both of us. You can go on with your life and so can I.'

## Chapter Sixty-nine

Liz hugged Sophie, the first to arrive on Sunday. 'How are you?' She looked into her eyes.

'So far so good. I haven't been doing any clubbing, just having a few drinks. Although now Robyn and Lucy are both thinking about cutting back which is great. It will make it much easier for me.'

'I'm glad to hear that. Have you been to one of the weekly meetings?' Liz asked gently.

'Yes.'

'And?'

'It wasn't bad.'

'Keep it up.'

'I'll try.' Sophie stared around her. 'There's so many things.'

'And more. I've tried to divide it up, but we'll just have to plough through it.'

'There's my old hockey stick with all the stickers on it.' Sophie picked it up.

'You can bring it home.'

'I'd love to.'

'Maybe you'd take it up again?'

'I don't think I'd be able to run around the pitch.'

'You're still a young thing, plenty of energy.'

She laughed. 'You weren't so bad in your day, what about joining the veterans?'

Liz raised her eyebrows. 'Do you want me to collapse altogether?'

'Not tonight, but you do need to keep fit.'

'I walk,' Liz insisted.

'I have to admit you are in good shape for your ...' Sophie said.

'Don't.' Liz wagged her finger, knowing immediately what she was going to say.

'All right, relax,' she grinned.

The front door opened. 'Hey there?' Luke and Brooke arrived together.

'Mum, how did you even manage to get it all down from there, you should have called me, I'd have helped you with it,' Luke asked.

'I was able to manage, thanks.'

'Is Peggy minding the children?' Sophie asked Brooke.

'She was only too delighted and the kids were all excited to have a sleep over.'

'That's great. Gives you a chance to have a night to yourself.'

'Hey girls, how does it feel?' Luke asked. 'Long time since we've all been together at home for a night. Want to go down memory lane?'

'Let's have a drink and you can look through some of the smaller boxes. What would you like? Wine, beer?'

'Beer for me,' Luke said.

'I'll have some wine.' Sophie held out a glass.

'Me too.'

'How's the restaurant doing?' Liz asked Luke.

'We were actually thinking of closing up recently, although in the last couple of weeks it's been really busy, it's extraordinary, we can't explain it. And suddenly, we have a crowd of young people coming in on the late nights and they're spending too.'

'I'm glad to hear that, Luke, I'd hate to see La Modena close,' Liz said.

'We're keeping our fingers crossed.'

'We should all get our friends to eat there,' Sophie said.

'We've printed up leaflets with special offers, we're trying anything now.'

'I'll take some and give them to friends, it might drum up some new business for you.'

They sat down around the kitchen table and raised their glasses.

'To our Mum and ourselves.' They made a toast.

'I can't remember when we were together like this,' Liz smiled at her children.

'It's been a long time,' Brooke said. 'And we have you to ourselves now, no interference from anyone else.'

'You mean Scott?' Liz asked. She couldn't help herself.

'I suppose I do. Can't hide how I feel.'

'You'll probably be glad to know we've broken up. He's no longer a part of my life,' Liz said slowly.

'I'm so relieved to hear that,' Brooke said. 'Thanks Mum, for thinking of us. You'll be better off without him. He could really hurt you, and none of us want that.' She hugged her.

Liz was disappointed that Brooke still felt the same way about Scott. But she said nothing.

Sophie looked at her brother. 'I can't say that I'm glad about it, what do you think, Luke?'

'Mum is entitled to be happy. This is her one chance and she deserves it.'

'Thank you,' she smiled.

Brooke didn't respond to their remarks.

There was an awkward silence.

'Now, you're all in your old rooms. Got your pyjamas with you?' Liz asked, reluctant to let the situation between herself and Brooke ruin the night.

'I haven't slept in that bed for years,' Sophie said, an emotional twist in her voice.

'Don't go all misty eyed on us now,' Brooke warned.

'Got my teddy bear?' Luke asked, laughing.

'Now you might be surprised, but close your eyes.' Liz got up and went into the hall. Rooted in a box, came back inside and put the soft teddy on his shoulder.

He opened his eyes. 'It's Rupert Bear. Oh God, I never thought I'd see him again.'

'This is turning into a right tear jerker.' Brooke wiped her eyes she was laughing so much.

'What age are you?' Sophie asked.

'Three.' Luke made a face.

'Let's eat, kids. School tomorrow and homework to be done,' Liz warned.

'Imagine having to do essays, or Irish translation, or maths,' Sophie groaned.

'Remember the arguments.'

'Fighting over space at the kitchen table.'

'I hated school.'

'There's a choice for dinner. Thai curry. Lasagne. Or Carbonara which I'm just making if anyone wants it.'

'That's for me, Mum, you know it was always my favourite.' Sophie stood up. 'Let me help you.'

'No, you relax and have a drink.' Liz didn't want them to do anything tonight.

They went through the boxes and bags carefully. Sifting through the things which had been collected as they grew up. So the girls found their old dolls. Prams. Games. Books. Both of them so happy to be reunited with their favourite toys.

Luke found a train set packed away in a box.

'I remember Santa bringing this. And it was all set out in my bedroom. Seemed like miles of track. And the engine was chugging around when I woke up,' he smiled at the recollection.

'Hey, here's one of Brooke's old diaries.'

'Give it here to me.' She reached to grab the one Sophie had opened. 'You can't read those.'

'Why not?'

'No-one's ever read them.'

'Let's have your secrets.' Sophie flicked through the first pages.

Brooke lunged towards her and there was a tussle between them each one holding on to a page of the diary.

'Girls,' Liz laughed out loud. 'Come on, you'll tear it apart, let's eat.' She served up.

'I don't want anyone to read my diaries.' Brooke was annoyed.

'Come on, they're only teenage scribbles,' Luke said.

'They're my deepest thoughts,' insisted Brooke.

'I really fancy this guy, I'm praying he'll call me,' Sophie giggled. 'He didn't, I'm heartbroken.'

'You're making a laugh of me.'

'No, we're not,' Liz handed dinner plates to each.

'I'm keeping a journal,' Sophie said. 'The counsellor suggested I should. They want me to keep a daily record of my life.'

'Have you started doing that?' Liz asked.

'Yes, although I was never a writer, and I'm not that interested in making a note of everything that happens in my life.'

'Maybe I should start keeping a diary again,' Brooke mused.

'You're doing really well, both of you,' Liz said, smiling. 'I'm proud of you.'

'This looks delicious. Better than anything you'd get in La Modena.' Luke tucked in.

Liz smiled at her children. So happy to have them all here with her.

They enjoyed the meal, particularly the desserts.

'Thanks for making treacle tart for me,' Luke leaned across and kissed her.

'It's a long time since I've had your bread and butter pudding, Mum, it's delicious.'

'You can all take whatever is left of your desserts home, and enjoy them.'

'If there's any left.' Luke had already finished his portion. 'What do you think I'll be having for breakfast?'

'I'd love a cigarette,' Brooke said longingly.

'Don't you dare,' Luke grinned.

'I won't,' she sighed.

'You've done really well,' Liz said. 'Congrats.'

Luke stood up, 'I'll get some more boxes. I'm really enjoying this. God knows what we'll find in the next one.' He went out into the hall and came back in. 'This is big. What does it say?' He read the label. 'Photographs.'

They spent a couple of hours going through them. Laughing at the odd poses, the clothes, the hairstyles.

'There you are, Luke, when you were about four.' Liz pointed.

'I remember that tricycle.'

'And me on my scooter.' Brooke looked at another.

'Jess is so like you.'

'Yea. The likeness is amazing isn't it?'

'And Cian is like Rory.'

'Let's go out into the hall and you can decide what you want to take.'

'I don't want those old football boots, they don't fit me any longer,' Luke said.

'Right, here are a few black bags.' Liz undid a roll. 'Take what you want and I'll throw the rest out.'

'I hate doing that, even if they're things we don't want.' Sophie was downcast.

'It has to be done, I must clear out this place.'

They took what they wanted, and the rest was left there.

'I'll order a skip.'

'It's like throwing a life away,' Luke murmured.

'Our lives,' Brooke whispered.

They looked at each other.

'Let's not get morose.' Liz left them filling black bags. 'I hope you enjoyed being back home tonight.'

'Yea, it's been wonderful.' Sophie was the one who seemed to enjoy it the most.

'Thanks for asking us over.' Brooke put her arm around Liz.

'Yea, Mum, it's been a great night. And I'm so glad I found some of my toys again, particularly the train set.' Luke picked up the green engine, and ran his hand over the shiny surface.

'And I'm going to really enjoy sleeping in my old bed again,' Sophie said.

*'Night night, sleep tight, don't let the bedbugs bite.'* Liz hugged them all, and then went into her own room. As if they were still her young children, instinctively she felt that she should go into them to check that they were all right. Tuck them in. Pull up the duvets. Kiss them goodnight. And turn off the lights. It took her back to those days long ago when they wanted her, and needed her. Now she felt an emptiness inside. A sudden missing of what they meant to her.

She picked up the photo of Ethan on the bedside table. He was gone now and if he had spoken to her through the medium then he had given her permission to step out of this cocoon and take a chance. She had done exactly that, and when her children had objected she stepped back in again. A cowardly move.

# Chapter Seventy

Liz was still going through some of the things which she had brought down from the attic. Now she took her time. Her nostalgic side deciding what to throw away and what to keep. Paper was loaded into the car and taken to recycling. Then furniture and any reasonable clothes went to the charity shop. She stood in the attic and couldn't believe the space up here now. Immediately she was reminded of the collection of landscape photos in her book, and wondered if those empty spaces were a reflection of her life?

The doorbell rang. She climbed down. Glancing into the hall mirror, she ran her fingers through her hair, and went to open the door astonished to see Scott standing outside.

'Hi Liz,' he smiled.

'Come in, Scott,' she stood back, her pulse racing.

He handed her a bouquet of red roses.

'Thank you, these are beautiful.' She ushered him ahead of her and closed the door. 'How are you?' she asked.

'Not so bad. To be honest, not so good either. And you?'

'The same.' She nodded. 'I'll just get a vase for these.' She went into the kitchen and busied herself arranging the roses. He followed and then she sat opposite him, anxious to keep him at a distance, afraid to get too close.

'I came up to tell you something, actually to show you ...' He took a document from a file which he had carried, and handed it to her.

She looked at him, and then she lowered her eyes to read the typescript. 'So Ciara agreed to divorce?' she asked after a moment.

'Yes, I'm selling the house and she will be given half the proceeds from the sale.'

'I see that here. Is she happy with the arrangement?'

'Seems to be,' he smiled.

'I'm glad for you,' she said softly.

'Liz, I don't know how you feel now, but are the family still very much against us?'

'Brooke is.' Liz felt self-conscious. Their conversation was stilted, as if they were total strangers who had never set eyes on each other. 'Although she's in better form.' She went on to explain what had happened with Rory.

'And Sophie?'

'She seems well, but it's still an uphill battle for her. She told me you paid for the treatment, and that you were there for her when she went to the clinic. Thank you, Scott, you're very generous, but I can't let you pay for it.' Liz stood up and went to the counter where she had put her handbag. She tore out a cheque from her chequebook, and scribbled her name on it.

'Liz …'

'I want you to take this, you can fill in the exact amount.' She held it out, hoping that there would be enough in the account as she still had to arrange a loan.

'This is something I wanted to do, and really, it's between me and Sophie.'

'You can't be out of pocket,' she insisted.

'I haven't even paid it yet, they haven't sent me the bill.'

'Take the cheque, surely you have some idea what it's going to be?'

'Liz, thank you for offering, but I'm not going to take a cheque from you. Tear it up,' he said firmly.

She sat down again, thinking how difficult it was to persuade him to do anything he didn't want.

'It will be all sorted, there's no hurry,' he said gently.

'I hope so. Anyway, the money isn't the most important thing, I just want Sophie to be well, that's all.'

'And I want the same, I'm very fond of her,' he insisted.

'There's nothing worse than problems with your children,' she said.

'Tell me about it. Ciara doesn't want to stay here any longer and she is going back to London. When she tells Cathal that then he will blame me. I didn't welcome her back, I didn't let her stay in the house. I'm insisting on a divorce,' he sighed and stared down at the floor with a defeated air.

'How do you deal with Cathal, how do I deal with Brooke?' she asked.

'We have to live our own lives, we can't allow them to control us.'

Her dark eyes met his in understanding. But what was there to say, she wondered. Only that she had to make a choice. Her heart was full as she looked at him. Could she let him leave? To live alone again. Days and nights. Empty. Unfulfilled. She shuddered.

A questioning silence stretched between them.

After a moment he stood up. 'I should go,' he murmured, and went out into the hall. At the front door, he turned to her. 'I'll always love you, Liz, never forget that.'

Slowly she moved towards him and leaned her body against his. Her head on his shoulder.

His fingers caressed her face gently.

She felt cherished by this man. Amazed that he cared so much for her.

Now she raised her head and touched his lips with hers. She tasted him. Smelled his skin. Knowing him. He was her life. She couldn't go on without him.

# TO MAKE A DONATION TO
# LAURALYNN HOUSE


Children's Sunshine Home/LauraLynn Account
AIB Bank, Sandyford Business Centre,
Foxrock, Dublin 18.


Account No. 32130009
Sort Code: 93-35-70


www.lauralynnhospice.com

# Acknowledgements

As always, our very special thanks to Jane and Brendan, knowing you both has changed our lives.

Many thanks to both my family and Arthur's family, our friends and clients, who continue to support our efforts to raise funds for LauraLynn House. And all those generous people who help in various ways but are too numerous to mention. You know who you are and that we appreciate everything you do.

Grateful thanks to all my friends in The Wednesday Group, who give me such valuable critique. Many thanks especially to Muriel Bolger who edited the book on this occasion also, and special thanks to Vivien Hughes who proofed the manuscript. You all know how much we appreciate your generosity.

Special thanks to Martone Design & Print – Yvonne, Martin, Dave, and Kate. Couldn't do it without you.

Many thanks to my brother Jimmy who allowed me to use his beautiful photographs.

Thanks to CPI Group and thanks to all at LauraLynn House.

Thanks to Kevin Dempsey Distributors Ltd. and Power Home Products Ltd., for their generosity in supplying product for LauraLynn House.

Special thanks to Cyclone Couriers and Southside Storage.

Thanks also to Irish Distillers Pernod Ricard. Supervalu. Tesco.

And in Nenagh, our grateful thanks to Tom Gleeson of Irish Computers who very generously service our website free of charge. Walsh Packaging, Nenagh Chamber of Commerce, McLoughlin's Hardware, Cinnamon Alley Restaurant, Jessicas, Abbey Court Hotel, and Caseys in Toomevara.

Many thanks to Ree Ward Callan and Michael Feeney Callan.

And much love to my darling husband, Arthur, without whose love and support this wouldn't be possible.

# CYCLONE COURIERS

Cyclone Couriers – who proudly support LauraLynn Children's Hospice – are the leading supplier of local, national and international courier services in Dublin. Cyclone also supply confidential mobile on-site document shredding and recycling services and secure document storage & records management services through their Cyclone Shredding and Cyclone Archive Division.

Cyclone Couriers – The fleet of pushbikes, motorbikes, and vans, can cater for all your urgent local and national courier requirements.

Cyclone International – Overnight, next day, timed and weekend door-to-door deliveries to destinations within the thirty-two counties of Ireland.

Delivery options to the UK, mainland Europe, USA, and the rest of the world.

A variety of services to all destinations across the globe.

Cyclone Shredding – On-site confidential document and product shredding & recycling service. Destruction and recycling of computers, hard drives, monitors and office electronic equipment.

Cyclone Archive – Secure document and data storage and records management. Hard copy document storage and tracking – data storage – fireproof media safe – document scanning and upload of document images.

Cyclone Couriers operate from 8, Upper Stephen Street, Dublin 8.

Cyclone Archive, International and Shredding, operate from

11 North Park, Finglas, Dublin 11.

www.cyclone.ie   email: sales@cyclone.ie  Tel: 01-475 7000

# SOUTHSIDE STORAGE
Murphystown Road, Sandyford, Dublin 18.

## FACILITIES

Individually lit, self-contained, off-ground metal and concrete units that are fireproof and waterproof.

Sizes of units : 300 sq.ft. 150 sq.ft. 100 sq.ft. 70 sq.ft.

Flexible hours of access and 24 hour alarm monitored security.

Storage for home
Commercial storage
Documents and Archives
Packaging supplies and materials
Extra office space
Sports equipment
Musical instruments
And much much more ....

Contact us to discuss your requirements:

01 294 0517   -   087 640 7448
Email: info@southsidestorage.ie

Location: Southside Storage is located on
Murphystown Road, Sandyford, Dublin 18
close to Exit 13 on the M50

# THE MARRIED WOMAN

## Fran O'Brien

### Marriage is for ever ...

In their busy lives, Kate and Dermot rush along on parallel lines,
seldom coming together to exchange a word or a kiss.
To rekindle the love they once knew, Kate struggles to lose
weight, has a make-over, buys new clothes, and arranges a
romantic trip to Spain with Dermot.

For the third time he cancels and she goes alone.

In Andalucia she meets the artist Jack Linley. He takes her with him
into a new world of emotion and for the first time in years she feels
like a desirable beautiful woman.

Will life ever be the same again?

Available now online
McGuinness Books
www.franobrien.net

# THE LIBERATED WOMAN

## Fran O'Brien

### At last, Kate has made it!

She has ditched her obnoxious husband Dermot and is
reunited with her lover, Jack.

Her interior design business goes international and TV
appearances bring instant success.

But Dermot hasn't gone away and his problems encroach.

Her brother Pat and family come home from Boston
and move in on a supposedly temporary basis.

Her manipulative stepmother Irene is getting married
again and Kate is dragged into the extravaganza.

When a secret from the past is revealed Kate has
to review her choices ...

Available now online
McGuinness Books
www.franobrien.net

# THE PASSIONATE WOMAN

A chance meeting with ex lover Jack throws Kate into a spin.
She cannot forgive him and concentrates all her passions on
her interior design business, and television work.

Jack still loves Kate and as time passes without reconciliation
he feels more and more frustrated.

Estranged husband Dermot has a change of fortunes,
and wants her back.

Stepmother, Irene, is as wacky as ever and is being chased
by the paparazzi.

Best friend, Carol, is searching for a man on the internet, and
persuades Kate to come along as chaperone on a date.

ARE THESE PATHS TO KATE'S NEW LIFE OR
ROUNDABOUTS TO HER OLD ONE?

Available now online
McGuinness Books
www.franobrien.net

# ODDS ON LOVE

## Fran O'Brien

Bel and Tom seem to be the perfect couple with successful careers, a beautiful home and all the trappings. But underneath the facade cracks appear and damage the basis of their marriage and the deep love they have shared since that first night they met.

Her longing to have a baby creates problems for Tom, who can't deal with the possibility that her failure to conceive may be his fault. His masculinity is questioned and in attempting to deal with his insecurities he is swept up into something far more insidious and dangerous than he could ever have imagined.

Then against all the odds, Bel is thrilled to find out she is pregnant. But she is unable to tell Tom the wonderful news as he doesn't come home that night and disappears mysteriously out of her life leaving her to deal with the fall out.

Available now online
McGuinness Books
www.franobrien.net

# WHO IS FAYE?

## Fran O'Brien

## Can the past ever be buried?

Jenny should be fulfilled. She has a successful career,
and shares a comfortable life with her husband, Michael,
at Ballymoragh Stud.

But increasingly unwelcome memories surface and
keep her awake at night.

Is it too late to go back to the source of those fears
and confront them?

Available now online
McGuinness Books
www.franobrien.net

# THE RED CARPET

## Fran O'Brien

### Lights, Camera, Action.

Amy is raised in the glitzy facade that is Hollywood.
Her mother, Maxine, is an Oscar winning actress, and
her father, John, a famous film producer. When
Amy is eight years old, Maxine is tragically killed.

A grown woman, Amy becomes the focus of John's
obsession for her to star in his movies and be as
successful as her mother. But Amy's insistence
on following her heart, and moving permanently to
Ireland, causes a rift between them.

As her daughter, Emma, approaches her eighth
birthday, Amy is haunted by the nightmare of
what happened on her own eighth birthday.

She determines to find answers to her questions.

Available now online
McGuinness Books
www.franobrien.net

# FAIRFIELDS

## 1907    QUEENSTOWN    CORK

Set against the backdrop of a family feud and prejudice
Anna and Royal Naval Officer, Mike, fall in love.
They meet secretly at an old cottage
on the shores of the lake at Fairfields.

During that spring and summer their feelings for each
other deepen. Blissfully happy, Anna accepts Mike's
proposal of marriage, unaware that her family have a
different future arranged for her.

**Is their love strong enough to withstand
the turmoil that lies ahead?**

Available now online
McGuinness Books
www.franobrien.net

# THE PACT

## THE POINT OF THE KNIFE
## PRESSES INTO SOFT SKIN ...

Inspector Grace McKenzie investigates the
trafficking of women into Ireland and is
drawn under cover into that sinister world.

She is deeply affected by the suffering of one
particular woman and her quest for justice
re-awakens an unspeakable trauma in her own life.

## CAN SHE EVER ESCAPE FROM ITS
## INFLUENCE AND BE FREE TO LOVE?

Available now online
McGuinness Books
www.franobrien.net

# 1916

On Easter Monday, 24th April, 1916, against the
backdrop of the First World War, a group of
Irishmen and Irishwomen rise up against Britain.
What follows has far-reaching consequences.

We witness the impact of the Rising on four families,
as passion, fear and love permeate a week of
insurrection which reduces the centre of Dublin to ashes.

This is a story of divided loyalties, friendships,
death, and a conflict between an Empire
and a people fighting for independence.

Available now online
McGuinness Books
www.franobrien.net

# CUIMHNÍ CINN
# Memoirs of the Uprising

## Liam Ó Briain

**(Reprint in the Irish language originally published in 1951)**

**(English translation by Michael McMechan)**

Liam Ó Briain was a member of the Volunteers of Ireland
from 1914 and he fought with the Citizen Army of Ireland
in the College of Surgeons during Easter Week.

This is a clear lively account of the events of that time.
An account in which there is truth, humanity and, more
than any other thing, humour. It will endure as literature.

When this book was first published in Irish in 1951, it was hoped
it would be read by the young people of Ireland. To remember
more often the hardships  endured by our forebears for the
sake of our freedom we might the  better validate Pearse's vision.

Available now online
McGuinness Books
www.franobrien.net